A Dan and Rivka Sherman Mystery

# *DEATH TAKES A MISTRESS*

## By Rosemary and Larry
# Mild

Magic Island Literary Works • Honolulu, Hawaii • 2016

Interior book design by **Larry Mild.**
Cover design by **Marilyn Drea,** Mac-In-Town, Annapolis, MD.

Library of Congress Cataloging-in-Publication Data
Mild, Rosemary P. ; Mild, Larry M.
**Death Takes A Mistress**
Mild, Rosemary P. ; Mild, Larry M.
ISBN 978-0-9838597-5-8

10 9 8 7 6 5 4 3 2 1

# Dedication

For our beloved grandchildren—
**Alena, Craig, Ben, Leah, and Emily**


**F**or our wonderful children—
**Jackie and Myrna**


**F**or our marriage—soul mates, partners, lovers


✳ ✳ ✳ ✳ ✳

## GOODREADS REVIEW - 5 STARS

"*Death Takes A Mistress* is a delightfully twisted tale of intrigue. The characters were fun and believable. I'm looking forward to reading more books by the Milds."

## Books by the Milds

Coauthors of the Dan and Rivka Sherman Mysteries
- *Death Goes Postal*
- *Death Takes A Mistress*
- *Death Steals A Holy Book*

Coauthors of the Paco and Molly Mysteries
- *Locks and Cream Cheese*
- *Hot Grudge Sunday*
- *Boston Scream Pie*

## Coauthors of the Adventure/Thriller
*Cry Ohana*

## Coauthors of Two Short Story Collections
- *Murder, Fantasy, and Weird Tales*
- *The Misadventures of Slim O. Wittz*

* * * *

## Books by Rosemary

- *Miriam's World—and Mine*
- *Love! Laugh! Panic! Life with My Mother*

## Acknowledgments

We could fill an entire volume with the names of all the family members, dear friends, and acquaintances who are loyal fans of our books. You are all precious to us and give us the ultimate push to continue our writing.

Our special appreciation to **Diane Farkas** for her judicious editing assistance.

## Disclaimer

***Death Takes A Mistress*** is entirely a work of fiction. The plot and the events therein are of the authors' imagination and invention. All characters are fictitious and any resemblance to living persons or persons having lived in this century or the past few centuries is purely coincidental.

# Contents

* * * *

# Special Credits

othic Leaf font was chosen by the authors of *Death Goes Postal* to represent what Gerheardt Koenig's floral font <u>might</u> have looked like, as in the illuminated first character in each chapter. The authors have chosen to continue the practice in ***Death Takes A Mistress***. Many thanks to **Rob Anderson** and the Flight of the Dragon organization.

"This font was created by **Rob Anderson** of **Flight of the Dragon**, using CorelDRAW version 5 and 6. This font is freely available, and may be distributed in any way as long as this message is included:

The author of the font makes no guarantee about the viability and usability of this font and is not responsible for any damages related to the use.

© All rights reserved. Copyright 1997, **Flight of the Dragon**."

# Chapter 1

## Mistress Lost
London, England—Wednesday, March 3rd, 1982

Nothing in the clammy London grayness seemed to herald that evening's terrible discovery. Following a full day's work at the law offices of Bleak and Fullbrite, solicitor Wayne Sachs set off for home to his wife and son in their fourth-floor flat. After rattling through six Underground stations on the crowded Central-Line Tube and walking several blocks, the thirty-five year-old bounded up the steps at 103 Devon Court. Passing 3C, he saw that the door was wide open. He hesitated for a moment and stuck his head inside his neighbor's flat.

"Lainee?" he called. No answer. Wayne pushed two steps inside and yelled her name once more. "Lainee Cohen!" Sweeping his eyes about the room, nothing seemed to be amiss, so he continued up the stairs to the next landing, taking with him a sense of foreboding. But even then, the worst had not occurred to him.

Janice Sachs stood just outside their door, waiting for her husband of eleven blissful years. Three-month-old Ivy Cohen nestled deep in the crook of her arm. Wayne kissed them both on his way into their flat, dropped his briefcase on the nearest chair, and hooked his suit jacket on the Bentwood tree in the corner. When his short, curly-haired wife didn't follow him inside, he again sensed the dread. Something wasn't right.

"What's wrong? Where's Ollie? Is he hurt?" Wayne pivoted toward her, anxious about their nine-year-old son.

"No, Ollie's still at school—at the cricket match," she answered. "He'll be home in an hour. It's Lainee I'm concerned about. She hasn't come by to pick Ivy up."

"Lainee's door is open," Wayne said, "and she didn't answer when I called to her."

"Dear, this is not good. I've been baby-sitting Ivy all day. Lainee told me it would only be for a few hours. She was going to break the news to her boyfriend that he'd become a father. And that was at nine this morning."

"Did she expect a problem telling him?"

"Oh, yes," Janice replied. "So much so that she brought all the baby's things upstairs with Ivy. I thought that in itself was strange, so I asked her why. She just said she wanted to tell the boyfriend in her own time and in her own way." Janice shrugged. "Not a very logical reason."

"A delicate situation, eh? Why haven't we ever met this boyfriend? I'll bet the blighter is married and diddling her on the quiet whenever he feels like it."

"You really think so?" Janice asked. "That could be. She hardly ever mentions him."

"Have you ever run into this lover boy? Do you know what he looks like or anything about him?"

"No," Janice answered. "That's weird, too. Especially since she just had his baby. And I always thought Lainee and I were so close. Wayne, honey?"

"Yeah?"

"Shouldn't we check up on her? After all, I still have Ivy on my hands, and there are only two nappies left. Besides, it's not like Lainee to go out and leave her door open." Janice shifted Ivy to her other arm. The baby nestled against her chest and kept slumbering.

"I agree," he said. "I'll go downstairs and give her flat a

thorough once-over."

"I'm coming, too."

They clomped down the carpeted steps to the floor below. Located opposite the staircase, Lainee Cohen's flat was the mirror image of their own. Through the wide-open door, the dining room appeared undisturbed. Wayne stepped into that room first and quickly faced the front of the house toward the bay window above the street and parlor. Still nothing out of order. With Janice trailing a few feet behind him, he moved down the hall to the kitchen and bedroom, only to find a few dirty dishes in the sink and an empty tossed bed.

Returning to the front of the flat, this time he stepped all the way into the parlor. Wrapping paper and gift boxes were strewn about one end of the ell-shaped room.

Wayne stopped abruptly. Two shoeless feet stuck out from behind the tapestried sofa. His heartbeat quickened as he stepped closer. Lainee's petite body lay on her back, legs apart, with bare toes pointed toward heaven and a salmon-colored robe thrown over her nude body. Strands of her shoulder-length coal-black hair lay matted and stiff against one side of her head. Dried blood, he guessed. Her expressive dark eyes, now glassy and dull, locked on to the ceiling. Her mouth gaped open, lips twisted in fear.

A chill gripped Wayne as he reluctantly knelt and put an ear to her chest, listening for signs of life. None. Lastly, he failed to detect any pulse. When he looked up again, he saw a wide-eyed Janice standing behind him with Ivy still asleep across her shoulder.

"Good Lord!" she gasped. "Shouldn't we call the police?"

"Absolutely," he said. "I'll call. You take the baby back upstairs with you."

* * * *

Ninety minutes later Scene of Crime Officers (SOCOs) moved about the flat like so many flies scouting new feeding fields. A tall woman in a tweed blazer was directing this assault on Lainee Cohen's apartment. Frequent photo flashes accented each potential clue.

"Aren't those photographers finished yet?" Inspector Jervis Harvey bellowed when he arrived eight minutes later. At first impression, he appeared to be a middle-aged grouch of broad girth and short temper, but he was a proven policeman and a caring human being.

"Yes, sir," replied a uniformed constable.

"Forensics? SOCOs?"

"Yes, sir, over there."

"Well?"

" 'Tis a toss between strangulation and a bop on the noggin. Maybe both. The SOCO doc said he couldn't rightly tell 'til he got 'er back to the lab. There's blood right here where she hit her head." The constable pointed to the red blotch on the steam-heated white radiator.

"Killer leave any signs?" asked Harvey, kneeling beside Lainee. Getting a negative answer, he probed on his own, noting the small amount of blood soaked into the carpet behind her head; the black-and-blue finger marks on her neck; both arms set at her sides; and a strange distortion in the doll-like face. *The body looks to have been rearranged, and certainly the robe should have come open when she fell, accident or not, he thought. It seems the killer was sensitive to her nakedness and covered her up.*

"Anybody else touch the body?" asked Harvey.

"None of us, sir. Just the bloke what discovered the vic'," responded the constable. "He tried to take her pulse. Nothing else."

"And where is *he* now?"

"Upstairs in 4B. The bloke and his missus both discovered 'er," replied the constable. Looking down at his notes, "Mr. Wayne Sachs and his wife, Janice."

"Any significance to all these presents or their packaging?" asked Inspector Harvey.

"Three things, sir," responded the senior officer of the SOCO team. "First, the lingerie items look expensive, and I'm betting they were intended for the victim. The sizes would be a close fit. Second, the merchandise is foreign—comes from several shops in Annapolis, Maryland, in the States. Three, they're extremely intimate-type gifts. Our perpetrator had to know the victim pretty well."

"Thank you, Miss . . . Mrs.?"

"Miss it is, sir. Felicia Anders, Forensics, SOCO team leader, sir."

"Well, Miss Anders, your people turn up any prints yet, other than our victim's?"

"No, sir. It appears that everything has been clinically wiped down. We did find a brand-new, unopened box of Pablum in a kitchen cupboard. Only the victim's prints on it."

Inspector Harvey frowned. "Can you place the time of death, Miss Anders?"

"Early afternoon, I would say, sir, but we won't know for sure until the autopsy."

Harvey nodded, satisfied with her answer. "Was the victim a mother?"

"I don't know. Other than the Pablum, it looks like Miss Cohen lived alone."

"Good job, Miss Anders. I'll be in touch."

* * * *

"What in the world are we going to do with Ivy?" asked an anxious Wayne.

"Exactly nothing," Janice said. Her voice trembled as she added: "You and I are going to take care of this darling infant as if she's our own. Lainee has no one else in the world, not a single relative. What if the bastard who killed her is Ivy's father? What if he lays claim to their baby? Well, he's never going to get her, not if I can help it." In her bulky sweater and skirt, Janice took on a protective, defending-the-barricades look as she gripped her tiny bundle more tightly.

A frown creased Wayne's high brow. "You want to lie to the police?"

"If I must," she snapped. "If it will keep Ivy out of the deplorable orphan and foster care system." She patted the baby on the back and rocked her from side to side, eliciting a pleasant, gurgling sound.

"Won't they find out anyway? Her things?" He held his hands to his forehead, feeling trouble coming just as surely as if it was a migraine.

"Don't you see? Everything belonging to Ivy is already in our flat. Lainee brought up two suitcases full of her things. She even dragged the portable crib up here."

"Where are we going to put it all? Besides, won't—"

"You wanted another child, didn't you?" she pleaded.

"Well, sure, but . . ." He followed her into the bedroom as she laid Ivy down in her crib for a nap.

"But nothing. You get this child free, no hospital or doctor fees." She turned out the light and pulled the door partly shut.

A flash of stubborn solicitor's logic shot through Wayne's brain. Suppressing it, he took a deep breath and held out his arms. Janice folded into his waiting embrace. That was all the answer she needed.

"I suppose we'll manage one way or another," he mumbled.

The doorbell rang, and the two of them looked at each other.

Inspector Harvey stood in the doorway. "Mr. and Mrs. Wayne Sachs? I have a few questions for you."

"Of course. Come in and have a seat," Janice said.

"Ma'am, I understand your husband called the police. Did the decedent have any relatives or close friends or even regular visitors that you know of?"

Janice shook her head, fighting back tears. "No relatives. I suppose we were about as close as anyone to her."

"And visitors?"

"She mentioned she had a boyfriend, but we don't know anything about him."

"Was Miss Cohen employed anywhere?"

"Not in the last six months," Janice said. "She was employed as a salesgirl at Harrod's department store in Knightsbridge before that."

"Did she ever mention any co-workers?"

"She did talk about Sally somebody, but I don't know a last name."

"Who paid the rent if she was no longer employed?"

"I really don't know. She did have that steady boyfriend, though. Maybe he paid it."

"Do you know his name?"

"We've never met him. For that matter, we've never even seen him. Lainee rarely talked about him and when she did, she used some funny nickname, beginning with an S, I think."

"Would that be Snooks?"

"Maybe . . . I think so. How did you know?"

"Our crime people came up with a diary. It was hidden under her mattress."

Janice froze. "Then you know about the baby."

"Of course." Inspector Harvey noted her reaction and made an instant decision not to grill her on why she and her husband failed to disclose this fact. Instead, he took a kindly approach. "Are you minding the child?"

"Yes. Lainee can't—couldn't—afford a nanny, and I loved helping her out," Janice confessed, her words catching in her throat. "It's so hard talking about her in the past. Ivy is such a sweet baby. She never cries."

Inspector Harvey's keen eyes swept over the orderly parlor. Solid, well-chosen furnishings. Polished wood tabletops. Shelves filled with books that looked read, not just for show. He made an on-the-spot appraisal of the husband and wife. "Are you both willing to take the child into your family on a temporary basis?"

"You bet," replied Janice. "Even on a permanent basis."

"Me too," chimed Wayne.

"I can't promise anything," the inspector said. "You'll have to face a bunch of social workers, solicitors, barristers, and eventually a judge." He moved his bulk into the hall.

Janice's cheeks flushed with relief. "Thank you, Inspector."

"Wayne, honey," she began when the door had finally closed.

"What, sweetheart?"

"About that extra child."

"Yeah?"

"There might be two of them. I've been having morning sickness for nearly a week now." She tried to smile, but couldn't. She was too worried about his reaction.

"How come I didn't notice?" he asked.

"My belly very considerately waited to throw up till you left for work."

"Wow! The more the merrier, I guess." He kissed her with enough passion to erase any of her concerns. "Hey, I almost forgot. My boss called me into his office today. He's pleased with my work, so there'll be eight and six more in my pay starting next check."

"That's wonderful, dear," Janice said as the two embraced again. "We'll need every bit of it."

*From one kid to three in the space of two hours?* Wayne's chin rested on the top of his wife's head, guaranteeing that she wouldn't see the hint of alarm in his intelligent gray eyes.

Chapter 2

## Mission Stated
Friday, October 14th, 2005

Four months after her graduation from Kings College London, Ivy Cohen emigrated to Annapolis, Maryland. Janice and Wayne Sachs had lovingly accepted, raised, and educated her, treating her just like their two natural children, although they never legally adopted her. Ivy appreciated their enormous kindness and adored them. No, she did not emigrate to run away from anyone or anything. On the contrary, she came to this city to find her mother's brutal killer.

There was no doubt in Ivy's mind that the murderer had been her mother's lover. She just didn't know why a beautiful love ended so tragically. Reading old press accounts led her to believe that Scotland Yard hadn't treated her mother's case as a priority. The detectives believed the killer had fled the country without a trace. So the investigation went cold all too quickly.

As soon as Ivy was old enough to learn of her mother's fate, justice became her obsession. Old police reports, plus clues in her mother's journal, pointed to Annapolis. Certain articles, supposedly gifts strewn about the crime scene, had been purchased there. The journal revealed hints of a lover belonging to a large Jewish family that had migrated to Annapolis to engage in a major family

9

business enterprise. Ivy knew the time frame, but without a family name, the city of London was far too immense to screen émigrés with any hope of identifying that particular family. Annapolis, the state capital, was a small city of only about 40,000, and probably more aware of any transplanted family businesses.

The scant tool Ivy had counted on working for her was the remarkable likeness she shared with her mother. She wanted to come face-to-face with the killer and see the overt shock he would experience upon meeting her. If it had been possible to observe Ivy and her mother side-by-side at exactly the same age, one might have sworn they were identical twins: right down to the petite build, oval face, soft voice, and large dark eyes. Indistinguishable, even to the way they wore their shimmering coal-black hair—straight, loose, and over the left eye. Their perky, jubilant personalities also seemed identical. One trait would not have been apparent in a photo: Ivy was a driven woman, rather than passive like her mother.

Fresh out of college and without teaching experience, she found it difficult to find employment in the Maryland school system. And without an advanced degree, she couldn't teach at the college level either. She had arrived in Annapolis three weeks earlier and was living in a Holiday Inn at the edge of town. At the current rate, her savings would last no more than a few weeks. She needed a job.

The circled want-ad in the folded newspaper had brought her to an elaborate four-story structure on Franklyn Lane. The Olde Victorian Bookstore sign hung high above the white veranda on the second story. To the right of the stairs leading up to that gingerbread veranda, an iron-strapped, wooden door, suspended inside a large stone arch, bore the name The Dungeon. Choosing The Dungeon entrance rather than the seven steep stairs up, she stepped inside  and hesitated a moment to get her bearings.

"Welcome! May I help you, young lady?" The warm soprano voice came from behind the counter next to her. And behind that voice sat a fifty-ish woman with dark brown hair, smooth skin, and sturdy body.

"My name is Ivy Cohen, and I'm here about your retail clerk ad in the paper."

"Yes, Ivy. I'm Rivka Sherman. My husband, Dan, and I own and manage the store. We're looking for someone who has excellent people skills. Literary knowledge and filing skills are also necessary, but we want someone who will stick with the job. The store is on four separate floors, so you will need a bit of athleticism to go with all that."

"Well, I do have a B.A. in English literature and I'm young and healthy enough to handle the rest. What about the hours, pay, and benefits?"

Rivka detected the accent, as well as a certain aggressiveness. *Already asking about benefits? Oh, stop being judgmental*, she told herself. *The girl needs a job.* She motioned Ivy around to a second chair on her side of the counter.

"You're English?" Rivka asked.

Ivy nodded. "Yes, from London. I've been here three weeks."

"Do you have a Green Card? And do you plan to make Annapolis your home? If not, I don't want to hire somebody who's only here for a few weeks."

*This is definitely a no-nonsense lady*, Ivy decided. "Yes, ma'am, I understand. I do have my Green Card. And I do intend to stay on and live here in Annapolis permanently."

"Do you have any references, Ivy?"

"I'm afraid not, ma'am. This is my first job. I'm right out of school. You could ring up my foster parents in London or my school. I'd pay for the calls, Mrs. Sherman. Here's my resumé. I know it's not much, but . . ." she said, handing it over.

Rivka scanned the single sheet. "That won't be necessary, Ivy. I see you got commendations as a student. I like to think I'm a fair judge of character. Our former clerk left to get married. Went to England, as a matter of fact. So here's what the job is. You'll work a forty-hour week mostly, and there's an opportunity for a little overtime just before the holiday season. We've only had the store a year, so we can't pay much—say, eleven hundred a month. And there's a modest health insurance plan we can review together later. What do you say to that?"

"When can I start?" The words came out louder than she intended.

"You can start any time. I'll show you the ropes. And please call me Rivka."

"Thank you, Rivka. I appreciate you giving me this opportunity."

Ivy watched her new boss ring up a cash sale. The electronic register vocalized a *ka-ching*. She slipped the receipt and a paperback copy of *Bartlett's Quotations* into a bag with the store's logo. The gentleman left the store with his purchase and change.

Rivka studied the young woman's data. "Ivy Cohen . . . You're Jewish, I gather. Are you a practicing Jew?"

"Oh, yes, I usually go to *shul* every week."

"Where are you staying?"

"The Holiday Inn." Ivy reddened, not wanting to appear too desperate. "It's quite expensive."

"I can imagine," Rivka said. She tore off a piece of paper and jotted down an address. "Mrs. Riley has a rooming house around the corner. I believe she has a vacancy."

"You're a Godsend, Rivka."

"By the way, Ivy, what brought you all the way to Annapolis from England? It is quite a leap, you know."

The question startled Ivy. She hadn't expected it, although she knew she should have. "I uh . . . came to find my birth father. I believe he lives here. I don't even know his name."

"Oh, dear, that's sad. Perhaps you'll join us for *Shabbat* dinner tonight. We close the store at five on Friday nights. Dinner's at six so we have time to get to temple for eight o'clock services. You'll come?"

"If you're sure I won't be a burden?"

"Of course you'll come. How much can a little bird like you eat?" Rivka grinned. "Now go get yourself some lunch, get moved in, and we'll see you upstairs in our apartment this evening." She pointed to the staircase leading to the next floors.

"May I hug you?"

Before Rivka could answer, she felt two arms, like fluttering wings, about her in a quick squeeze. Ivy headed for the door. "See you later," she sang. The door jingled shut behind her.

Rivka heard the back door slam a few minutes later and peeked down the aisle to see her husband approaching from the rear of the store. Daniel appeared pleased with himself and proceeded to hum along the way. As he passed the third book stack section, a furry black cat leapt down and fell into step behind him. Approaching the front of the store, it suddenly ran ahead, jumped into Rivka's lap, and snuggled into a comfortable niche. Lord Byron tilted his head to one side as though he expected her fingers to rub behind one ear. He wasn't disappointed.

"And where have *you* been?" she asked as Dan dropped his tall, gangly frame into a folding chair. Rivka still appreciated her husband's bushy, black hair with its traces of gray and horn-rimmed glasses; they gave him a look both scholarly and sexy.

"Out back, breaking down the cardboard from those eleven cartons of books that arrived yesterday. Took almost an hour. They ought to put rip strings under the tape to make the job easier."

"Is that another one of your *Whydon'tchas?* You could write a book about all your inventions."

"You bet, and my rip string wouldn't cost much either. It could be manufactured within the tape itself." He stretched out his long legs. "Did you miss me?"

"Of course I missed you, Dan. I had to interview the new employee all by myself."

"New employee! Rivka, you've already hired her without consulting me?"

"A-yup, as you would put it."

"Why didn't you call me?"

"You would have hired her on the spot without even an interview."

"That cute, eh?"

"Uh-huh. Besides I didn't know where you were, Dan."

"When do I actually get to meet this beautiful chick—I mean clerk."

"I just knew I had to hire someone young enough you couldn't catch or old enough you wouldn't bother."

"Verr-ry funny, dear. When?"

"Tonight, sweetheart. I invited Ivy Cohen to *Shabbat* dinner."

* * * *

Ivy stepped out of the store into the bright spring sunshine and marched around the block as instructed. *At last*, she thought, *I've landed a decent position*. She glanced up at the street sign and down to the piece of paper that Rivka had given her. The address matched the third house in: a charming, three-story Victorian place, gray with white trim and lots of curlicued wood accents like so many others on this street arched by oaks and elms. Crossing the five steps to the lace-curtain door, Ivy pushed the bell and waited.

A short, white-haired lady with unusually thick eye glasses answered. "Yes, young lady, what is it that you want?"

"I understand you have a furnished flat to let," said Ivy. "Rivka Sherman at the bookstore sent me round."

"They're actually single rooms, two of them up on the third floor. Both have been empty for awhile. I had trouble with my last tenant. I'm not anxious to rent to just anyone."

"My name is Ivy Cohen, and I've only been in America a short time. Mrs. Sherman also hired me to work in the bookstore."

"Well, then, my name is Irma Riley, Mrs. Irma Riley. There isn't any Mr. Riley anymore. He passed on, nine years this August."

"I'm sorry, it must be terribly lonely for you," offered Ivy.

"That's life. You sound British. Educated British?"

"Yes, ma'am. I have a degree in English literature."

"I guess you look fit enough to climb two flights of stairs

several times a day."

"Is it at all private up there?" Ivy asked.

"Perfectly private," Irma assured her. "I rarely go to the third floor in my condition. So you'll have to clean up properly after yourself and send your laundry out. I'll provide two sets of linens and such. Bathroom's got a combination tub and shower. No meals in the room and no cooking. I won't tolerate a smelly house and I can't abide someone else's food in my refrigerator."

"Would I have to share the bath with a stranger if you rented the second room?"

"Possibly, but it's not likely that I'll rent the second room. It's never happened before—both rooms being rented at the same time, that is."

Ivy followed as Mrs. Riley laboriously climbed the two flights of stairs. She looked at both rooms, but immediately preferred the larger one that faced the rear of the house. "I'll take this one if your rent is fair enough. I can't afford very much right now."

At first, Irma regarded Ivy with a cautious look, then softened. "Normally, I charge $235 a month, but because I like you, you can have it for $200, and I'll want one month's deposit in advance from you."

"Done," said Ivy with excitement in her voice. "You're just being so nice."

"Would you care to join me in a cup of tea?" said Irma as she hobbled down the stairs to the living room.

"That would be lovely," replied Ivy. "And here I thought everyone in America only drank coffee."

"Not everyone," said Irma as she motioned Ivy to follow her to a seat at the kitchen table. She donned an apron, put a copper-bottom kettle on the stove to heat, and set a pair of flowered mugs on the table. "There's a selection of tea bags in the covered bowl in front of you. Take an Earl Grey out for me, please."

Ivy selected the tea bags, then removed a checkbook and pen from her purse. "By the way, will a personal check do?"

"A local bank?"

"I'm afraid not." Ivy hesitated. "But it's a major London bank, Barclays. It might take an extra week for the check to clear but they're secure and good for it, ma'am."

"I suppose so," agreed Irma. "Go ahead and write it, Ivy. That's $400 even."

The kettle screamed, and Irma poured the hot water while Ivy finished writing the check. Irma scrutinized it and tucked it into her apron pocket. As the submerged tea steeped in their mugs, Ivy inquired about the trouble Irma had with her previous lodger. The landlady took a deep breath as though ready to start a major epic.

"Didn't Mrs. Sherman tell you about her ordeal?" She set a plate of sugar cookies in front of Ivy.

"I'm afraid not. We only met this morning," said Ivy munching on a cookie. It was one-thirty, and she hadn't had anything since breakfast.

"Well, my sister Agnes was having an operation, and I had to go up to Albany and take care of her during recuperation. I'd been gone two weeks when it all happened."

"What happened?" asked Ivy at the edge of her seat.

"Mr. Kravitz, my lodger, went absolutely berserk and kidnapped Mrs. Sherman right out of her own backyard. Kept her hostage in my bedroom. Tied her up in *my* bed, mind you. Messed up the whole house—blood, lipstick, and junk all over the place. Threatened to kill her, too, if she didn't tell him about some artifacts that belong to a museum. The police told me he had already killed some professor in England to get a hold of those things. Anyway, as I understand it, he escaped to Savannah, Georgia, taking Mrs. Sherman with him. She was all bound and gagged and everything."

"Please go on," Ivy urged. "How did Rivka get free?"

"I guess Kravitz must have let her go. I don't really know the end of the story. You'll have to ask the Shermans that."

Ivy gulped the last of her tea. "Oh-oh, it's two-twenty already. I have to get my things from the motel before checkout time. I can't afford to get charged for another day. I'm assuming I can move in right away?"

"Yes," said Irma. "That will be fine."

"Thank you," Ivy called over shoulder as she fled through the front door.

* * * *

At five minutes to six that evening the doorbell rang upstairs in the Sherman kitchen. Rivka was sliding two pre-roasted, store-bought chickens in the oven to re-heat. "Dan, could you answer that, please?" Dan bounded down two flights to The Dungeon level, where the sci-fi, fantasy, and horror fiction resided amid *trompe l'oeil* doors, tunnels, spider webs, and ladders. He opened the door for Ivy and introduced himself. She followed him upstairs into a large reading room at the next level. A massive dark wooden table nearly filled the room. Permanent scratches, nicks, and dents lived within its otherwise slick surface, attesting to its long literary service. It was flanked on two sides by travel bookshelves and related posters. One end faced the wide-open Sherman kitchen, and a three-panel bay window overlooking the street occupied the other. Shorter bookcases under the window extended the travel materials. The aroma of roast chicken abounded.

"Yum!" said Ivy. "Everything smells so delicious."

Dan pulled back one of the fourteen non-matching, upright chairs for Ivy. She exchanged smiles and "Hi" signs with Rivka who remained busy in the kitchen. A linen tablecloth covered only a quarter of the monster table. There were three places set, complete with wineglasses. A colorful napkin covered yet another plate with a hint of shiny egg-bread challah showing at one end. A crystal decanter and two silver candlesticks with short candles stood beside it.

Dan took his seat at the head of the table. Rivka hung up her apron and joined them. Still standing, she lit both candles and, covering her eyes, recited the blessing in Hebrew and then in English. "Praised be thou, eternal God, ever-present in our lives, who has sanctified us by thy commandments and commanded us to kindle the lights of *Shabbat*. May the lights bring you Sabbath peace. May the lights bring you Sabbath joy. Amen." Dan mouthed the words to himself. Halfway through, Ivy joined them. Then Dan stood and led them in singing the *Kiddish*, the blessing thanking God for the fruit of the vine. Afterward, he placed two hands on the challah and everyone sang the *Motzi*, the blessing thanking God for the bread. He ripped a chunk of challah from one end and tore it into three pieces, two of which he distributed to the two women. Rivka chewed hers on the way back to the oven.

"Rivka tells me you've transplanted yourself all the way from London to confront your birth father. I'd say that required a good deal of courage on both counts."

Ivy's breath caught in her throat. Her new employer's blunt remark startled her. Were all Americans so outspoken? The English didn't talk that way. They circled around, hinted, implied, hemmed and hawed—which she'd often considered an annoying national trait.

"I don't think of myself as courageous," she said. "But thank you for the compliment. About moving here, I mean. It's just that I relied on my foster parents for so many years that I didn't want to be a burden to them any longer. Wayne and Janice have two of their own sons they still have to put through college. Coming to the States seemed to be a way to make a clean break of it."

"Did you leave on good terms?"

"Oh, yes, the best of terms. They're a loving family."

One by one Rivka transported bowls of hot chicken soup with rice to each place setting and then occupied the chair closest to the kitchen. "Did Irma Riley fix you up with a room okay?"

"Oh, yes." Ivy replied after a few sips of delicious thick soup. "On the third floor. My room overlooks the rear of the bookstore. In fact, all the backyards on the block, including some lovely gardens."

"What did you think of Mrs. Riley?" asked Dan.

"Nice. Quite chatty. I sense that she's a bit lonely."

"Anything of particular interest?" Dan prodded further as he spooned up his soup.

"She complained a lot—something about a former tenant and that she would never rent to a strange man again."

"Did she explain what that was all about?" asked Dan.

"You stop that right now, Daniel Sherman," Rivka burst in. "She doesn't need to know about Emil."

"Who's Emil?" stammered Ivy.

"See what you've gone and done now, Daniel?" cried Rivka, gathering the empty soup plates and heading into the kitchen. "Now you'll have to tell her."

"Tell her what?" Dan called after her. "You're the one who mentioned his name." Then turning to Ivy, "Whenever Rivka's angry with me, she calls me Daniel."

Rivka stuck her tongue out at him and returned to the table with a platter conveying juicy, brown chicken quarters.

"Are you going to tell me who Emil is or not?" asked Ivy.

*Aggressiveness again*, Rivka thought as she set down platters of steamed carrots and parsley-buttered potatoes. "Was," said Rivka. "He's dead now." She forked a quarter roasted chicken part into each of their plates and took her seat. "Sure he'll tell you. He'd better, if he knows what's good for him."

Dan didn't reply immediately. He was always blindsided by her sudden mood changes; at this moment, the edge of bitterness in his wife's tone. It cropped up occasionally, unexpectedly now, since the kidnapping. With his keen sensitivity, he recognized that no one, not even his plucky Rivka, could emerge from those terrifying days without aftershocks. He passed the potatoes to Ivy and helped himself to the carrots. "Emil Kravitz was a vicious murderer, thief, and kidnapper, who disrupted our lives for several weeks last spring. He killed one of your countrymen in Bath and kidnapped my wife for four days. All of this in order to get his hands on some print-founding artifacts."

"Print-founding?" Ivy parroted.

"It's how old-time printers manufactured the tiny moveable type characters they used in books and newspapers," Rivka explained.

"It must have been terrible," said Ivy, "being kidnapped, I mean." She tried to tread lightly, careful not to reveal how much Mrs. Riley had already told her. But she wanted very much to hear all the ugly details.

"It was, especially in the beginning. He drugged me, tied me up, and left me on the floor. Later on, he began to trust me some and made things somewhat easier, but it was no picnic, I assure you."

"What happened to him?" Ivy persisted, forking a chunk of chicken thigh.

"When the police had him surrounded, he chose not to give up and stepped into their line-of-fire without a weapon," replied Dan.

"Where are these relics now?" Ivy inquired.

"The murdered man had bequeathed them to the British Literary Museum, along with some rare academic tomes," replied Dan. "So that's where they are. Thank God it all ended well."

"Rivka, I think you were very brave. I can't begin to imagine what you went through," Ivy murmured with a bite of drumstick tucked in her cheek.

Rivka went silent, anxious to change the subject. "So, Ivy, how do you propose to go about finding your birth father?"

"I'm not sure. I'm afraid I'm counting on too much."

"On too much what?" Rivka asked.

Ivy was almost wishing she hadn't started this conversation. "On getting the right reaction out of him when he sees me for the first time. You see, my mother and I look very much alike." She fumbled around in her purse and extracted a remarkably clear photo of her mother. She handed it to Rivka, who then passed it to Dan.

"Wow, I see what you mean," Rivka said. "What a likeness."

"I could swear that's a picture of you," agreed Dan. "I don't know quite how to put this, but your method sounds a little on the lame side." He handed back the photo. "You might not be aware of that first encounter. How would he know you're in Annapolis? Let's say he does know. What if he sees you first and takes evasive action? What if the man has already moved on?"

"That's what I'm afraid of." A prominent tear trickled down Ivy's cheek, and she dabbed at it with her forefinger. "But it's all I have to go on right now." A second and third tear appeared.

"There, there, dear." Rivka reached out and patted their guest's arm. "Perhaps Dan could help with your search. As you can tell, he has great detective instincts. Without him, the FBI could never have rescued me."

Ivy's fair complexion turned scarlet. Her blue-gray eyes clouded over with confusion and anxiety. How would her host and hostess—her new employers—take what she was about to reveal? Would it queer their relationship, especially after the trauma that Rivka had been through? *Will I lose my new job before it even begins?* Her heart seemed to suspend its beats. Then she plunged ahead as if diving into an icy lake. "I'm afraid I haven't told you the whole story. It's painful for me. But I guess I can't avoid it. My mother was murdered when I was three months old. The police never found the killer."

The Shermans sat frozen in their chairs for a few moments. Dan broke the silence, framing his reply with an engineer's logic, based on the profession he had only recently left. "That's terrible. How old are you?"

"Twenty-three."

"So it's a twenty-three-year-old cold case. But what made you target Annapolis in the first place?"

Ivy, looking sparrow-like in the tall Victorian chair, knew she'd opened Pandora's box. The details came pouring out. "The police searched my mum's apartment, every nook and cranny, every drawer. They found some gift boxes—personal stuff like lingerie—with wrappings from stores here in Annapolis. And . . . they found Mum's daily journal, very detailed, written in her lovely script. It revealed that her lover, my birth father, intended to move to Annapolis to work in a brand-new family business venture with several other family members. The only other clue I have is that he was Jewish."

"How do you know that?" Rivka asked.

"The diary has some references. They lit Chanukah candles together, and at Pesach, they went to a Seder at the synagogue."

Dan glanced at his wife. Rivka's curly bangs, impudent and unruly, nearly touched her wire-rimmed glasses, hiding the frown on her high forehead. He knew her so well, he could almost see the gears meshing in her overactive brain cells; they never shut off, even while she slept. He rather worried at what was coming next, and with good reason.

"Ivy," she said softly, "how do you know your mother's lover is also your birth father? What if she had some kind of fling, like a one-night stand?"

Dan groaned inwardly.

Ivy bristled. She drew her cable-knit sweater tightly around her slight body, as if to fend off the onslaught of questions. "My mother would never have done such a thing. The journal proves it. Her lover was the only one she ever mentioned, and she wrote about him almost every day, obsessively."

"Oh, dear," Rivka said. "I apologize. I'm not trying to give you the third degree. Sometimes my imagination goes overboard."

"Are there dates in your mother's journal?" asked Dan.

"Oh, yes—a good deal more than your ordinary diary."

"Do you still have this journal?" asked Dan.

Ivy sighed. "No. It's so frustrating. Scotland Yard still has it. They allowed me to copy from it, but they wouldn't let me take it because it's still evidence in an open case. Also, there wasn't a last will and testament, so they couldn't release the diary to me or anyone else, even after twenty-three years."

"Just maybe," said Dan, "I can get a photocopy of the entire diary made and sent here."

"And how would you go about accomplishing that miracle?" asked Rivka.

"Well, now, the good constable or his chief inspector just might be grateful enough for our help in solving Abner's murder last spring to come to our assistance in this matter. Also, it might lead to closing one of their own cold cases."

A small smile crept across Ivy's face with the arrival of new hope. Dinner ended with babka, a pound cake filled with chocolate chips and diced apples. Ivy helped clear the table; Rivka loaded the dishwasher; Dan stored the leftovers in the fridge.

It was time to leave for temple. Ivy declined the offer to accompany them. She was too exhausted—from the day and her revelations. At The Dungeon door Dan called after her, "We open at nine. See you tomorrow."

Chapter 3

## Register, Books, and Aisles
Saturday, October 15th

At twenty minutes to nine, Ivy showed up. She found The Dungeon door locked and the lights out on the next floor. She knew she was early, but wanted to make a good impression on her first day of work. *Do I ring the doorbell and disturb their breakfast or do I wait it out here?* She decided to wait and sat down on the steps leading up to the veranda. Ten minutes later she heard the massive door of The Dungeon being unbolted and swung back on its rusty hinges. It sounded like a crypt being opened for the first time in a century.

"Hello," she called. "May I come in now?"

"Who's there?" said Daniel poking his head out the door. There was no one in his line of sight. "We're officially not open 'til nine."

"Ivy Cohen," she replied, coming around the end of the staircase banister. "I'm ready to start work, Mr. Sherman."

"Come on in, Ivy. I'm glad you're punctual. You can call me Dan. We don't stand on ceremony here. Rivka's upstairs doing the breakfast dishes and tidying up a bit. You wouldn't happen to know how to ring up a sale by any chance?"

"I worked in a confectioner's shop one summer at home. I

suppose it's quite a lot like that." She followed him around to the cashier's counter and stood behind him.

Dan grabbed a random book off the shelf behind him. "Then you evidently know how to use the cash register." He waited for her to nod her ascent and picked up the bar-code scanner. "Ever use one of these?"

Ivy shook her head and watched him wave the scanner wand over the coded portion of the book's rear cover. The title, ISBN number, author, locator code, list price, discount, tax, and total appeared on the computerized register's plasma screen. A blinking reminder of "CASH OR CHARGE" also appeared.

"The ISBN number is some kind of stock inventory number, isn't it?" she asked.

"ISBN stands for International Standard Book Number. It's a unique numeric commercial book identifier based upon either a ten or thirteen-digit code," Dan replied. "The ten-digit code is older. The potential sale doesn't actually ring up until you either swipe a credit card across the reader like this or hit the ENTER key." He demonstrated with successive waves of his hand. "The printer will knock out two identical copies of the sales slip. One always goes in the bag with the purchase. We keep the second one on the printer roll. If it's a charge, you then get the customer to sign the credit receipt. The credit blanks are under  the counter right here. The original and one copy of the credit receipt go into the metal box here." He pointed to the green cashbox with a lid. "The remaining copy goes to the customer."

Then Daniel hit the CANCEL TRANSACTION key, and the screen went into its screen saver mode. "Think you can handle that, Ivy?"

"Looks easy enough, Mr. Sher . . . Dan."

"Good! It's extremely important that you learn to find your way around the store. Not only will you be expected to assist customers in finding what they're looking for, you'll need to stock and restock the shelves so that everyone can find books on their own."

"Restock?" questioned Ivy.

"Yes, people take books and periodicals into the reading rooms and leave them there. We prefer they don't return them, as they are easily misplaced on the shelves. We have a library cart for that purpose. It's parked next to the stairs. You can load it and run up and down the aisles with it."

"What system do you have for locating books?" she asked. "Is it like a lending library?"

"In some ways similar, but we've added our own innovations. As soon as Rivka comes down, she can walk you through the whole scheme and the store as well."

"If a customer has a title and/or genre I don't recognize, how do I know where to look for it?" she asked.

"Type in the title, ISBN, or principal author if it's a coauthored book: last name first; and look for the locator code on the screen. It will generally get you a list of books and their locator codes. The leading number of the locator code, one through four, is the floor it's on. The letters, A through D, following that indicate the room it's in. The front room facing the street is always A. Then B, C, and D clockwise from A."

"Wait," she said, as she fumbled through her purse for a little spiral notepad. "I need to get all of this down on paper." She began to write furiously. "Right."

"The next two digits give you the stacks, clockwise around the perimeter of the room starting at the door; then parallel stacks in the middle of the room, again with the numbers continuing from near the door. The final three letters are acronyms for the genres. For example, MUR is murder, SHK is Shakespeare, NOF is nonfiction, REF is reference, ROM is romance, and so forth. Once you're there, the stack is arranged by authors' last names and then titles." He pulled a sheet of paper from the drawer under the counter and said, "This is what I use as a cheat sheet."

Ivy took the sheet from him, walked to the nearest stack, and checked out the small rectangular labels on the book spine. She used the sheet to translate the five-digit code found on the label. She smiled.

"Eureka, it works," he said observing her expression.

They heard Rivka bouncing down the stairs into the aisle where Ivy stood. "Good morning, Ivy. Ready to get started?" She waited for the nod and continued. "Let's take a fifty-cent tour of the store. And, by the way, our dinner table last night? That's actually the official table where our mystery critique group meets. A bunch of us get together every Thursday evening to exchange manuscript drafts, story ideas, and helpful hints on writing and getting published. We read aloud from our new work, too. Dan is the current leader." Rivka's voice grew more animated. "You're welcome to join us. Especially if you have a story in progress. The atmosphere is quite tame, and we tend to be more helpful than critical."

Ivy's face lit up. "I'd love to. I've started a story and I'd like an opinion on it."

"All the more reason to join us," Rivka said. She grabbed her purse from under the counter. "I've got a short errand to run, and Dan's on the second floor repairing the magazine stand. Think you can handle the store while I'm gone?"

Ivy nodded eagerly. "It's all quite under control. Besides, Dan just finished giving me a smashing good lesson on the register this morning—before you came down. So don't you worry."

*Maybe 'smashing' isn't the best choice of words*, Rivka thought. "If Dan asks, tell him I went to the drugstore."

* * * *

Phil's Pharmacy still had that old-time corner drugstore charm: a soda fountain; two wrought-iron tables with matching chairs; a candy case complete with tilted, wide-mouth jars and scoops; magazines and out-of-town newspapers. Rivka entered and went directly to the pharmacy window. She laid her prescription on the counter in front of Phil Papas, the pharmacist.

"Hi, Rivka," he said. "How are you?" He picked up the prescription and read it. "Should be ready in about thirty minutes. Do you want to wait or stop by later?"

"I'll wait, Phil. I want to get a few personal things from the shelves."

Rivka turned and started down the nearest aisle. About half-way through the cough-and-cold aisle, she noticed a woman with long, auburn hair, reading the label on a box of cough syrup.

"Heather Germain," said Rivka. "What are you doing out of school?"

"Actually, it's Saturday, but I'd be taking a day of sick leave anyway. I have this cough that sounds like a bull moose bark. It's distracting in the classroom. The kids probably won't learn any *Français* with a substitute, *mais c'est la vie.* Maybe this will help my cough."

"Then you surely have time for a cup of coffee, you gold-bricker, you."

"I suppose so," said Heather. "We can sit at one of the tables at the front of the store and let Merry fix us a brew. Maybe I should have hot tea instead. Better for my cough."

Phil's wife took their orders at one of the glass-topped wrought-iron tables.

"I got some good news on Friday," said Rivka, squirming her pear-shape figure to a more comfortable position on the hard chair.

"Good grief, Rivka, don't tell me you've gone and gotten yourself pregnant at your age?"

"No, no, nothing like that," she chuckled. "Do you remember the short story I wrote last February? The one with the mother-in-law and the son's nagging wife?"

"The one where the old gal gets her sweet revenge in the end?"

"Yeah, that's the one," said Rivka. "Prune Ink Press is going to publish it online in their next quarterly edition."

"I liked that story a lot," said Heather. "Do they pay anything?"

"Fifty bucks for five-thousand words. Hey, don't sneer. All donations accepted."

"Congratulations," said Heather. "Maybe I should try them for my stories. By the way, I have a little news, too. You'll never guess who I received an e-mail from yesterday. Constable Sergeant Fenton Thorwal. Can you imagine that? All the way from London?"

"You mean Vernon . . . Vernon Levant?"

"*Oui*, Vernon was the undercover name he used last spring when the police were after the guy who kidnapped you."

Rivka took a long sip of her coffee. "So what did he say in the e-mail?"

"He has some vacation time coming and wants to spend it here in the States with me."

"Apparently, you made quite an impression on the good constable. You never mentioned that you two had something cooking."

"We had a few drinks. Then I . . . that is, we . . ."

A grinning Rivka leaned forward and touched her friend's hand. "So what happened?"

Heather squirmed in her chair. Puckering up her face, her freckles joined in a pout. "You know what? This just isn't a good time. I don't want to talk about it right now."

Rivka's cinnamon eyes narrowed. She hated being left in the dark. "I understand—I think."

The pharmacist approached and set a small white paper bag on the table. "Here's your prescription, Rivka. Have a pleasant day." He returned behind the counter window once more.

"Well, Heather, I'd better get back to the shop." She picked up her coffee cup and drained it.

"Have you found a new clerk yet?"

"As a matter of fact, we have," Rivka said. "She's a quick study, but a little new to leave on her own for long. She's from London, too. Now isn't that a coincidence?"

The two women parted outside the door and each went her own way.

Chapter 4

## Delving In
Tuesday, October 18th

oward the end of an interminable day, Ivy began restocking books and periodicals left out on the reading room tables. Striving to be efficient, she carried far too many at once. Cradling a stack of science fiction books up to her chin, she couldn't look down to see where she was going. Her shoe snagged on a small loop in the carpet seam. Her right arm shot out and grasped a nearby shelf. The stack of books flew out, and within a second or two, one end of the shelf she'd grabbed gave way, thereby thumping Ivy hard on the floor. Only a muffled cry of surprise emerged from her lips. She listened for a moment. No one came running.

Scrambling to her knees in the narrow aisle, Ivy heaped the tumbled books into several piles and proceeded to examine the damaged shelf. The broad board had survived intact, but the pins and pin slots in the vertical panel that supported the shelf had not. A quick search located the two missing pins, but the holes they came from were splintered and would not sustain even the pins alone. She would have to tell Dan. *Good grief, I'm not even here two days, and they're going to dismiss me.*

Just then, Ivy saw Dan pass the end of the aisle. "Dan?"

she called meekly. What surprised her most was that her mentor never asked how it happened. Neither a word nor an emotion. One glance and he disappeared to fetch his toolbox. Returning, Dan removed a small pre-drilled and pre-stained bracket and fastened it to the bookcase side wall over the splintered pin holes, driving home the two screws with a battery-powered drill. In minutes the shelf had a brand new end support. He stayed on to help her re-establish order in the Science Fiction section.

Dan was about to leave her to finish her work when he stopped and turned halfway down the aisle. "See me when your finished. I'd like to have a talk with you."

*Oh God,* she thought. *Here it comes. He's about to give me the sack. Why do I have to be so dreadfully clumsy?*

Ivy finished the overall restacking, this time using the tea cart. It was nearly six o'clock. She found Dan doing the daily cash-out at the register.

"Here, have a seat. I'll be finished in a minute."

He finally turned to face her once more. "I've been doing a lot of thinking about your situation."

"Please don't give me the sack. It was an accident and, really, none of the books were damaged."

"Whoa, there," he said. "It's nothing of the sort. I wasn't talking about firing you. Collapsing bookcases occur all the time and are easily fixed. A good bookstore clerk is hard to find. No, I was thinking more about the search for your birth father."

She sighed with relief. "I'm so grateful, Dan. I do love working here. Have you found out anything yet?"

"Of course not. I did go through the envelope you gave me, but I haven't had a chance to act on any of it. First of all, I'd like to contact the detective in charge of your mother's case and see what I can get from him. Do you happen to remember his name?"

"Of course I do," she replied. "It was Homicide Inspector Jervis Harvey."

"How old a man was he? Do you think he'd still be on the force?"

She thought for a minute. "I'm not a good judge of age, but I'd venture to say mid-forties. The man was clean-shaven, a bit on the portly side, but he seemed pretty spry."

"Do you know which police precinct or district he came from?" asked Dan.

"Devon Court was in the county of London district. That's not the same as the city of London district. I assume that's where he came from. It's all part of Scotland Yard, though."

"Good," Dan said. "I plan to call first thing in the morning and try to locate the man. If you have any questions for him or insights for me, let me know beforehand."

* * * *

"G'morning," Dan greeted Ivy at the cashier's counter with his hand over the telephone mouthpiece. "I've been on the damn phone with London for almost an hour trying to locate your Inspector Harvey. I just found out the man retired eighteen months ago. I'm ringing up his home in Brighton now. Ah!"

"Inspector Jervis Harvey? . . . I've had a hard time reaching you and just learned that you're retired. My name is Daniel Sherman and I'm calling from Annapolis, Maryland. I'm assisting Ms. Ivy Cohen in trying to learn more about her mother's brutal murder case, specifically, why the case went cold. Nothing official. Just acting on behalf of a friend. . . .That's good of you. Of course I'll wait."

"He's gone to get his personal notes," prompted Dan with his hand over the mouthpiece.

"Yes, Inspector." Dan spoke in a raised voice at first, repeating everything the inspector said for Ivy's benefit. "You concluded from the victim's diary that the killer, a lover she referred to only as Snooks, would have fled the country, most likely to Annapolis. But without a proper name or description, there was little else to trace."....But Dan quickly realized how annoying this process must be for the inspector. With a legal-size yellow pad in front of him on the desk, he began furiously taking notes. After fifteen minutes, he said, "I appreciate all this information, Inspector. Thank you very much for your help."

After hanging up, Dan swung around in the swivel chair and faced Ivy, relaying everything he'd learned, checking his notes often. Her small body sat ramrod straight at attention, so tense she looked like she might break in half. He spoke softly, gently. "The crime scene had been wiped clean, no fingerprints, nothing, except for the victim herself. As for the presents, the police checked the store wrappings and logos on the boxes and looked for register receipts. Inspector Harvey said the gifts came from two stores in Annapolis, both on Main Street. Both were cash sales. One was lingerie, a teddy, but the sales slip proved unintelligible. The other gifts were a black dress and purse from Brenda's Dress Shop, but with no corresponding sales slip." He paused, studying his jumbled handwriting. "Then I asked Inspector Harvey if they'd found out anything from Passport Control. He said literally thousands leave England daily, and without a name, a description, or an exact date there was no way to cull those lists."

Ivy asked, "Did he say how long they kept the case open?" "Yeah," said Dan. "Six months, and then it went cold for lack of information." His demeanor and voice brightened. "Hey, don't get discouraged. I have some other avenues to explore. Boy, Rivka sure is going to be ticked with me for spending so much on phone calls. Maybe we should get to work and sell a few books to pay for them." He winked at her.

* * * *

Dan checked out the scrap of paper he'd slipped into the folds of his wallet. He wanted to be sure he had the correct address on State Circle, a tight thoroughfare that ringed the oldest U.S. state capitol building still in use. He was a tad early for his 1:30 appointment with Joel Wise, so he took a few minutes to absorb the capitol's sunlit green and impressive white colonial-era architecture across the street. He shaded his eyes as he looked up at the scaffolding surrounding the dome and the brave men working up there. After another glance at his watch, he spun around to the red-brick brownstone and climbed the steps to Joel's second-floor office.

"Good morning, Mr. Sherman. Mr. Wise will be with you in a few minutes," said the matronly secretary.

"And a good, good morning to you," Dan said. A smiling Joel opened the door to his inner sanctum and motioned Dan in. The two old friends shook hands and sat—Joel behind the desk and Dan in an armchair purposely pulled in next to him.

Joel slid out a single sheet of paper from a green file folder and handed it to Dan. It was a list of family names, dates, and addresses. "I had my secretary spend a whole morning down at the courthouse archives looking through the real estate tax records. It amounts to three billable hours at her rate of $75 per hour, but I'll only charge you for two. She went with the March 3rd, 1982 date you gave me and did a search, spanning three years before and one year after that date to produce this list. An entry had to appear on the rolls for the *first* time in the '79 through '83 tax year, but not before or after."

Dan took out his checkbook, filled in the amount, and signed it. He handed the check to Joel. Scanning the list for himself, he recognized the name Reubens right off: Herschel, Meyer, and their business in the '82 tax year. He also knew Leo Schwartz and Abe Guzeman. Only two names appeared in the '81 rolls. Four additional names appeared in '82 and three more in the following year. Dan knew he could eliminate some of these, but thought it would be better if he and Rivka did it together.

Joel's next appointment had arrived. They said their good-byes.

* * * *

"Rivka?" Dan called.

"I'm right here," she replied from a nearby aisle. "Where have you been hiding since lunch?"

"I had an idea, so I went to see Joel Wise."

"So what's your idea? And why did we need his legal services?"

"Well, Joel had his secretary scour the tax rolls for new payers a few years before and after the March 3rd date, the day Ivy said her mother was murdered." He held a folded sheet of paper, but before he had a chance to open it, Rivka interrupted.

"Wait just a cotton-picking minute, Buster. And Joel had her do this out of the goodness of his heart?"

"Not exactly. She was at it a whole morning, but he only billed us for two hours."

"How much, Dan, how much?"

"A hundred fifty."

"You realize we didn't take in that much all day yesterday."

"So we had a bad day. We took in ten times that last Monday."

"Just deduct it from my salary," came Ivy's voice from the cashier's counter. "Oops! I couldn't help overhearing."

"No problem," Rivka called back, then murmured, "Sorry, hon, I shouldn't go off the deep end like that."

He gave her a squeeze. "It's okay, Rivvie."

"So what did this hundred fifty buy us?"

"A bunch of names and addresses that just might narrow the field on who killed Lainee Cohen." He spread out the page on the table before them. "Maybe you can help me eliminate some of these people. Excluding the large supermarkets and big chains, there were only five new businesses started during that period. I think we can eliminate Sue's Card Shop. She's a sole proprietor."

"And Mike's Bar and Grille," said Rivka. "Mike and Sally are long-time Annapolitans. And Marie's Style Salon, that's an all-female operation."

"What about The Smoke Shop? Rivka, do you know anything about that?"

"That's the little place off Church Circle, but I can't imagine it being a family business."

"I guess I'll have to put my money on the Reubens Brothers Electrical Merchandising Company. Herschel and Meyer Reubens, plus Leo Schwartz and Arnold Katz. From these names we might assume Snooks is Jewish."

"At least it appears so. What about the individual names,

hon?"

Dan read the first name on the private rolls. "1979: Lazarus, G.A."

"Yeah, that's Gilbert Lazarus's. I had a class with him once. I think he's gay."

"What's that got to do with anything?"

"Just that gay men seldom keep mistresses, Dan. Who's next?"

"1979: Potts, L.L. I bet that's Loretta Potts who runs Plants and Potts over on West Street. The next one in 1979 is Morgan, S.E."

"Dan, I know Stan Morgan from the post office. I bring him all our packages for mailing."

"Well, Rivvie, there are two in 1980: a Portnoy, P.E. and a McCarthy, J.J., and Patricia Portnoy is a customer of ours. You know, the roly-poly woman with the ten-year-old, Holly."

"I remember the little girl very well. She's a cutie and so polite, too. The mother is kinda quiet and reserved. They usually hang out in the children's reading room. I don't know anything about a J.J. McCarthy, though."

"Nor I," said Dan. "There are two more in 1981: a Benjamine, M.A. and a Wilson T.J. I don't recognize either name."

"What about '82?" asked Rivka.

"Well, there are the Reubens—Hersch and Meyer—and Leo Schwartz as expected, and Abe Guezman, who died last year, but I expected Arnold Katz's name to be there, too."

"He must have come later," Rivka said. "But Abe was in his nineties, so I think we can eliminate him."

"Yeah," Dan agreed. "In '83 there's Stash Walenski, who I know from flag football and a Maxwelly. That's the end of the list. That leaves four unresolved names: Maxwelly, P.J.; McCarthy, J.J.; Benjamine, M.A.; and a Wilson, T.J. Where are you going, Rivvie?"

Rivka slipped out to the cashier's counter, retrieved the phone directory, and returned to the reading room. Flipping through the pages, she declared that two of the four names, Max-welly and Benjamine, were unique in the Annapolis directory and could be eliminated.

Dan shook his head. "Uh-uh. Two reasons. One, not all the owners of a family business need have the same last name. And two, not all of them need to live within the coverage of the phone book. I'm afraid we're stuck with four unresolved names until we find another criterion to eliminate them."

"Rivka? Dan? Could I have a little help in here, please!" It was Ivy calling to them. Business had picked up.

Without saying it aloud, both husband and wife were hoping they hadn't hit a dead end.

# Chapter 5

## Bad Break
Thursday, October 20th

hursday morning. Irma Riley had been using the feather duster to rearrange the dust on her furniture when she heard the doorbell ring. *Don't tell me Ivy forgot her key.*

"Hi, Mrs. Riley," said the youngster in a Yankees cap. "It's that time of the month again. Twenty-six weekdays at fifty cents and five Sundays at a buck fifty each. That's $20.50."

"Oh, my goodness. Wally Frazer. Wipe your feet and step inside on this little throw rug while I fetch my purse from upstairs. I can't have you tracking dirt into my front hall, can I?"

Wally, knowing Irma and the drill, religiously followed her orders. She laboriously climbed the steps, fetched her purse from atop her dresser, and turned to retrace her steps. On the third stair from the top, the heel of her shoe snagged on the stair-runner carpeting, causing her to tumble, twisting mostly sideways, down to the front hall. Near the last steps, her right leg got caught up under her midsection. She felt a snapping sensation. Then nothing. She passed out.

Irma lay unconscious for only a few moments, but when she awoke, Wally stood above her with a glass of water. "Kin I help ya, Mrs. Riley? Are you okay, ma'am?"

"No," she whispered. "The pain's excruciating." Wally helped her roll off the twisted leg and tried to straighten it into a less critical position. Irma shrieked, blubbering complaints, epithets, and instructions. He finally comprehended enough to sit her back against the railed balusters, dove for the landline phone on the little table across the room, and called 911.

Two paramedics arrived shortly and collected her vital signs. They determined they were dealing with a broken leg, but no internal bleeding. In three minutes they'd immobilized her in a mesh body basket ready for transit. Wally stood by and watched as they carried Mrs. Riley out the door, down the steps, and into the back of the ambulance. His eyes followed the vehicle as it sped away from the house. Returning to the scene of the fall, he collected all the items that had spilled from her dumped purse and tucked them back in. He considered extracting the money she owed him from her wallet, but then thought better of it. He could be accused of taking more than he was entitled to. Wally looked around once more before turning out the lights and locking the door. He had other customers to collect from.

* * * *

Rivka untied the string of her blue smock and glanced over at her new assistant collecting magazines from three tables. "Are you coming tonight, Ivy?"

"Tonight? What's tonight?"

"It's the mystery writers' critique group. We meet every Thursday at seven o'clock upstairs in the reading room. Won't you join us?"

"Oh, yes," replied Ivy. "Would there be time enough for me to read something I've written?"

"Perhaps," said Rivka. "Let's see, Dan's reading a chapter from his hardboiled detective novel. Then there's Frieda with her horseracing mystery; her chapters are short. Yes, there should be time. They're the only two readers scheduled. You can grab a bite with us upstairs, if you like. We're only having sandwiches. You can choose from tuna, Swiss and cheddar cheese, lox, and chopped egg.

There's lettuce and tomato, and we have borscht to drink."

"Oh, Rivka, I'd love to. You've both been like family to me, and to think I've been here less than a week."

"We're just pleased that you're working out so well. You've latched onto every aspect of the job. A member of the family couldn't have fit into the picture any better. Dan says I'm acting like a mother hen with you. I guess it's because we don't get to see our children and grandchildren that often."

The phone rang and Ivy answered. "Olde Victorian Bookstore—how may I help you?" She listened for a long time and said, "Yes, I will," then slowly returned the phone to its cradle.

Rivka came hurrying down the aisle toward her. "What's wrong, girl? You look so serious."

"That was Anne Arundel Medical Center. Mrs. Riley fell down the stairs and broke her leg. They've set it, but they're keeping her overnight just to be careful. A social worker called and asked me to bring a few things for her. She wants her own nightgown and bathrobe. Toothbrush, too. Apparently, the paperboy was there at the time and he called the ambulance."

"Poor Irma," said Rivka. "You run along."

"I'll be here tonight. I might be late, but please save me some reading time." Ivy grabbed her purse from under the register and rushed out.

Dan suddenly popped up behind his wife.

"So what've you been doing this morning, hon?" she asked.

He pumped up the desk chair at the counter to suit his long legs. "I've been trying to figure out a way to get hold of Lainee's diary. You know, Ivy's mother's diary. If we're going to be of any help in finding Ivy's father, we'll need it."

"Uh-huh! Now you're sticking your nose deeper into someone else's business. I admit I'm as curious as you are, but I wonder if it's taking us away from time we could be spending together or even time when we could be doing our own writing."

Dan crossed his arms over his chest. His hazel eyes met hers in dead seriousness. "Think of it this way, Rivvie. We're mystery writers. You're getting close to starting your own novel. Helping Ivy? This is real life, babe, and if we succeed in helping her find her father—and maybe eventually even the murderer—for crime writers it doesn't get any better than that." He raised one bushy eyebrow. "Does it?"

Rivka's round cheeks flushed as she allowed herself a surrendering smile. "You're right. I guess I've let myself get too obsessed with making a success of this place."

"It's our first year, hon. We're doing pretty well. Now . . . I tried several times today to reach that British Chief Inspector we spoke with last year."

"Correction, dear, *you* spoke with him. Remember, at the time I was tied up in a car on the way to Savannah. But wasn't it Winston or something like that?"

"Oh, jeez. Sorry, babe.  But you're right. It was Chief Inspector E. Howard Winston I spoke with. The number isn't his anymore, and no one at the Bath Constabulary seems to know of his current whereabouts."

"You gave it the old college try," she said, opening *Anna Karenina* in her lap. "Maybe you'll think of something else. That reminds me, sweetie. I ran into Heather Germain at Phil's Pharmacy the other day."

"So what's new with Mademoiselle Germain?"

"She's been corresponding with that Thorwal fellow by e-mail. It seems he wants to spend his vacation here with her, and she's a little unsure whether to let him or not."

"Wait, you're not talking about Vernon Levant, the constable from Bath, are you?"

"Yes, dear, I am. But Levant was his undercover name in the investigation of Professor Fraume's murder. His real name is Fenton Thorwal. Constable Sergeant Thorwal."

"I didn't know he had the hots for Heather. What's she doing about it?"

"She didn't say. I don't even know if there's anything going on between them. She got all upset when I asked her for details. Dan, she just shut down. Refused to talk about it," replied Rivka.

"Oh. But, hey! Maybe *he'll* know what happened to the chief inspector."

Chapter 6

**Critique Group Meeting I**
Thursday Evening, October 20th

n the reading room of The Olde Victorian Bookstore, Frieda Forrester read aloud:

. . . . Clara awoke with a start and sought out the clock. 3:10 a.m. Had she heard a noise outside? The sleepy youngster threw back the covers and staggered to the rear window overlooking the unpainted barn and white-fenced corrals. The barn door appeared to be left ajar. Unusual. Had she forgotten to close it after feeding Ginger and Max? She pulled on jeans, tucked in her nightshirt tails, and slipped into her mucking boots. Rumbling down the stairs, she bolted out the back door, just catching it before it slammed and woke the entire household.

Quietly shutting the back door behind her and stepping off the rear veranda, Clara was immediately struck by a thought. *Locked out.* She'd forgotten to unlatch the door. *Oh well,* she reasoned, *I'll sleep with the horses 'til breakfast.* Sliding the barn door shut behind her, she continued into the barn—past the tack room, with its saddles, bridles, and miscellaneous equine accessories—to the two stalls housing Snap Ginger and Grand Max. Max was her father's quarter horse and Ginger was her Morgan. *If the sun cooperates maybe Daddy and I can squeeze in a ride this morning after*

43

*chores.*

Ginger had her head over the stall gate when Clara arrived. After the two hugged, patted, and nuzzled a bit, she grabbed a couple of horse blankets from the tack room and bunched up stray hay into a suitable bed in an unoccupied adjacent stall. The youngster fell asleep quickly and would have slept until the neighbor's rooster crowed, except that she awoke with the sense that someone else was in the barn. She sat up and listened. No, it wasn't the horses. Clara peeked out of the stall and saw that the barn door was open again. She was sure she had closed it this time. Someone else *was* in the barn with her.

Clara's first thought was to hide, so she lay back silently and pulled the top blanket over her head. The prolonged silence broke with two heavy shoes crunching dry hay in the passage between the stalls. The footsteps continued—slow, careful, measured, stopping in front of the stall next door. She heard the clink, the sliding bolt on Ginger's stall lock. Someone was trying to steal her horse. *Who? Why? What can I do about it?* . . . .

#

Frieda gathered up her manuscript pages. "Well, people, what do you think of the ending to Chapter Three of *Ginger's Secret?* I read you the start of it last time."

"So who's the intruder?" asked Arnold.

"You'll find out when Clara does, wise guy," returned Frieda with a half-sneer.

"Good for you, Frieda, keep 'em guessing," said Heather. "Nice suspense. Sounds like the plot is taking shape now."

"Thanks. It's coming a little easier now since *our* three daughters have taken over the chores." Frieda gave Garry Posner's shoulder a playful shove to accent the word *our*. "In case you don't know, Garry and I are engaged. His daughter, Phyllis, will be joining my girls, Marcia and Trudy, after the wedding."

"I hate to be the picky one," said Esther, "but didn't you mention the word *door* quite a number of times? I counted five."

"A door is a door," retorted Frieda. "There's not a lot you can substitute for it. The open barn door is why she goes to the barn in the first place. The locked back door is why she spends the night in the barn. The newly opened barn door explains why she knows there's an intruder."

"Frieda, you don't have to be so defensive. You might try to vary it a little," Esther said. Several agreeing nods around the table snuffed out any other comments for Frieda's horse mystery.

Dan picked up his pages and began to read.

.  .  .  . Patsy worked her way up cobbled Maryland Avenue toward the Statehouse. The petite, dark-haired woman of thirty wore a lightweight camel coat, brown slacks, and deck shoes without sox. Dreamily, she was enjoying her pleasant afternoon walk soaking up downtown Annapolis, yet perceiving nothing in particular. That is, until she saw the silk scarf, awash in stunning pastels, in Fanfair's window. Patsy Worth simply had to have it. She couldn't afford a whole new wardrobe. But around the neck, across one shoulder, or puffed out of a pocket—that little piece of fabric would do wonders for the wardrobe she already had.

So intent on the scarf, Patsy only now noticed the reflected face in the glass next to her own. Georgio Gianetti was stalking her again, despite the restraining order. *My God, what do I have to do to get that man off my back?* she thought. *Should I pay no attention to him, confront him, go to the police, or try to evade him some way?* Deciding to ignore him altogether, she entered Fanfair and sought out a saleswoman. The only one there held a cell phone to her ear, seemingly more an appendage to her body than a useful tool.

Patsy waited patiently for the woman to complete her obviously personal phone call. This was fine with her. She reasoned: the longer the wait, the more likely Georgio would give up his recurring pursuit. Twenty minutes later, Patsy purchased the scarf and confidently left the store with the boutique shopping bag in tow. So enthralled was she with her new purchase that she'd forgotten about Georgio for some minutes. But not for long—slowly, a consciousness of him returned, and tension burrowed deep into her lower back. But her stalker was nowhere to be seen. *Maybe he's given up*, she thought.

Patsy reached State Circle and turned the corner. Briskly, she walked another short block and turned onto Fleet Street, downhill toward the water and away from the capitol building. No sign of him. Patsy kept glancing over her shoulder, each time feeling more secure. At the end of Fleet, she turned right toward Main Street and darted behind the bustling Market House. Something sharp jabbed at her heel. She stopped to lean against the side brick wall of Maria's Italian Restaurant to remove the offending pebble from her deck shoe.

Suddenly she felt heated breath on her neck.

"You shouldn't have called the police on me, Patsy. They came for me at the shop, and as a result, I lost my job. I'm very angry with you. You'll pay for this, you little bitch. I'm not at all through with you yet."

The message left little doubt of Georgio's intent. Patsy knew the man could be vicious. Without looking back, she pushed off the wall and darted toward a nearby street café table, overturning a pair of wrought-iron chairs in her way. Then she sprinted to the corner and out into Main Street, teeming with strolling tourists and locals. And nearly bumper-to-bumper traffic. She urged herself on. *I must get to Kasper Brasse's office. It's only a block away. I can do it.* A car screeched to a halt in front of her, but not before its right fender delivered a heavy thump to her left hip. Patsy bounced into the street, miraculously unhurt, and landed upright on two running feet. Over the curb on the other side, she scrambled uphill at an exhausting pace toward her target. Pushing, shoving, bumping through the lolling throngs, she couldn't afford to be polite. Neither could she take the time to look over her shoulder. But she knew Georgio wasn't far behind. Finally, she saw a shingle hanging from the second-floor office up ahead. Dark wood with gold-filled letters: Kasper Brasse, Discreet Inquiries. Could she make it there? . . .

#

Dan sat down to a round of modest applause. The excerpt was from *Shadows of Fear*, his second Kasper Brasse novel. He was still shopping the first one, hoping to find a publisher, but at least his Kasper Brasse was proving popular with the critique group. In fact, Dan turned out the most work of anyone in the group.

"Dan, why did you have Patsy spend so long in the store?" asked Garry. "It seemed to stop the action, don't you think?"

"I used the time to prolong what the reader wanted to know most at that point. Who is Georgio? Why would he want to harm Patsy, and how would she evade him? It's my attempt to inject a little suspense."

"You built Patsy's anxiety to a peak," said Joel Wise. "I assume she makes it to Brasse's office or there wouldn't be any more novel."

Dan grinned. "You'll just have to wait for the next chapter to find out now, won't you?"

The group heard the front door jingle, and a light set of footsteps ascending to the second floor. Ivy Cohen appeared at the top of the stairs with a brown cardboard accordion file under one arm.

"Hey, everyone," Rivka said from her place at the head of the mammoth antique table. "This is Ivy Cohen. She's our new clerk. She's late of London and eager to join us. Why don't we just go around the table and introduce ourselves."

"Hi, I'm Frieda Forrester," offered the chunky woman with the short, wiry, gray hair. The voice had a friendly rasp to it. In her mid-fifties, she wore an open-collared shirt. "Mostly, I wait tables at the Double T Diner at the other end of West Street. In my spare time when I'm not being a mother, I write horse-related mystery stories."

"Hi there! I'm Garry Posner. That's Garry with two r's. I'm a residential plumber, formerly of Baltimore," said the man with a black GI buzz cut. "I write police procedurals between fixing leaks." Garry, in jeans and blue chambray shirt, put his arm around Frieda and squeezed her shoulders. "And were gonna be married soon."

"Hello, Ivy," piped up the round-faced man with a smile. "Welcome to the fold. I'm Joel Wise, attorney at law. And in case you're so inclined, I've heard all the lawyer jokes." The jacket of his charcoal suit lay open to reveal a vest of many buttons and pockets.

"Oh, and my writing remains a mystery to me. I've got several short stories to my credit that still require some critical tinkering."

"Pleased to meet you, Ivy," said the fortyish busty woman with a studied Goth look. Her ear-length pageboy had blonde and white streaks running through jet-black hair. A rhinestone dog collar encircled a thick neck and rested on an ink-black sweater. "I'm Peggy Fraume and, believe it or not, I'm Garry's half-sister. I've started a historical mystery with a— you guessed it—Gothic twist. Welcome."

"Hi, Ivy. Esther Reubens," said a forty-two-year-old woman with a squared, kindly face. "I also emigrated from London—when I was nineteen, twenty-three years ago. I haven't any writing credentials as yet, but I'm learning an awful lot at these critique meetings. I actually have a story in mind." A jeweled Star of David rested on a stylish print dress buttoned to the neck.

"*Enchanté!* Heather Germain, high-school French teacher," chirped the smiling woman with long auburn hair and a myriad of harmonizing freckles. Even her eyebrows and lashes matched. An emerald-green scarf, the color of her eyes, swirled stylishly around her neck. Full breasts inflated her frilly blouse to its limit. "I write romantic mysteries. My *Mona Vain* will appear in the next on-line issue of *fortheloveofmurder.com.* It's a quarterly e-zine."

"Arnold Katz here," claimed the tall man with the thinning blond crop. "Mostly I play the guitar and write music whenever I get a chance. I did get a story published once in *Ellery Queen Mystery Magazine.* Beginner's luck, everyone tells me, but they're just jealous. I'm hanging out with this talented bunch waiting to get inspired again." His deadpan expression made it difficult to tell whether he was serious or not.

"Katie Silvers here. Former Londoner, formerly related to Esther. After my divorce we remained the best of friends. We still see a lot of each other. I've always written poetry, but now I'm fascinated with the mystery genre, so I intend to get all I can from these meetings until I make the transition. I believe I will start with the short story." The dark-haired, tiny-voiced individual wore a floral blouse and black slacks.

"Hello, everyone," said Ivy, wriggling into the chair between Dan and Katie. "I'm so very glad to be a part of this literary group. Thank you."

"What happened at the hospital, Ivy," asked Rivka. "Is Irma okay?"

"Quite! But the poor woman fell down nearly a full flight of stairs. Her leg is in a fiber cast and will be for the next six months. She's sedated, resting comfortably tonight. They're keeping her overnight."

"That's good news," said Dan. "The old broad could have done a great deal more damage, a woman of her age."

"Stop! Mrs. Riley isn't some old broad," scolded Rivka. "That's disrespectful, Dan. She's our neighbor and she's been through a lot lately. I'm glad you were able to help her, Ivy."

"Yes ma'am, but there is a bit of a problem though."

"What's that, Ivy?"

"Well, Mrs. Riley's going to be out of sorts for the next six weeks. I can do the shopping, tidy up a bit around the house, and I can fix her breakfast and dinner and the like, but it'll be terribly tight to get home and back in a half-hour at noon."

"Don't worry about that. We'll work something out."

"Can't the old penny-pinching magpie afford outside help without enslaving Ivy here? Oops!"

Dan was already sorry for his outburst. The embarrassing stares from the rest of the group were tame compared to the two bolts of lightning that shot from Rivka's eyes. His loving wife looked like she would explode.

"Daniel Sherman, That was a horrible thing to say. I know for a fact that Irma has to watch her pennies. The woman lives on Social Security and what's left of her late husband's pension." She punched him sharply in the ribs with her right elbow.

"Aw, that hurt, woman," Dan said. "Rivvie, why don't we save this private conversation till our critique group friends have gone home. Not that there's anything left to say. I believe Ivy has a contribution she'd like to read. Ivy?"

Rivka reddened, but knew her husband had a point.

Ivy unstrung the accordion file and pulled a sheaf of papers from it. "What I'm about to read is a true story that took place more than twenty years ago. It's about a murder that's never been solved, a true mystery. The victim was my mother, so I have more than a passing interest in seeing this case solved. I have extracted as many facts as I can from her diary and the news media accounts of the police investigation. The rest is a bit of fictionalized filler to make the story readable. Here goes."

<h1 style="text-align:center">Chapter 7</h1>

<h2 style="text-align:center">Love Turns Ugly</h2>
The Same Evening

vy Cohen selected the first page and began reading her story.

It was Wednesday, March 3rd, 1982. Lainee Cohen darted about her second-floor London flat, picking up any visible sign of her three-month-old daughter. Waves of shiny coal-black hair floated high with Lainee's every step. The petite twenty-seven-year-old bent over to retrieve a crib toy from among the settee cushions. Her dark eyes scanned the room. Satisfied at last that she'd hidden everything from view, her thin lips formed a slight smile. His last letter said he'd arrive at ten that morning. She looked at her watch—9:05 already. Could she pull it off?

Lainee had transported her infant, whom she'd named Ivy, to her friends' flat on the fourth floor. She knew her baby would be safe with Wayne and Janice Sachs. They had a preteen son and were expecting a second child.

Perhaps one day she could tell her lover that he had a beautiful daughter. But not just now. During their last date, just before he'd gone overseas on business, she'd told him about the early pregnancy. He had reacted horribly, ordering her to have an immediate abortion. She had politely refused, but he had insisted so vehemently that she

51

felt bullied, compelled to promise, so as not to spoil their last night together. A crossed-her-fingers lie, so to speak.

Snooks is what she called him, her playful *nom d'affaire*. Better than Arthur, the name she knew instinctively was an outright lie. At the onset he'd told her he was "a very private person," a term she always considered a synonym for secretive. Yes, they'd been lovers on and off for nearly three years now. His mistress, nothing more. All she really knew about him was that he had another life: a wife; maybe even a family; an ill-defined family business; but no last name or address. He had warned Lainee not to pry, or their affair would end.

For her there could be no one else. She'd never met anyone like him. It started with a strong attraction to his good looks, fit figure, and fine manners. He was enormously generous. Money flowed freely for rent, expenses, and extras. So what was there to complain about? She had no family left, and her job as a retail clerk was keeping her poor.

Snooks had been overseas for ten months, a place postmarked Annapolis, Maryland. *Somewhere in the eastern U.S.*, she thought. She never bothered with maps; they confused her. He'd explained it was to promote a new branch of an expanding family business. The money for her keep never stopped, and they'd been communicating by mail every few weeks—passion-filled missives, but nearly nothing about what filled his days. Perhaps she was just as guilty. Lainee had neglected to tell him that she actually had had his love child. She couldn't. There was no way to contact him.

Lainee was confident he'd come around once he got to know Ivy, but for now she'd spare him any anxiety and let him enjoy his homecoming. *I wouldn't expect him to accept Ivy into his family*, she thought, *but I would expect him to see and respect her as our child with my last name. No extra demands. I can live on less,* she justified.

A quiet knock on the door roused Lainee from her anxious thoughts. She spun around for one last look at the flat and straightened her powder-blue skirt. At the door Snooks stood there, arms full of packages, presents for her. Once inside, he dropped everything on the floor, and Lainee jumped into his arms. He swung her about him, her outstretched circling bare feet barely missing the Oriental floor lamp. Stopping, her slight frame slid slowly and sensually down his body until her toes touched the carpeting. Two lips now aligned, they kissed long and sensuously, breaking only for a much-needed breath of air.

"I came straight from the airport. I haven't even been home yet. I couldn't wait any longer to see you, sweetheart."

Their eyes met and they exchanged silent tender words. Snooks slipped his arms behind her back and knees, lifted her, and conveyed her to the bedroom and the queen bed there. Clothes soared about in a flurry, and the two embraced once more; kissing, fondling, and searching until the lovers found exactly what they'd missed most. Exhausted, they both fell into a contented nap.

Lainee awoke first and began to daydream of the life the three of them would have together. Still in his strong arms, she could feel his heart beating. Turning her head to admire his handsome face, she listened and watched for several minutes. Then she slipped out of bed and padded into the front room to the presents on the floor. She slipped off the ribbons and removed the wrappings to find what he'd brought her: a black evening dress with spaghetti straps; a frilly see-through teddy in pale violet she knew wouldn't stay on her body for long; and a Gucci clutch bag with the softest gray leather.

Lainee heard a noise behind her. It turned out that Snooks had settled into an armchair and had been quietly observing her all the while she opened her goodies. He wore a white terry robe she'd given him. She glowed at him, and he appeared pleased with the results. He held out his arms and she went straight to him, nestling on his lap.

"I'm just bursting with happiness, darling," she whispered.

"Sweetheart, I can see you like the gifts."

"Oh, yes! They're wonderful." Lainee thought for a moment. *Is this the right time?* "I've got something to tell you."

"What is it?" He noticed a frightened expression travel across her face and drew her closer to him.

"While you were gone, I gave birth to a baby girl, our love child," she blurted out.

"What?" He screamed, choking on his one word. "What did you just say?"

"I had your baby."

Snooks struggled to his feet, dumping Lainee on the floor in a heap. "Noooo!" he yelled. "I told you to abort that thing."

"She's not a thing. Ivy is a beautiful little girl. Your little girl."

"That's it. We're done. Through! I'm leaving you for good." Snooks headed for the bedroom, gathering his clothes as he went.

"Please!" She pleaded with him, tugging at the back of his terry robe belt.

He slashed her hand from his waist, spun around, and pushed her away. "I don't want anything to do with you or the child. Get away from me and let me finish dressing."

"You can't leave me like this." She grabbed him around the waist and try to nuzzle his back.

"No?" he cried. "Just you watch me."

He wrenched her arms loose, turned to face her, and backhand-walloped her across the face, a blow that carried her halfway across the room. Lainee lay there on her back stark naked with her mouth agape, stunned by the blow and shocked even more by his words. She saw hatred in his eyes each time he glanced at her while he finished dressing. *How could this man turn into a monster in a split-second? Where did all the love go? Did he ever love me?* From simmering seconds of helpless despair, anger boiled up. "You bastard. I'll tell your wife about us."

"You little bitch, you don't know anything about me, let alone my wife. I've been very careful."

"That's what you think," Lainee lied. "I've had the goods on you for some time now, mister."

He stood above her, looking down, deciding if she knew more than she should. He had too much to lose. *Would a one-time settlement do the trick or would the little bitch continue to blackmail me?* He suddenly became aware of her nudity, and hidden in his trousers, a stirring. He began to think money wouldn't do the trick.

Lainee sprang to her feet and grabbed his undone tie with all her strength, trying to strangle him with it.

An infuriated Snooks bent over, first to relieve the strain on his neck and second, to position himself to land another blow. This time his fist contacted her chin with such force that her body snapped back, and her head struck the hardwood floor. She lay there, eyes shut, unmoving for several minutes until he pulled back one of her eyelids with his thumb and saw her staring eerily back at him. Snooks knelt and then straddled her nude body, first trying to grab her flailing arms. Unsuccessful at that, he wrapped his muscular fingers around her neck and began to squeeze.

Her arms began to beat at him. Her beautiful dark eyes grew larger and the white face of fright slowly turned blood red. Tighter and tighter he gripped until her pretty mouth distorted and her arms quit moving altogether. Putting his ear to her bare chest, he listened to detect her breathing. None heard. He felt for a wrist pulse. Nothing there either.

Suddenly seized by panic, a cold shiver traversed his spine. He'd committed murder. He'd taken a precious life. As he looked down at Lainee's body, it was as though someone had rearranged her face, torso, and limbs to bring out her ultimate beauty. Regret arose in him and he covered her nakedness with the terry robe she'd lent him. Snooks began to shake uncontrollably. It was an accident, he tried to convince himself. But who would believe him? The spasm of panic passed as quickly as it came. Rationale arrived next. He had to save himself, look out for number one. But how?

Snooks didn't really love Lainee, but hadn't meant to kill the best sex and comfort he'd ever had. He still loved the woman he'd married, but she'd made it clear she was unwilling to give him the intense lovemaking he demanded. Starting a second family was so repugnant to him that he couldn't bear the thought of another child. He hated whiny, demanding kids. It was the very reason he regularly left his wife and their son and daughter for Lainee's bed. *Damn! Such a convenient arrangement, too.*

The man called Snooks spent the next ninety minutes cleansing the flat of his presence and scanning her personal journal for mention of his name. He eased out the door and completely shook himself free from three years of pleasurable distraction. He was in no shape to go home and face his wife. Not yet. Perhaps a drink would help, but not in this neighborhood.

Six hours later, as prearranged, the fourth-floor friend, Janice Sachs, walked downstairs to return baby Ivy Cohen to her mother. Letting herself into the flat, she discovered Lainee's body in the ell-shaped front parlor and, sick at heart, returned to her own flat to call the police.

Afterward, Janice and her husband, Wayne, accepted Ivy into their own home and lovingly raised her like one of their own, seeing to her needs and education.

The police did the best they could with so little evidence. Their report indicated the poor woman was strangled. There was head trauma where it had struck the floor. The bruise marks about the throat revealed only partial fingerprints. The small amounts of DNA and fibers collected were of no use to them unless they had a suspect to work with. No one in the building ever remembered a male entering or leaving the Cohen flat. No particular cars or cab drop-offs were discovered. The name Snooks in Lainee's journal meant nothing to any of the interviewees, nor any of the investigators. So, in the course of six months, the investigation became a cold file.

#

Ivy laid down the last page of her story and turned over the sheaf of papers. She stacked them upright. The room was silent—altogether too silent. Ivy looked up and encountered a number of eerie expressions. *They don't like my story? It isn't real enough?*

"What?" she asked.

"It seemed so real," said Frieda. "Like being in the room at the time of the murder."

"I agree," added Esther. "It's a tidy bit of writing. So sad, too."

"I can see why you'd like to see your mother's murder solved," said Peggy. "But really, twenty years plus is an awfully long time. What would convince the police to suddenly open the case now?"

"I don't expect Scotland Yard to get involved," explained Ivy. "That is, unless I find new evidence. No, I plan to pursue a few clues on my own and see where they take me. Dan here has a few ideas and promised to help."

"Ivy?" Joel's legal engine now in gear: "Just what do you propose to do when and if you discover who killed your mother?"

Ivy's dark eyes burned with resolve. "Without hard evidence, all I can do is expose the man to his family, friends, and all the world for what he is: a brutal killer. I'll do it in the context of this novel."

"Without hard evidence, young lady, you'd be subject to libel," persisted the attorney. "How would you go about handling that?"

"I plan to continue my story, a chapter at a time, as I learn more about him and include the details, step by step, of how I learned those facts. I *will* publish this book eventually. I might change some names to ensure the story's fictional appearance, legally, but the killer himself would never mistake either the incident or setting. And, of course, he could never challenge the veracity of the story in court without admitting some sort of guilt."

Joel shook his head. "All I can say is, this man is dangerous. He's killed at least once that we know of. So be careful, my dear."

Chapter 8

## Second *Shabbat*
Friday Evening, October 21st

Ivy squirmed in the desk chair at the cash register. "Dan, have you seen Rivka? It's getting almost closing time, and I want to prepare Mrs. Riley's supper before I head to *Shabbat* services tonight. Rivka needs to ring up the day's receipts and close out before I leave."

"I haven't seen her since early afternoon," answered Dan. "But I can cash out for the day, and you can run along. I assume she's still up in the kitchen cooking and baking her heart out. I know Rivka has *Oneg* duty tonight."

"Ivy, wait! I've got supper for you and Irma," called Rivka from the foot of the stairs. "It's a vegetable barley soup with meat. Careful, the pot's steaming hot. I simmered it all afternoon to make sure the meat's tender enough for Irma. Meat is hard to chew with her two removable bridges. Ivy, I think it's so sweet of you to volunteer as caregiver, so I wanted to help out, too." Rivka set the pot down on the counter and handed her the two insulated stove mitts.

Ivy took hold of the porcelain pot with the mitts and headed for the door. "It smells yummy, Rivka," she said over her shoulder. "Thanks!"

* * * *

An hour after the delicious soup and meat dinner for two, Irma Riley sat in the parlor facing the television set in her transport-style wheelchair—her arms not being strong enough to propel a big-wheeled chair on her own. A pair of aluminum crutches rested on the coffee table next to her, with water and Kleenex within easy reach.  Irma pointed her remote at the set and selected her favorite game show, *Wheel of Fortune*.

Ivy approached from behind and leaned over to say, "I'm going to temple for services, Irma. I'll be home in a few hours. The dishes are washed and in the rack drying. I'll put them away when I get back. Is there anything else I can get you?" She felt Irma's hand grasp her own.

"No, sweetie. Dear Lord, I don't know what I'd do without you, young woman. You're an absolute angel."

"I'm pleased to be able to help, Mum." Ivy had already taken a step toward the door when she thought to return and plant a kiss on Irma's cheek. A salty kiss at that, intercepting a runaway tear there.

* * * *

Some fifty or sixty of Beth Israel's faithful congregants, and a number of random visitors, met Friday evenings in Annapolis in the 110-year-old red brick and stone masonry synagogue. At the top of twelve steps leading up from the sidewalk, a handsomely carved wood door led into a foyer and cloakroom. The sanctuary, with its raised bema and Holy Ark, left scant room at the rear of the building for the rabbi's office, an administrative office, and a modest library. The area beneath the main floor was dedicated to a social hall, restrooms, and tiny kitchen that was kept kosher—allowing milk or meat dishes, but not both at the same time. Though most members didn't keep kosher at home, all respected the synagogue's semi-strict conventions.

Three or four congregation ladies volunteered each week to serve on an *Oneg Shabbat* committee to furnish and dish up light refreshments for an informal get-together following the evening services. They arrived ahead of time in the social hall to set out the goodies, covering them in Saran wrap, and hastening upstairs in time for the service. Afterward they remained to clean up. Generally, they were a hospitable bunch with cheery greetings for all comers. This week's offerings were supplied by Rivka, Thelma Katz, Anna Reubens and her sister-in-law, Esther Reubens. Anna's seventeen-year-old daughter, Julie, usually accompanied her, and tonight Anna's son, Stuart, joined them. He had volunteered to be one of the ushers, who helped with the greeting and seating and the distribution of prayer books.

Rivka arrived first and stacked up her rugulah ("little twists" in Yiddish) on two large platters from the kitchen cabinet. She'd cut the wedges from a large, flat circle of dough covered with a diced mix of raisins, walnuts, currant jam, and cinnamon. Then she'd rolled up each wedge into a horn shape for baking. Thelma set out brownies, while Esther positioned two glass bowls of fruit salad.

Anna arrived bearing a perfect German chocolate cake under a plastic dome. Julie balanced a large tray of pound cake slices and tried to nudge it into a narrow space between two loaded platters near one end of the island counter. Instantly, the platter on the far right sailed over the edge, crashing to the tile floor in an irretrievable splash of rugulah and china shards.

"Julie! You clumsy ninny," bellowed Anna, churning up a facial hue of overripe tomatoes. "Why don't you *ever* pay attention to what you're doing?"

"I'm so sorry," whimpered Julie in her soprano squeak. "I didn't think anything would happen if I gave it an ever so tiny nudge. Really!"

"That's just it," said Anna, a tall, imposing woman in a gray wool suit. She stamped her foot like an impatient horse to punctuate her message. "You never think, you never look. Your mind is always filled with theatrical garbage."

Gawky and plain-faced, Julie spun around in her peasant skirt and blouse. Her single braid, the color of tree bark, flopped about her back. "It's not garbage, Mother. Theater is my chosen profession."

"It doesn't seem to help your ability in the kitchen, does it?"

"Hey, Anna, aren't you being a little tough on the girl?" asked Esther. "It was an accident."

"I'll thank you to keep your long, bumpy proboscis out of my private business, Esther Reubens. In short, butt out!"

Julie, choking back sobs, ran into the arms of her Aunt Thelma, who just stood there aghast, not wanting to take sides in a family squabble. Thelma gave Julie a comforting pat, then disengaged herself to fetch a broom and dustpan.

"Don't you dare insult my nose," said Esther. "I'm just defending my niece. There's no need to get that bent out of shape over a little spill."

"Stop it, please," begged Julie. "Please!" She held the dustpan while Thelma wielded the broom.

"Girls, girls," cried Rivka. "Remember where you are and why you came here. *Shabbat* is a time to reflect—on your faults and omissions of the prior six days and how you might improve for the coming week."

"Jeez, Rivka!" said Esther. "You're beginning to sound like Rabbi Moshe Goldstein."

"Mama, Auntie Esther," said Julie between sniffles. "Either the two of you kiss and make up now or I'm going straight home."

"A little blackmail never hurt," murmured Rivka. She had witnessed the two women in their recurring tiff, a familiar performance. The slightest provocation and the two proud ladies were off to the races. They usually ended it with hugs. Rivka couldn't help but smile at Julie. Klutzy, yes, but at times quite adult and take-charge, all rolled into one. She reminded Rivka of her own daughter, Jenny, at the same age. Now Jenny and Leonard had families of their own in far-away cities. Rivka and Dan sorely missed their grown kids and grandchildren.

Checking her watch, she called out, "Hey, ladies, let's get

upstairs. Rabbi Goldstein hates for us to be late."

* * * *

Ivy slowly climbed the stairs to Congregation Beth Israel. She noted that each step bore a chiseled symbolic shield, specifying a different tribe of Israel. A small window in the high brick façade held a Jewish star in stained glass. Stepping inside the grand front doors, she heard the rabbi chanting the candle-lighting prayer, leading a group of ladies. Ivy was late and embarrassed. Taking a white doily from a wooden box, she affixed it to her hair with a bobby pin from her purse. As she passed through a second door to the sanctuary, she was handed a *siddur*, a prayer book, open to the current page. In a fleeting glance, to see who had provided it, Ivy discovered an extremely handsome young man in a dark, well-cut suit, a blue and white striped tie, and a black yarmulke. Tall and lean, he proved worthy of an extended look.

The young man let his eyes roam over the pretty new arrival in high heels and a sleek, form-fitting tan dress. "Good *Shabbos*," he whispered.

"*Shabbat Shalom*," Ivy whispered in return, pressing the open *siddur* to her chest. She nodded her appreciation and took a few steps deeper into the sanctuary to search the rows of pews for a familiar figure. Daniel and Rivka sat on the left center aisle in the eleventh row; there were a number of empty seats beside them.

As Ivy walked down the aisle, heads turned—a newcomer to the congregation and an attractive one at that. She slid into the Shermans' row and Rivka wiggled her bottom, making room between them. During the ninety-minute service, they joined in both the responsive and collective prayer readings, both in Hebrew and in English. Ivy found the service surprisingly familiar. After all, most *Shabbat* services throughout the world contained Hebrew, the language that provided the universal common bond, as well as prescribed content and order. Allowing for differences in time zones, Jews throughout the world were praying together, and that was a comfort to her.

The rabbi's sermon was a treatise on this week's Torah portion or *parshah*. Each week throughout the year, a different portion is read and each takes its name from a prominent initial word therein. Following the *Aleinu*, or prayer of hope, the service turned to prayers for healing, and finally, the *Kaddish*, remembering those loved ones who have passed on. A hymn and benediction brought the service to a close, and the congregants flowed toward either of two staircases to the social hall below.

The rabbi waited to greet and shake hands with many individuals. "*Shabbat Shalom, Shabbat Shalom*" As Dan Sherman took his turn, he introduced Ivy, and she received a warm, two-hand welcome from him.

White tablecloths covered several long tables filled with the baked goods and fruits. Rivka was still adding platters as Dan and Ivy approached. Dan snatched up a paper plate and shoveled a large slab of chocolate cake onto it. Ivy nibbled absently on an oatmeal-raison cookie, but her real attention had strayed to the far end of the table, where the young usher stood. "Who's that gorgeous hunk of a young man?" she asked Dan. "He was the usher in the sanctuary."

"That, my dear," said Dan, "is the catch of the congregation. His name is Stuart Reubens. He's an associate in a local law firm: Fenner, Fenner, Levin, and Johnson. He was an athlete at Annapolis High School—football, I believe. Yale undergrad and law school, too."

"Now you've got his whole pedigree, Ivy," grinned Rivka, leaning across the table. "What else does she need to know?"

"An introduction would be nice," said Dan. He took Ivy's arm in his and together they strolled toward the Reubens. "Hi, Anna, Julie, Stuart. I'd like you to meet a protégé of ours from the store. This is Ivy Cohen, and she's new to Annapolis and our congregation, a recent arrival from London, as a matter of fact. Rivka has asked me to introduce her around."

"Welcome, my dear. Welcome to Beth Israel," boomed Anna while scrutinizing Ivy at mach speed. "This is my son, Stuart, and my daughter, Julie. You'll have to excuse the dejected expression on her face. She's still sulking, making a mountain out of a slight mishap in the kitchen earlier."

"Mu-therrr!" whined Julie, her thin, five-foot-eight body slumping into an S-curve.

An embarrassed Dan turned to talk with someone else, while Stuart and Ivy, oblivious to the family bickering, drifted away.

"How long are you here?" he asked.

"Let's see," replied Ivy. "About five weeks, six next Tuesday."

"Did you leave family behind in London?"

"Oh, yes, the Sachses who raised me. They're my foster parents, but somehow they've never let me feel like an orphan."

"And friends?"

"Of course, friends," Ivy responded with a giggle. "I'm not exactly a recluse."

"Sorry. Anybody special you were dating?"

"My, aren't we the expert in third degree," she quipped. "All my friends are special, but no, I'm not promised to anyone, if that's what you mean."

Stuart decided he'd gotten too personal. He tried to switch gears, but couldn't shift out of his ingrained interrogating mode. "Mr. Sherman said you were a protégé at the bookstore. What does that mean?"

"It means that I'm a lowly shop clerk. I graduated college as an English literature major, hoping to teach, but unfortunately I have no accreditation here in Maryland."

"So the bookstore is only a temporary stop for you."

"I haven't given that a lot of thought yet. I suppose I'll pick up the necessary evening courses and eventually, certification. I'm in no hurry. There are some things I have to do. Meanwhile, I'm enjoying the book world and learning a terrible lot. And of course, Daniel and Rivka have been wonderful to me. There's no way that I can repay them for their kindness, except to be their lowly clerk, and a good one, for at least a little while."

"So what brings you to Annapolis, anyway?"

"I came here to look for my father."

"Your father? I thought you said you were an orphan."

"For all practical purposes, I am," she declared. "I never knew either one of my birth parents."

"Oh-oh!" said Stuart, "I'm getting the evil eye from my mother. That means it's time to go. I'm the designated driver."

Sure enough, Anna stared steely-eyed at the couple, her prominent chin drawn deeply against her thick gold necklace. Stuart nodded and turned to Ivy once more. "Can I come calling on you soon?"

"I guess so. Sure, except that I take care of an elderly lady sometimes. We'll see."

Ivy watched him join his family and start to leave the room. But before he did, Stuart offered a tentative wave and a sheepish grin in her direction. She couldn't help but wonder: *Is he a mama's boy or just a nice, sensitive son?*

Searching out Dan and Rivka, she said goodnight.

* * * *

Before Ivy left for the synagogue, she'd switched on Irma's hall and porch lights. Now at ten o'clock both were out. She fumbled through her clutch purse for the keys and the elusive keyhole. Slowly pushing the door open, she heard a strange, excitable male voice. *Who in heaven's name?* Ivy stepped into the hallway. With hand trembling, she tucked away her keys and flipped the hall switch. The twenty-five-watt bulb cast a pathetic light. Peering into the parlor, Ivy's eyes strained to adjust to the silent room, coal-black except for the eerie blue-green glow of the telly. *So that's where the male voice is coming from.* Ivy had deliberately turned on both porcelain reading lamps before leaving the house. In the flickering glow of the TV she made out the shadowed profile of Irma's wheelchair, but where was Irma? No way could an old lady with a broken leg get up a flight of stairs to bed on her own. Even if someone had helped her, why wouldn't the wheelchair be at the foot of the stairs?

Near panic led her to grope for one of the lamps and switch it on before venturing all the way into the parlor. Moving closer, she discovered Irma lying in a heap at the foot of her wheelchair amid an array of foot cushions and rugs. Her crutches lay a few feet away. There was no blood visible, and placing her fingers against Irma's neck revealed she had a reasonably strong pulse.

Ivy raced into the kitchen for a roll of paper toweling, soaked a large wad with cold water from the fridge and returned to the old woman. Gently washing Irma's face brought her to consciousness. At first Irma was disoriented, mumbling incoherently. Ivy sat patiently on the floor, cradling the old woman's head in her lap.

"Are you hurt, Irma? Shall I call 911?"

"Don't be silly, girl. Ambulances cost money I can't rightly afford."

"What happened? What are you doing on the floor?"

The old lady looked away, trying to hide her embarrassment. "I'm fine, dear. Except that I'd been sitting in that damnable wheelchair so long my behind was sore. Besides, those annoying lamps in the back of the room were reflecting into the television. I got up on my crutches and turned them both out. Then I took a spin through the downstairs, where I found the hall and porch lights on. I turned them off, too—gotta save on electricity, you know. I had every intention of turning them back on again for you when *America's Funniest Home Videos* was over. When I got back to my chair, I felt light-headed and then nothing. I guess I needed one of them sugar fixes, a candy bar or cookie or something."

"You gave me a fright," Ivy said. "I'll get you a cookie."

Irma's back straightened. "Make it three, dear. Those delicious lemon bars."

"Will do." Suppressing a smile, Ivy slipped two hands under Irma's arms, lifted the old lady to her feet, and maneuvered her back into her chair.

After packing away the rich cookies and a little glass of orange juice, Irma whispered "I'm so tired, dear. Would you put me to bed now?"

"Of course."

Ivy parked the chair at the foot of the stairs, and steadied Irma up to her bedroom. Helping her into a flannel nightie, she tucked her in for the night.

Chapter 9

## Tainted Visitor
Saturday Morning, October 22nd

The one-bedroom Germain apartment on West Street was furnished in a mélange of Danish modern and Early American. Heather was in such a deep sleep that she didn't hear the doorbell. On the second ring, she stirred enough to eyeball the clock on her nightstand: 6:05 a.m. *Who would come calling this early on a Saturday, a no-school day?* It wasn't until the third ring that she threw back the covers and hit the floor in a dash to the bathroom, where she slipped into a flowered cotton robe. Whoever the caller was got sick of ringing and began insistently knocking on the front door.

"Coming!" Heather shouted. She undid the deadbolt and turned the knob until she had an opening to the extent of the security chain. At first peek she couldn't believe her eyes. Fenton Thorwal. Her e-mail response to him had been extremely cool. So cool, she hardly expected to ever hear from him again. She unlatched the chain and swung the door wide. "What on earth are you doing here?"

"I took the red-eye flight out of Heathrow," he said. There was a rugged look about his tousled, wavy, walnut-brown hair and angular face. An open sport coat revealed a garish orange polo shirt tapered to a trim waist. A black wheeled valise stood at attention by his side. "I thought you were expecting me, Heather." Her pillow-ruffled red hair and matching fiery freckles glistened in the early morning sunlight. The lines of anger in her face attracted him even more. He smiled, thinking she was only joshing with him.

"You really thought I was expecting you? I was not! And you woke me up! I thought I had sufficiently discouraged you."

"Then you're not glad to see me." He spun the valise around toward the street and started down the steps.

"Wait," she called. "Come in."

He hesitated, turning his head slowly to look back at her.

"Fen, please come back. I want to have a word with you." He continued down the steps.

"Damn it, Fenton Thorwal, you come back here." She stomped her foot, but her fake-fur slipper made no sound.

Fenton trudged back up to her door and stepped inside, leaving his bag out on the concrete step. He stood with arms crossed, staring intently at her. "What?" he asked.

"Please sit down. Fen. You took me completely by surprise. You show up at my door at the break of dawn, expecting to move in with me. In a way I suppose it's my fault. A little too much wine and I let you have your way with me last spring. But you didn't even have the decency to spend the whole night with me. You didn't wake me or explain why you left. When I saw your real name in the wallet you dropped, I thought you were Abner Fraume's killer. I wanted to scream."

"But I thought I explained all that in my e-mail," he said.

"An e-mail almost a year later?" She pulled the belt of her robe tighter, as if to defend herself.

"I was doubly embarrassed. I thought I had botched my investigation into Abner's killer by exposing my cover. I didn't know how to patch things up with you."

"And it took almost a year to apologize? *Mon Dieu!* And I thought my students were creative with excuses for not doing their homework."

His look turned grim and he shook his head. "I wanted to write a letter and tell you why I left so abruptly and how I really felt about you. I started it at least a dozen times over the past eight months. Each version was either too mushy and gushy or too trivial. My work got the better of me, and in the end, I compressed everything into one unemotional e-mail. I guess it didn't quite make the grade."

"Mushy, gushy, trivial, and unemotional." she repeated. "This sounds like a long explanation. I think I'd better get dressed before you continue." She was feeling awfully vulnerable in her flimsy robe. *This is so weird*, she thought. *I haven't even brushed my teeth.*

"Of course," he replied.

"Help yourself to some coffee in the kitchen," she yelled through the bedroom door. "The pot's all primed and ready to go. Just plug it in. The cups are in the cabinet above the pot. I won't be able to hear you in the shower."

Fen headed for the kitchen and started the coffeepot. He also found an inviting frying pan on the countertop. The refrigerator yielded all the ingredients for scrambled eggs, toast, and jam. By the time Heather returned to the kitchen, the food was ready, and the table was properly set.

"My my," she said. "You *do* make yourself at home." She wore a Kelly-green sweater, jeans, and sandals. A lime-green ribbon pulled her hair back in a ponytail, making her look even younger than her thirty-one years.

"I'm sorry," he murmured. "Did I presume too much? Neither of us has had breakfast. I thought—"

"You thought it would put you in my good graces," she said. "And quite frankly, it did." She sat in one of the two ladder-back wooden chairs and allowed him to pour her coffee. "But this doesn't let you off the hook, bub. I want that full explanation you promised me."

He returned to the stove. This time he came back with the frying pan and slid half the scrambled eggs into each plate. "And so you shall, my dear Heather," he said, settling into the other chair. He took a bite of the eggs and a swig of coffee while he buttered and smeared his toast with jam.

"Apparently," he began, "you dropped something on the sink that night while you were in the bathroom. The noise woke me. As you now know, I had two wallets. I went to get a picture for you from my real wallet and discovered it was missing. I panicked, thinking my cover had been blown. I thought maybe I'd dropped the wallet in the Brew Moon Pub, so I got dressed and rushed back there to retrieve it. I planned to explain to you in the morning. The problem was, the bar was closed at 3 a.m."

"So why didn't you at least call me to let me know?" she asked. "I would have told you I had the wallet. You treated me like a piece of trash, a one-night stand to be discarded. Like I didn't deserve an explanation. You could just return to England and forget me. Well, Mr. Constable Sergeant Thorwal, I don't do one-night stands. I have never gone to bed with a man on a first date before or after that night. I have had only one prior relationship in my life." She picked up her coffee cup and angrily gulped. "Wow, that's hot." It only made her more angry. "You bastard," she yelled in his face, "you had your conquest."

"It wasn't like that," he claimed. "I never meant it to happen that way. I don't do one-night stands either. The only prior sex I've had was with my fiancée, Susan, four years ago."

"So you're engaged to be married? You're a bigger bastard than I thought."

"No, no, that was years ago. Susan wound up marrying my second cousin. I swear to you I'm unattached. I have had no other sex. The closest I get to women is when they're dead."

"When they're dead? Gross!"

His keen eyes bored into hers. He was getting pretty sick of the third degree, even though he knew he deserved it. "Or when they're a witness to a crime."

Heather shrugged. "You still haven't told me why you didn't at least try to reach me in the morning."

"I called the chief inspector to report the loss of my wallet. He had me go to Baltimore to pick up new credentials. There was no time in between. From there I was sent to Savannah, and then the kidnapping case heated up. As soon as things were finished there, I was sent back to Bath on the first plane. A transcontinental phone call seemed so lame after that. You're shaking your head. Why?"

"All those things are excuses, and not one of them tells me why you couldn't pick up a phone or send a note. And why are you here *now?* Are you trying to renew your membership in the friends-with-benefits vacation club just so you can return home after a fortnight vacation, brag to your womanizing friends, and forget me all over again? Sure, I find you extremely attractive, but there's no way I want to play that game." She jabbed her fork into a clump of scrambled egg.

"I'm here because I have strong feelings for you. All right, I'll spell it out for you. I think I'm in love with you." He was almost shouting at this point, matching her attack on him. "I came here to find out whether those feelings are strong enough to ask you to marry me. If I weren't eighty-five percent cocksure already, I wouldn't be here."

Heather suddenly giggled. "Cocksure? That's a strange choice of words, Fen."

He smiled grimly. "I guess so. But let me finish. The thought of living without you has been driving me crazy. I've been imagining what our life would be like. The two of us living either in Bath or here in Maryland. I know I've made a bloody mess of *us*, but I want to set that right."

"But Fen, we've only had one date. How can you be that sure of me or even of yourself in that little time?"

"Dear Heather, I just know that I want—no, need—to be with you. I've had this feeling the whole time I've been away. I've never felt like this before, not even when I was engaged to Susan."

"Fen, dear," Heather responded in sweeter tones, "I'm practically speechless. I also can't explain my own fondness for you after only one date. But let me be clear. That fondness is a long way from being in love. We know so little about each other—likes, dislikes, stresses, commitments, quirks." Her lips turned up at the corners in a tentative smile. "You do make a good breakfast, I'll give you that. Actually, there's only one way to learn how we really feel about each other. Go get your bag and put it in the living room. I'm willing to let you stay here for the two weeks, but you're going to bunk in the living room and you're going to abide by my rules. We'll see where our relationship goes from there."

"And maybe you'll come to me for a few weeks, too."

"Let's not get ahead of ourselves, Fen."

The eggs had gone cold, along with the toast and coffee, but neither minded the food. They ate in silence, both pondering the new situation they had just committed to, each equally unsure.

* * * *

Rivka and Dan hadn't quite finished their Saturday morning breakfast when they heard the doorbell. "I'll get it, hon," said Dan as he noisily pushed his chair backward. "Probably Ivy." He bounded down the stairs and threw open The Dungeon door. "Good morning," he said cheerily. Ivy's return greeting appeared so low-spirited that he had to ask, "What's wrong, dear?"

"I had my hands full when I got home last night. The house was unexpectedly dark except for the television." She spilled out her landlady's latest crisis. "She wouldn't let me take her to the emergency room. She insisted she couldn't afford to go to the hospital. Finally, we compromised. She promised I could take her to the doctor this morning. I hate to ask for time off, especially during inventory, but—"

"Don't worry, Ivy. Rivka and I will manage a few hours without you. Wait, how'd you get a Saturday appointment with a doctor? What time is your appointment anyway?"

"It's at 10:45 with Dr. Yuu in the Wayson Pavilion at Anne Arundel Medical Center. We were lucky. She has Saturday appointments one weekend a month. Let's see, it's 8:15 now, so I can work until 9:30 and then I'll call a taxi to pick us up at the Riley house. That all right with you?"

"Why don't you take the entire morning off and come in after her appointment is finished and you get the old bird home again. It's a noble enough cause. I'll see that it doesn't affect your paycheck."

Ivy threw her arms around Dan in an appreciative hug. "Thank you, Dan, and you too, Rivka." Then she quickly disappeared through The Dungeon door.

"What doesn't affect her paycheck?" asked Rivka, standing in the stairwell behind Dan.

"Ivy's taking Irma to the doctor. She found the old bird lying on the floor in a heap last night and promised to get her to the doctor this morning."

"So you gave Ivy the morning off with pay?"

"Yup! That's it in a nutshell, my love. I figure it's our contribution to *tzedakah*, to charity, for this *Shabbat*. She should be back around noon."

*Fine*, Rivka thought. *But does she have to throw her arms around my husband?*

Sales at The Olde Victorian Bookstore that Saturday morning were even better than usual. The Shermans were kept busy, mostly with their regular nonfiction patrons wanting biographies, memoirs, historical accounts, and assorted how-to's.

Around ten Rivka discovered Stuart Reubens rummaging among the used law books. He appeared to be admiring the excellent leather bindings on each of the volumes of a collection on Maryland tort law. He didn't seem to be pursuing anything in particular, except every so often he'd thumb past a few pages and read for several moments.

"Good morning, Stuart. So nice to see you," Rivka said.

He looked up with a start and broke into a smile. "Hi, Mrs. Sherman."

"I can give you a good price on that set," offered Rivka. "It's complete through 2004. It was a part of old Judge Gibbons' estate.

His widow is selling off her husband's law office assets. There's a good chance I could get my hands on more of the same."

"You know I'd love to have them, only I share a cubicle with three other associates. And the firm's library is kept quite complete. But thank you."

"I might set them aside for you for a small deposit."

"No, no," protested Stuart. 'It'll be some time before I set up my own office." He had an easy, confident manner, and looked her square in the eye behind wire-rimmed glasses.

"Then what can I do for you today?" Rivka asked.

"I'm sort of embarrassed to say . . ."

*He doesn't look embarrassed*, Rivka thought.

"I was hoping to run into Ivy this morning."

"She'll be in this afternoon. Can I give her a message for you?"

"Sure. Just tell her I came by to see her." Stuart replaced the last law book from the set in its place on the shelf and headed out of the reading room.

Rivka returned to the front of the store to relieve Dan at the register. "That young man is smitten already."

"All it takes is a little meddling," said Dan, sporting a crooked grin.

"Well, Dan, I guess you did a *mitzvah*, a real good deed last night by introducing Ivy to Stuart. She's all alone here and needs friends." Rivka laid one hand affectionately on her husband's shoulder.

* * * *

"Oh, thank God you're here," Rivka pounced on Ivy as soon as she came through the door. "In the last hour the place has become a veritable madhouse. There must be a herd of tourists in town today."

"Isn't that a good thing for us?

"Sure is. I sent Dan to the post office. He's not back yet."

"Where can I help you most?"

"Take over the register so I can at least grab a pee and a

quick bite to eat upstairs. "Oh, by the way, you had a visitor this morning."

"And who might that be?" asked Ivy.

"Stuart Reubens, the young man you met last night. You must have made quite an impression on him."

A line of customers formed at the counter, so Ivy didn't have time to react. The register must have *ka-chinged* a dozen more times before Dan came in the door and took over.

"So what did the sawbones say was wrong with the old broad?" asked Dan.

"What?" Ivy drew a blank.

"Mrs. Riley. What did the doctor have to say about her keeling over?"

"Oh. She was just dehydrated. That's why she fainted when she left her wheelchair to walk around the house on her cane. She's supposed to be drinking six eight-ounce glasses of water every day."

"That's a lot of water." Dan shook his head in sympathy.

Ivy nodded. "There's an accumulation of books in all three reading rooms. I had better get them back on the shelves before the place turns to bedlam."

Between her job and her landlady, Ivy wondered whether she would ever get back to the real business that burned in her heart day and night.

# Chapter 10

## The Herschel Reubens Family
### Saturday Evening

"You want another heart attack, Herschel Reubens?" cried his wife, Anna. "That's the second piece of carrot cake you've snitched tonight. You want me to tell Dr. Frost that you cheat all the time?"

"I won't squeal if you don't." There was an impish smirk on Herschel's face. A dab of butter-cream frosting and a few cake crumbs sat there, too.

"Stop that nonsense. You were 273 pounds on the doctor's scale, and he warned you about your diabetes. If you don't lose eighty pounds soon, you're likely to start losing limbs. See if you can make light of that fact."

"I've already lost four pounds, and the cake doesn't even weigh a quarter-pound."

"That kind of logic will be the end of you. Of me, too," said Anna.

"I'm still the man you married, dear."

"No, you're twice the man I married. You used to cut a fine figure. I remember well."

He couldn't resist getting in the last word. "There's more of me to love now."

She refused to answer.

Anna and Herschel made a handsome couple when they emigrated from England to the States twenty-four years before. They had been married only three years when Herschel and his brother, Meyer, sold out their interest in the London store and started the new business in Annapolis. Leo Schwartz, a cousin, invested in the new enterprise as well. Anna had been pregnant with Stuart at the time. The fledgling company did well right from the start. Still, it took eleven years to return enough of the original investment so that Anna and Herschel could make a down payment on a house.

During those early years, they lived in a cramped apartment upstairs from the business on Fleet Street. Stuart was born there, and seven years later Julie arrived there, too. It was a struggle, four people in three rooms. Yet Herschel always had money in his pocket. He gambled some and traveled on his own a bit. She suspected there was some inheritance he withheld from her and nagged him incessantly about it. He cleverly managed to keep mum on the subject.

Yes, she remembered Hershel being more attentive and affectionate then. He brought gifts home without rhyme or reason; he said he just felt like it. They both seemed happier during those years. Long before the emigration, before Herschel began expanding his waistline, Anna learned to withhold her sexual favors, and doled them out only on those occasions when she wanted or needed something from him. She never knew whether he looked elsewhere, nor did she want to know as long as his dalliances didn't become scandalous.

Now they lived on Prince George Street in Annapolis, in a three-story brick house with Georgian columns out front. It took nearly two years for Anna to decorate the four bedrooms, three baths, spacious living room, and formal dining room—all to her Victorian taste. She felt an almost sensual pleasure in her sumptuous kitchen with its walk-in pantry and stainless-steel appliances. An excellent cook and baker, her desserts at *Oneg Shabbat* always disappeared from the table first. Herschel observed all too often that the kitchen held more passion for her than their bedroom.

Spidery lines radiating from the corners of her mouth and a premature graying of her brown hair made Anna appear somewhat older than her forty-six years. Coloring it would be against her old-school principles. Honesty, modesty, and conservatism guided her way of life. She stood a mere inch shorter than her husband's five-foot-eleven. If slightly on the chunky side, it had to be attributed to her robust but well-proportioned figure. At 165 pounds Anna never varied more than a pound or two. She managed a tight household. Not that there was any real shortage of money to run it these days; more of a habit from their apartment years.

Herschel, quiet for several minutes, took another impulsive bite and handed her what little was left of the wedge of cake. "Must you berate me all the time? You're nagging me to death, woman. I'm trying, you know I am."

"If I don't nag you, you'll kill yourself before your next birthday."

"So why are you always seducing me with these delicious rich desserts? Maybe you are trying to kill me."

"Don't be ridiculous, dear. I know how you love my baking. I just like to please you. You want me to give you sugar-free Jello?"

His moon face turned into a pout. "Maybe. No." Anxious to get off the heavy-weight topic, he asked, "Where are the kids?"

"Stuart's still at work and Julie is staying over at Maurine's. The girls are practicing their parts in the Children's Theater of Annapolis summer musical, *Guys and Dolls*."

"Well, well. Does Julie have a big part or not?"

"Fifty lines and three songs to learn."

"Anna, where've I been during all this? I didn't know she'd even auditioned. When and where is this nonsense to take place?"

"In the new CTA theater on the twenty-sixth of July. And yes, we'll both be in the audience supporting her, whether we're happy about it or not."

Herschel grumbled to himself for a minute. "Stu's been

working late a lot recently. What's going on in that sweatshop of an office, anyway?"

"It's a law office, and they do lots of after-hours work because that's when people come in. He's only a first-year associate, so he catches all the grunt and gofer work. What do you expect one year out of law school?"

"I haven't seen the kid in a week," Herschel complained.

"He's a grown man now! And when he was at home more, you never had time for him."

"Now Anna, you know that's not true. We went to ball games together. Even overnight hikes."

"Yeah," she giggled. "I remember the time you split your pants and you made him walk behind you so the others wouldn't see your southern exposure."

"Sure, you'd remember that," he said. "Didn't I help him with his high school homework?"

"Yes, until the teacher said he should look elsewhere for help. You immediately got insulted and took it out on poor Stu. After that you mostly spent your time in the den with work you brought home from the office. I was the one who sat there with both of them at the dining room table, pressuring them to do their homework."

The Prince George Street house came with a den, which Herschel used as both an office and a hiding place. Outwardly, he was an aggressive businessman, always searching for new customers and new products. He knew the product line inside and out. "Hersch," as he was known to everyone, enjoyed conversation and basked in the knowledge that he could manipulate any topic around to the one he wanted. He loved to tell stories, especially the off-color ones. At fifty-one years this made him the congenial, consummate salesperson. He dressed the part, too, wearing sharply tailored $500 suits and $75 ties. Hersch had a handsome, round-cheeked face except that his friendly eyes sat a bit too far apart. His hairline had disappeared, leaving a shiny bald swath over the top of his head and three-inch fringes with touches of gray on either side.

Only Anna saw through him and managed to stifle his glib tongue. But never in public nor in front of his friends or business colleagues. She smothered him with unwanted town gossip and ran through his faults on a regular basis, so the den became his main refuge—no henpecking allowed. A small TV, a stereo collection, and a personal computer became his regular companions in there.

"You don't know what I have to put up with in the office, Anna. It's a wonder Reubens Brothers makes any profit with all the incompetence that goes on down there. If things ran more smoothly, I wouldn't have to bring work home."

"You needn't apologize to me. I'm satisfied. You've got an MBA, Meyer has his CPA, and your cousin Leo is a master electrician. What the hell else do you need to run a wholesale electrical merchandising business? A magic wand, maybe?"

"Now don't go getting sarcastic, Anna banana."

"Don't call me that, Bushel. See? How do you like it?"

"Enough! Perhaps I should fire that lazy, good-for-nothing brother of yours. Arnold disappears for hours on end. He needs supervising all the time. If we don't check on his work, someone has to redo it. I'm getting tired of it. One more screw-up and he goes, I'm telling you."

"Calm down, Hersch. Calm down, or you'll put your blood pressure in a boil. I'll speak with Thelma tomorrow. She'll know how to bring Arnold in line. Some wives do that all the time."

"Tell me about it," he said, sinking into a chair.

* * * *

World Series, Game Two thundered along in the living room, the Chicago White Sox vs. the Houston Astros, on the 54-inch flat-screen TV visible from the dining room. But there was much more going on in Meyer Reubens' dining room. In the center of the table was a messy pile of multicolor poker chips. Cousin Leo Schwartz was dealing the fourth card to five-card stud. It was a quiet weekly game whose participants were the male family members.

"A five, pair showing. A deuce—no help. A jack-ten-nine—possible straight. And a six of clubs for me—possible flush. The pair of fives bets. Hersch?"

Herschel tossed two blue and one red chip on the pile, "A quarter to stay," he said.

"A big spender, my brother," said Meyer as he threw two clacking white chips down. "Wrong. It'll cost you fifty cents to see the last card."

Arnold and Leo each kicked in the required amount and Leo began to deal around once more. "An ace. A pair of lovely queens. An eight, straight still alive. And a king of spades—right color, no cigar. The ladies get to bet." Leo turned over his five cards. "I'm out."

Meyer quietly pushed two white chips into the center. A roar erupted from the other room. Chicago had scored another run.

"Your four bits and four more," said a grinning Arnold as he contributed to the growing pile in the middle of the table.

"Arnold, you dawg you, you're bluffing," declared Herschel as he tossed four white chips in. "So I'll raise you another fifty cents." He pushed in two more white chips. "Up to you now, brother."

"Hersch, the five of hearts is right next to my queens, so I don't believe you have the five of spades in the hold," said Meyer. "So I'm gonna call you." He slid the other two white chips into the pile and turned over his hold card, a seven of hearts. "Two pair, queens over sevens. Arnie?"

"I got bubkis, guys." He folded all five cards so no one would see them.

"Rats," said Hersch, feinting a loss. "But I *do* have the elusive five of spades, dear brother. I'll turn over just that card for you all to see and weep."

"I don't know how you do it week after week," said Meyer. "Are you really that good at cards or do you cheat?"

"Careful, Meyer. I never cheat. In fact, I give poker lessons every Sunday night," Hersch said with a big meaty-red smile.

"Don't give me that *never* crap, Hersch. We both know you've been cheating ever since we were kids. Dad knew and used to take his belt to you. You've cheated on your wife, you've cheated on your business expenses, and on your taxes, too. How's that for never?"

"Screw you, Meyer," bellowed Herschel, pushing his armchair away from the table. "And I suppose you don't cheat on Esther. You've screwed us out of every secretary we've ever had down at the business. How many have there been? Four? Five? You're not exactly the model of innocence either, mister." He scrambled up, grabbed his coat from the hook in the front hall, and slammed the door behind him. The inlaid glass rattled.

Arnold turned to Leo. "I suppose this is our cue that the game is over."

"You're a master of the understatement," said Leo. "Come on, Arnie, I'll buy you a cup of coffee and a doughnut. Goodnight, Meyer."

"Good night," chimed Arnold as the two men left an unsettled Meyer alone in his dining room.

"I suppose that's the end of the Sunday night poker games," said Arnold as they reached the sidewalk.

"No, no, of course not," replied Leo. "The two of them have been at each other's throats since they were old enough to insult one another. The itch to agitate must have been implanted as a gene when they were embryos, but the inherent desire to quickly bury the hatchet and the short-memory gene appear to be even more dominant. By morning, Hersch and Meyer will have forgotten all about tonight's debacle. It's a good thing too—there's a business to be run tomorrow."

"Wow! That's real brotherly love," declared Arnold.

"Believe it or not, there's a hell of a bond between those two. Don't ever come between them," warned Leo.

# Chapter 11

## The Meyer Reubens Family
Monday, October 24th

eyer Reubens had been examining the several accounting journals and checkbooks spread across the steel desk in front of him. Numbers had long been his true friends. They had never lied to him and often revealed truths about themselves not readily seen by others. Before his alert mind, dynamic data exposed itself—sometimes like an indecent flasher, revealing all he needed to know to arrive at astute business decisions.

Meyer pressed down the TALK lever of the intercom. "Leo, would you bring me last week's register tapes?"

"Yeah, yeah, I'll get the damn tapes for you. It'll take four or five minutes, though," came the return message through the speaker of the wood-grained metal box.

Meyer didn't bother to answer the insolence. It wasn't necessary. He had a problem, and like a ferret, needed to burrow deeper until the solution appeared in its simplest form. Like that rodent, burrowing was in his ruthless nature. As comptroller of Reubens Brothers, Meyer oversaw an annual cash flow of $2.4 million. From the standpoint of inventory, their wholesaling business was always at risk. Too little stock and they couldn't meet deadlines; the competition would eat them for lunch. On the other hand, too much stock tied up precious capital and exposed them to excessive inventory taxes. Also, space was always at a premium. Thus the flow of merchandise required the expertise of an air traffic controller.

Meyer, comfortable in inexpensive two-piece suits and ten-dollar ties, would do nothing to fix his jaundiced pallor or crooked teeth. That came with aging and he accepted it. He doggedly shunned the outdoors and despised dental offices. He was otherwise a reasonably good-looking man of medium build, and dignified posture as befitted an executive of their firm. He captivated everyone with his command in the kingdom of facts and figures, but fell quietly short in the realm of group socializing.

Meyer's office, like the other three at Reubens Brothers, doubly served as a storeroom extension. Floor-to-ceiling shelves surrounded each of those office spaces, as well as the main warehousing area outside their doors. The eight-foot-high stacks of shelves covered all but the packing, shipping, and receiving areas. Meyer didn't mind sharing the office with stock, but there were a lot of interruptions while storing and pulling inventory. One bright spot: he had the only window, although a small, high one at that.

The office door flew open, and his cousin, Leo Schwartz, approached and dumped five curled paper strips on his desk. Meyer thought he heard a grunt before Leo turned to leave.

"Wait, Leo. We need to talk."

"What now?" Leo already had his hand on the doorknob. The giant of a man turned to face Meyer. A layer of perspiration covered his shaven head and well-muscled body, at least the parts left exposed by coarse jeans and sweat-soaked T-shirt.

"Aren't we a bit grouchy today?" asked Meyer. "All I wanted was the tapes, like every other week. Is that so much to ask?

"Sorry," Leo replied in his muted, raspy voice, "but every time I'm in the middle of putting an order together, someone else wants something and I have to start counting all over again."

"Can't Arnold be doing some of that work?" asked Meyer.

"Sure, if I knew where to find him," replied Leo.

"Didn't he come to work today?"

"I thought I saw him earlier."

"So where can he be now?" asked Meyer.

"I don't know. Why don't you ask Hersch? It's his brother-in-law."

"Okay, okay, I get it," said Meyer. "Just don't take it out on me."

"By the way, what did you want to talk about? Arnold?"

"No," said Meyer. There's nothing to talk about there. Leo, we've got a shortage problem again. I got an e-mail from Beeman and Beeman Electric this morning. It seems that each of the four reels of Number Twelve copper building wire was short by sixty feet. It forced them to buy an extra reel at retail price. They're totally pissed at us and are threatening to pull their business and transfer it to a company in Baltimore. We're talking 60 feet missing per 300-foot reel; 240 feet at $4.10 per foot wholesale. That's almost a thousand bucks. Can you blame them?"

"Of course not, Meyer. I thought I noticed that two of the six reels in stock didn't look quite as full as the others, but I thought it was a matter of winding tightness. I'll send them a whole reel, one of the short ones, free of charge."

"Thanks, Leo. Do you think someone out there is stealing again?"

"Appears so, but who? There're only two stock handlers and a driver. The rest is family."

"Don't forget about the new office manager, Leo."

"You suspect Ceila?"

"No," said Meyer. "I was just finishing the employee list, and I was thinking . . . Could one person alone handle reels that size?"

"I don't see how, Meyer. They're just too big to muscle by yourself. I'm sure we've got a conspiracy on our hands."

"This is serious. Let me know what you find, Leo. I promised Esther I'd take her to the doctor this afternoon." He looked at his watch. "I hate to dump this on you, but I've got to get going in a few minutes."

"Go ahead, cousin. I'll handle it."

* * * *

Meyer Reubens parked the Cadillac Escalade in the circular driveway of his sprawling Beards Creek waterfront home. Although it appeared to be a brick-trimmed ranch style from the street level, its rooms tiered down a cliff toward the water and dock forty feet below. The site, sprawl, and frequent alterations—all of it was, unfortunately, his wife's preoccupation; her hobby, although she insisted it was essential, and to this day, the house remained wholly in flux. Before their emigration, the four-room flat in east London had left little room for her creative changes.

Esther had always enjoyed athletics, dancing, and the great outdoors. Her well-toned body and eternal tan added to her basic good looks, which included sparkling green eyes, a slender nose, and a small mouth. The agile blonde with blush cheeks showed little or no sign of motherhood, nor her fifty years. Her attractive children, Josh, twenty-two, and Abel, seventeen, were excellent swimmers and boat handlers, but only mediocre students. Although Meyer and Esther led very separate lives outside their home, inside the master bedroom they enjoyed a hearty relationship. They were definitely in love, soul mates according to Esther. But there were a few times in their marriage when Meyer had strayed; most recently, with va-va-va-voom Sandy, the office manager. The fling lasted three months before he had to send her packing with a cash bonus. Esther had never confronted him, so he presumed she never knew.

Briefcase in hand, Meyer headed up the four steps to the front door and stepped inside. "Hello! Anybody home?" The storm door snapped closed behind him. He searched through the house and finally found Esther sitting on the lower veranda, asleep, all bundled up in her favorite rocking chair. He released the rear storm door, and let it slam intentionally.

Esther sprang to life as he bent to kiss her hello. "Hi, dear, I didn't hear you come in."

"Just arrived," he said. "We have an hour before we have to leave. Perhaps we could have a little lunch beforehand."

"I set a plate in the fridge with some chicken salad sandwiches for you."

"Aren't you joining me, sweetheart?"

"I'm not too hungry," she said. "My stomach gets tied up in knots whenever I have to see a doctor. Never fails. But I'll sit with you anyway."

"But you said it would be just a routine checkup at your gynecologist."

"I wouldn't even have needed you to drive if I hadn't had my license suspended for speeding last month. Six months. So foolish of me, but he could have given me a warning instead."

"The judge gave you that warning last time," he said as he took a bite of his sandwich and followed with a sip of coffee. "Besides, I don't mind driving you. Are you okay? Is there something you're not telling me, sweetheart?"

"I guess I'm fine," she replied. "Well . . . nothing I can put my finger on. It's like I have this gloomy, foreboding feeling." She used her napkin to dry a tear from the corner of her eye.

"Nonsense," he said between bites. "You look fit as a fiddle, the picture of health."

She sighed. *Clichés, clichés, but he means well.*

* * * *

Rivka heard the doorbell tinkle and looked up to greet the newest customer, who turned out to be Stuart Reubens. This time Rivka had no doubt about his purpose in the store. *Rather unlawyerlike*, she thought as she silently pointed to the poetry section on her far right. She watched him approach the stack where Lord Byron lay stretched out atop the volumes of William Wordsworth, his regal realm. She noted his amber feline eyes pick up on Stuart and his head swivel like a locked-on gun-control radar as the young man walked past him while entering an aisle between the stacks.

When Stuart lifted a hand to pet the shiny ebony fur, Lord Byron rose up and emitted a low-pitched motorboat sound to discourage the gesture. He pulled his hand back in a hurry and mumbled something under his breath.

"Don't worry. Lord Byron won't attack unless I tell him to," Ivy piped up, kneeling and straightening the books on the bottom shelf. A mischievous smile accompanied her words. A clipboard full of inventory paperwork lay beside her.

"Hello down there," Stuart said. "I came by on Saturday, but you weren't here."

"I took my landlady to the doctor in the morning." She brushed a few strands of silky hair away from her left eye and looked up at him. "Sorry I missed you. Was there something I could help you with?"

"Yes," he replied. "I came to see you, of course. I'll be a little late this morning going into work."

"In that case, you won't mind giving me an assist to get up." She picked up the clipboard with one hand and extended the other toward him.

He pulled up the 126-pound Ivy with hardly any effort at all. Standing, her head came up to a little below his shoulder; he was just over six feet.

"Did you have anything specific in mind, Stuart?"

"I want to get better acquainted if you don't mind my being forward," he replied. "But please call me Stu. Everyone else does."

Ivy cocked her head. "You know what? I don't want to call you Stu. It sounds too much like peasant food. 'Stuart' is so much stronger and more elegant."

The athlete in him broke into a huge grin, exhibiting near-perfect teeth, except for a couple with small chips, souvenirs of his college football. "In that case I'm fine with you calling me Stuart."

"Oh good. So how do you propose we get together? I'm at work now, and I've already blown off Saturday morning."

He couldn't shut off his playful side. "Propose? It's a little early for that. Anyway, there's dinner, the theater, a movie, dancing, picnics, sports events, biking, and hiking. I know so little about you, I don't know what you'd like."

"Why don't we start with something simple like a movie and a cup of tea or coffee afterward?"

"Sounds great," he said. "I'll pick you up at six. But I'm not sure where."

"Whoa! I didn't know you had tonight in mind. I won't be through in the store until we close at 7:30. Then I have to go home and feed my shut-in landlady and get her ready for bed. Maybe we could go somewhere for dessert around nine."

"Swell," he said with a hint of disappointment on his face. "I'll pick you up at nine. I still don't know where you live."

"That's easy enough." She jotted down her address on the last page of her clipboard pad. She tore it off and handed it to him.

"Thanks!" He took the note, folded it in half, and tucked it in his tiny black day book, which he returned to his hip pocket. "I'll stop by at nine, and we'll go for supper."

"Dessert," Ivy said. "I'm having supper with my landlady."

"Correction, dessert it is." Stuart took a few steps backward to leave and stumbled over the book cart. He quickly left before he made any more goofs.

* * * *

Meyer Reubens absorbed himself in *Sports Illustrated*. He'd brought his own copy, knowing that a gynecologist's office would hardly have anything for him to read. Meanwhile, Esther had begun thumbing through her fifth fashion magazine in ten minutes. Mind and body seemed on divergent courses. She scanned the waiting room. Three other women. Meyer was the only man. Esther heard the inner office door creak and swing open. The nurse stood there motioning for her to come inside.

"I'll wait out here for you, dear," said Meyer, not comprehending that she actually wanted him to accompany her.

90

Rather than make a scene, Esther disappeared inside and he resumed his reading. Some minutes later, Meyer looked up when he sensed movement across the room. He noticed an attractive blonde, perhaps in her early thirties, with exceptional legs, slinking across the room for a magazine on a corner table. Bending slightly in a body-clinging dress, she selected a periodical from the middle of the pile, causing several others to slip to the floor. Bending more deeply, she retrieved the errant magazines and looked over at the only man to see if he were watching. She knew by the hesitant grin on his face that she had his attention and winked at him.

"Lovely day," she said.

"Oh, yes." he answered. "Verrry nice."

The woman perceived his double entendre and moved into the chair next to him, the one that Esther had vacated. He could hardly say no, but he worried what Esther might think of the two of them sitting so close together. After all, there were plenty of other empty chairs. It was an amusement, an embarrassment of sorts. This woman had taken control.

"I assume you enjoy sports," she said, noting the magazine in front of him.

"Oh, yes," he replied. "I'm an avid fan, especially football and tennis. How about you?"

"Not so much the sport as the professional men who play them," she replied, intentionally bumping his elbow on the armrest. "I simply adore the athletic body, the bubbling muscles, the chest expansion, the sheer power. Did you ever play?"

He could hear her breath, now faster and deeper. "Uh, no. I was never quite skilled enough. I stuck with tennis and swimming."

The woman twisted her body, leaning closer. He felt her heated breath as she spoke directly into his ear—a deep throaty voice, dripping with overtones. "Maybe you didn't try hard enough as a young man." Her hand had casually fallen upon his knee.

He turned to face her and found himself leering down into her outrageously low-cut cleavage. His mouth dropped open, and when he realized what was happening, he turned to see if anyone else had perceived their risqué behavior. The two other women in the room certainly had. They were staring, at least until he glared at them. He turned back when he felt a gentle squeeze just above his right kneecap. His face had assumed a pink glow.

"My friends call me Maisie," she offered. "I have lots of friends." The flashy woman pressed her business card into his right hand.

Meyer wanted to refuse the card, but helplessly took it anyway. He wanted to tell her that she was being entirely too friendly, but couldn't vocalize the words. From the smirk on her face he suddenly realized that she'd been entertaining herself at his expense. To make matters worse, the door to the inner office opened and Esther stood there agog, watching him.

Esther reacted by huffing and walking right past him to the outer door. Her form was just a blur to him, but her muttered words were clear enough. "You son-of-a-bitch. You can go straight to hell."

Meyer stood up and flew through the doorway after her. He caught her at the elevator and turned her around to face him. "Wait, you don't understand."

"Apparently I don't," she scolded. "Were you trying to arrange some late-night orgy for yourself? I'm not servicing you enough? Is that it?"

"Sweetheart, let me explain."

Esther snatched the woman's business card out of Meyer's hand and glanced at it. She read aloud: "Maisie and a phone number—nothing else. What's to explain? She's a prostitute, not an interior decorator."

"But—"

"Never mind 'but,' that's what got you into this mess."

The elevator door opened and Esther stepped inside. "No!" She held up her hand. "You can get your own elevator."

Meyer shoved his body between the closing doors and caused them to reverse. "I swear to you that I did nothing to encourage that woman in any way. She was just trying to embarrass me." He stepped all the way in and pressed the LOBBY button. "What would a hooker be doing in a gynecologist's office? And how do you know she's a hooker?"

"A business card with only a first name and phone number? Come on," she sneered. The elevator door opened to the lobby. They both got out and walked through the front door to the street.

"Don't respectable ladies have calling cards these days?"

She had to chuckle. "Respectable ladies? Are we in a Jane Austen novel? Not calling cards, Meyer. Legitimate business cards, but they wouldn't be passing them out to strange men they meet in a gynecologist's office."

At the car he held the door. "I love you," he said with the most serious face he could muster.

Esther relented. "Get in, you damned fool."

"What did the doctor say?" asked Meyer.

"Don't go changing the subject. I'm not through with you yet, you masher."

"Now who's sounding like Jane Austen?" He stopped for a red light. "I never wanted anything to do with that bitch. Now tell me what the doctor had to say or I'll strangle you." The light changed, and he continued driving.

Esther remained quiet for the next five minutes while she mulled everything over in her mind. When she couldn't hold it in any longer, she said. "All right, he wants me to schedule an appointment to have a D and C done. He'll decide then whether I'll need a full hysterectomy or not. He said not to worry, as that kind of surgery is quite common in women of my age."

"Jeez," he said. A worried look pained his face. "How long will you have to be in the hospital?"

"Probably just outpatient surgery unless I need to have the hysterectomy and then it might be several days. Damn it, Meyer, why do you have to go astray when I need you most?"

"I'm telling you I never went astray. I only spoke when spoken to. I was only being polite. I didn't get out of *my* chair to sit next to *her*. I'd apologize, but there's nothing to apologize for. Honest."

"All right, all right. I won't say any more about it. It's just that I don't want you to ask me to bail you out again."

"But that was so many years ago in another world, Esther darling."

* * * *

"Ivy, I hear the doorbell," said Irma. "It's ten to nine. Your young man must be here. You hurry along."

Ivy pulled the covers up to Irma's chest, kissed her on the forehead, left the lights on for her to read, and left the door slightly ajar. The doorbell rang again. "Coming," she called. At the bottom of the stairs she straightened her white blouse, brushed a bit of lint from her black slacks, and donned the gray cardigan she had thrown over the banister earlier.

When she swung open the front door, Stuart stood there in a light blue dress shirt with an unbuttoned collar and tan sport jacket, looking just as handsome as he did Friday night. They exchanged greetings and Ivy slipped out of the house, looping her arm through his in one smooth move. Stuart helped her into the passenger seat of his Toyota Corolla and headed toward West Street, where he turned left and continued into the Parole section of town.

"Where are we going?" she asked.

"For dessert, as promised," he replied.

"I mean what's the name of the place?"

"It's called the Double T Diner, and they have at least two display cases filled with spectacular cakes, tortes, and pastries. You won't be disappointed, I assure you."

The Corolla zipped into a space, and while they waited to be seated she saw the array of mouth-watering pastries on display. "I see what you mean. I've got my eye on those adorable chocolate mice. Yum." She followed the hostess and settled into a booth next to Stuart.

"Don't they have pastry shops in London?" he asked.

"Oh yes," she replied, "but I didn't frequent them. Too expensive."

"I'll bet you didn't know my parents came from London, too," he said.

This remark caught Ivy by surprise, and she managed somehow to conceal it. "And how long ago was that, Stuart?"

"Twenty-six years ago. My mother was pregnant with me at the time."

A shock wave passed through her. *My God, could Stuart's father be Snooks? Moreover, could Stuart be my secret half-brother?* A shiver ran down her spine, and she visibly shook it off by pulling her cardigan closer about her.

"What's wrong, Ivy?" He had sensed a change in her demeanor.

"Nothing," she replied. "I felt a little chill, that's all. The air conditioning's set a little low for me."

"Would you like my jacket?"

"No. No thank you, Stuart. I'll do up another button here and I'll be fine. What were you saying about your family coming to Annapolis?"

"My father and three uncles moved the family business to Annapolis from London just before I was born. The Reubens Brothers Electrical Merchandising Company. That's the name of the family business. Wholesale."

"Must have been a major undertaking," she commented. "I guess it took many trips across the Atlantic and some time to accomplish." *Four men*, she thought. *Could there have been more? Another family, perhaps?* Finding Snooks could be more difficult than she had ever imagined.

"What's it gonna be, folks?" A waitress stood at their table, where both menus lay unopened. "Need a little more time?"

"Two coffees, please, and . . ." Stuart looked up. "Oh, hi, Frieda. I didn't notice it was you."

"Stuart Reubens and Ivy. I didn't realize you guys were a twosome."

"I like the sound of that," Stuart said.

"It's just our first date, Frieda," returned Ivy sternly. *Oh my,* she thought, *this really is a small town. Waitresses and customers so chummy. Never happen in London. Are any secrets safe here?*

"What can I get you besides coffee?"

Ivy said, "You get something, Stuart. I'm not very hungry."

"Nonsense," he answered, Turning to Frieda he ordered two chocolate mice.

"Two coffees and two chocolate cream-filled mice coming up," Frieda jotted on her pad, then crossed the room on short, speedy legs.

"So how do you like being a solicitor?" Ivy asked.

"I'm a law school graduate, but I haven't had much of a chance to do any real lawyering yet. I'm a first-year associate, one step up from a gofer. It's not very exciting."

"I'm sure it will get more exciting as time goes on."

They chatted amiably until a humming Frieda set the two desserts in front of them. Ivy's eyes widened, and she exclaimed, "My goodness. This fella looks a lot bigger than he did in the case. She tweaked the mouse's gumdrop nose off and popped it in her mouth. "But I can't eat all of him," she said between munches. "It's so wasteful."

"They have those cutesy take-home doggy baskets," said Stuart. "You can surprise that shut-in old lady you keep telling me about."

Despite her protests, Ivy speared one of the large ears. While savoring the velvety frosting in her mouth, her thoughts turned back to the possibility that her date might be her half-brother or that he might be related to Snooks in some other way. She had to admit she was fond of this young man. She should be hating him. But she couldn't seem to conjure up that emotion. She heard a clicking sound and saw Stuart tapping his empty dessert plate with his fork. It was his way of bringing her back to the here and now.

"Sorry, I was just daydreaming. It's getting to be my bedtime. We do both have to go to work tomorrow."

*She's sounding a little like my mother,* Stuart thought. He nodded and caught Frieda's attention for the bill. He left a tip, and on their way to the cashier a voice called to him.

"Stuart, darling." The voice belonged to his Aunt Katie Silvers. The other woman at the table was his Aunt Thelma Katz. After an early movie they had come to the diner for coffee and a chat.

"You can't go anywhere in this town without bumping into someone you know," he whispered to Ivy. "It's the penalty you pay for having a large family in a small town." He introduced her as his new friend from London, then smoothly said, "Hope to see you both again soon," and waved goodbye to avoid getting the third-degree.

The Corolla delivered the two of them to the Riley home. On the porch Ivy gave his hand a warm squeeze, then ducked in the door, leaving him wanting.

## Chapter 12

## **The Arnold Katz Family**
Tuesday, October 25th

Yo, Arnie! Wake up! Leo's looking for you."

"Wha . . .? What?" moaned Arnold Katz as he shook himself awake. He nearly fell out of the folding chair he'd propped between the wall and the last stand of merchandise pallets opposite it. It was the perfect hiding place, a section of the warehouse rarely frequented. He'd spent a lot of time researching this goldbricking haven. And why not? He wasn't a shareholder in Reubens Brothers. He wasn't even a Reubens. His sister, Anna, was a Reubens by marriage, and he had a job by virtue of his brother-in-law's generosity. He was constantly reminded of this generosity by both his sister and his wife, Thelma. But Arnold didn't like the work. He'd been a shipping clerk since he started and knew he'd never get promoted; there was no specific job to get promoted *to*. At the age of forty-nine, he didn't exactly see himself as lazy. He just had no motivation to work harder.

"Leo's looking for you," George Hernandez, the elderly stock clerk repeated. "He sounded kinda pissed, man."

Arnold scowled as the realization hit him that he'd been discovered. With a forklift, George had just removed the pallet of Square D breaker boxes that had concealed his current hiding place.

Arnold dragged himself to his feet, stretched his long arms in a full yawn mode, and rubbed the sleep from his eyes. At six-foot-three and slightly over 200 pounds, the wannabe musician/poet had comical ears that stood away from his face and thinning blond hair. He was born in Suffolk, England, and at age twenty-eight, moved to London, next door to Herschel and Anna in the same apartment house. A year later the Reubens emigrated. He stayed behind.

Arnold met Thelma Fitzwaller at a birthday party for one of her girlfriends. He'd brought along his guitar, and when he softly sang folksy-like along with his chords, the party's groupies gathered around, and he became the center of attraction. Before the end of the evening Thelma remarked to the birthday girl that she would marry that guitarist. Arnold walked her home that night and kissed her at the doorstep. The top of her chestnut-brown head only came up to his shoulders. He fell in love with her high-pitched little voice, bouncing pony tail, and pert breasts. Her small, turned-up nose didn't hurt either. It didn't take long for him to get over the fact that she was a *shikse*, a non-Jew. With Anna and the rest of the Reubens clan already in America, her religion wasn't a factor.

Three months later, Thelma moved in with him, and before that year ended, they married. They had to; she'd gotten pregnant. It was as though she had accomplished this all by herself. Arnold resented the early marriage, and when baby Maurine arrived, he felt the trap close completely. Thelma had eyes only for the baby, driving a wedge between them. He viewed the child as one more obstacle in the way of his happiness and success. The fatherly instinct never even occurred to him. It just wasn't there.

Arnold lost interest in his waiter's job at a local restaurant in London and eventually got sloppy with his appearance. Soon he was without employment. But Thelma didn't know he'd been canned. He passed the workday hours experimenting with other women, lavishing gifts and favors on them. In time Arnold realized that the small inheritance he and his sister had split couldn't last much longer. He wrote to Anna for money. She couldn't send much because her share of the inheritance had gone into her husband's business. Instead, she invited Arnold and his family to come to the States and furnished the fare to get there. Reubens Brothers had a job waiting for him.

That was fifteen years ago. Today, Arnold, Thelma, and Maurine, who was now seventeen, lived in an upstairs apartment in the Eastport section of Annapolis. The building was old and badly in need of renovation, but it was all they could afford. He sang and played in a nearby pub for extra cash, often writing original music and lyrics for these gigs. His sing-a-long karaoke style music had become popular with the local crowd. Hardly a financial success, but the music did seem to fill the deep gap in his life. During some of those interludes at the Reubens warehouse when his colleagues thought he was asleep, Arnold was actually composing music with his eyes shut. He couldn't really complain. Thelma appeared happy. So there was no need to change his way of life. *It ain't likely someone's going to fire me, so long as I do a minimum of the daily work expected of me. Besides, I'm family.*

"You still here?" questioned George, returning on his forklift for another load. "You see Leo yet?"

"Nope. I'm headed over there right there now. Lickety-split even." He grinned pleasantly.

Arnold strolled over to the last office on the right. The door was open, and he could see Leo bending over a crate of sump pump motors. He was copying numbers from the name plates into a notebook.

"You wanted to see me, Leo?"

"Yeah, where the hell have you been?"

"There weren't any orders to fill, so I was straightening up the cases on Aisle 18 so you could read the labels. What do you need?"

"Two weeks ago we got a big shipment of wire from Lightning Wire and Cable. There were eight reels of Number Twelve/Four-Wire and four reels of Number Ten/Three-Wire. You were in charge of the unloading."

"Yeah, Leo, I remember. Bummed my damn playing fingers on the reels doing it. So?"

"Did you notice anything unusual about the reels?"

"No. Why do you ask?" Arnold drew back, expecting to be accused of something petty.

"One of our good customers is complaining of shortages."

"So now you're accusing me of stealing?"

"No, no, Arnie, nothing like that. I'm just trying to figure out whether the reels were already short when we received them. We have to determine whether those reels were completely full when they came in."

"Leo," Arnold said, "there's only one way to find out. Let's go check out the reels still in stock."

The two men cut through Aisle 9 and stopped in front of the wire inventory. The four reels of Number Ten appeared to be filled correctly: to the rim of the reel. The ends were machine-sheared on a bias, painted blue, wrapped with shiny black electrical tape, and stapled to the wooden carrier reel, along with the specifications tag. Leo and Arnold turned their attention to the remaining four reels of Number Twelve wire that came in under the same order. Two were as full as the Number Tens with normal cut, paint, tape, and tag. But when they reached the last two reels, Leo jerked to a stop. "My God!" On those reels, the top ring was at least three inches shy of the rim and had square ends as though the wire had been cut off with a hacksaw.

He pulled a thick triplicate form from the clipboard under his arm and handed it to Arnold. "This order has to go out tonight. You go ahead, get it in the works. I'll be here awhile." Arnold sauntered off. Leo began checking the reel tag information against what was written in his green accounting book. When Arnold was out of sight, he knelt down on the cement floor and ran a finger across it to see if the floor had been recently swept. It hadn't been. Neither had any of the adjacent flooring. Using a foxtail brush, Leo swept the floor directly under the reels, first into a dustpan and then onto a clean sheet of paper from his clipboard. Holding the paper directly in front of his face, he gently blew away the lighter dust matter before carefully folding the paper around the remainder. He would analyze it later. Leo headed back to his office, deep in thought.

* * * *

Ivy spent the entire morning sifting through the inventory, taking up from where she had left off the day before. On the one hand, inventory was a bastion of monotony, and on the other hand, it was definitely the best way to learn about what the store was all about. At 12:15 she sat down in the ground floor reading room and poured hot English tea from a Thermos into its lid. She munched on half an egg salad sandwich and quietly sipped tea until Rivka passed by the door. Ivy called, "Rivka, do you have a minute?"

"Sure, Ivy. What's troubling you, dear?" Rivka drew up a chair. She'd noticed her young  protégée's drawn expression.

"What do you know about the Reubens families?"

"Not very much, I'm afraid. Why do you ask?"

"Stuart and I had our first date last night, and I learned that his family emigrated from London just about the time my mother was murdered."

Rivka's back straightened imperceptibly. "So what are you thinking?"

Ivy answered perhaps too quickly. "I'm thinking that maybe Stuart's father had something to do with Mother's murder. But his two uncles and a cousin emigrated at the same time, and I don't know how many other strangers also came at the same time. If Stuart's father did have something to do with the murder, then that makes Stuart my half-brother. I have this upsetting dilemma and I'm not sure what I should do. Do I discourage Stuart as a possible suitor because his father might be complicit and we would be too closely related? Or do I play dumb and play the spy to learn all I can about the family? I feel so guilty because I'm fond of Stuart. I'm not sure whether to admire or abhor him."

Rivka adjusted her square glasses with their bronze-colored steel rims. They had a habit of slipping down her slightly bumpy nose. In her purple turtleneck shirt and cargo khakis, she appeared, at first glance, more casual than the owner of a thriving business, but her no-nonsense demeanor exuded intellect and authority. "This is quite a stretch, Ivy. You're really leaping to conclusions. The Reubens family might have nothing at all to do with your mother's death. And don't forget, false accusations can destroy innocent people. I'm not sure I'm the one you should be talking to about this, but Dan did promise we'd try to help. For the moment I'll humor you, if you'll forgive the expression, by following your logic.

"Let's say there is a possibility that Stuart is your half-brother. He could also be your second or third cousin by one of the two uncles. I think Leo Schwartz is a first cousin to Herschel and Meyer, so that would make you two either second or third cousins. In any case, your young man is guiltless, and presumably, ignorant of the crime. There's no reason for you to despise him. You may someday want or even need him as a friend or possibly something closer. However, you should guard against developing any romantic feelings toward him until you know more. As you said, there might be others who fit the same time-and-place criteria. And if one of those so-called others were the murderer, you would miss an opportunity to grow a relationship with someone you're already fond of."

Rivka pressed her line of reasoning. "However, I'm not so sure you should continue on a track to pursue your mother's murderer. It could prove to be very dangerous. Remember, the treed animal will fight for its life. After this much time and distance, I doubt if you'll get much help from the authorities. You really have to wonder whether justice will prevail. Don't let on what you already know, and above all, stop telling everyone *why* you emigrated to Annapolis. It will only set you up as a target." Rivka paused as she assessed the impact of her words. But she wasn't finished.

"If you truly intend to stay on this terrible course, it would probably be best that you maintain the status quo with Stuart. I only suggest this because you will need him to learn more about the whole family. You needn't make an enemy of him. I'm more friendly with Esther and Katie through the critique group. Anna, Julie, and Thelma are mere acquaintances from the *Oneg* committee. I know nothing of their men-folk except maybe Anna's brother,

Arnold. I understand that he's something of a wastrel. I've even heard Esther call him lazy." Rivka stopped herself, thinking, *Oops. I shouldn't be such a gossip.* "But he is good-natured and he does have some musical talent. I've listened to him play guitar and sing at one of those Eastport pubs a few times."

Slumping slightly, Ivy said, "I hadn't realized how hazardous my quest might become." She emptied her cup and reassembled the Thermos.

"Let's talk to Daniel about what your next step should be." The two women stood and walked to the cashier's desk where Dan had just finished ringing up a sale. The only other customer in the store was still browsing in the magazine aisle. Rivka encouraged Ivy to explain her dilemma, then added her own words of concern.

Dan listened intently. "I agree completely with the status quo part and all of the cautions as well. First of all, we have to get hold of your mother's diary. If the included dates are good enough, we might be able to eliminate some of these men by correlating those dates with tax and voting records, as well as possible ship or plane manifests. Perhaps immigration records would be the most helpful. I called Scotland Yard in London, and they refused to release any information on an unsolved case."

"Have you had any luck reaching that Chief Inspector fellow yet?" asked Rivka, leaning her plump backside against the counter. "Didn't he run the show in Bath?"

Dan said, "Yes and no. Winston did run the show, and no, I haven't reached him yet. Almost no one in the Bath constabulary I've talked to seems to know anything about him. One sergeant recognized the name and said Winston was transferred out of the Bath region, but didn't know where to. When I asked if there was some sort of police directory, I was informed Yes, but it was an internal document and he couldn't release any information from it. I even tried calling Sergeant Thorwal. Rivka, you remember him by his undercover name as Vernon Levant. I was told he was on leave and couldn't be reached for a fortnight. Just my luck."

"Dan, I think I know where to find him."

"And how do you propose to do that, m'lady?"

"Remember when I told you I'd run into Heather at Phil's Pharmacy?"

"That's right! The Thorwal chap wants to spend his whole vacation with Heather. Isn't that what you said?"

"Yeah," said Rivka. "I thought it was kind of brazen of him to think he could just move in on her for two weeks after more than a year of no communication. Maybe I should give Heather a call when school lets out this afternoon."

"You two are wonderful," offered Ivy. "Especially when you put your heads together. But I wonder how this constable sergeant can help us retrieve my mother's diary after so many years."

"I'm hoping," Dan said, "that Thorwal can lead us to Chief Inspector E. Howard Winston or someone else with enough pull to release or copy it. Personally, I can't see why they still think they can solve a case that's been a dead-end for twenty-three years. I think even we may have a better chance at solving it."

"It's 3:30 now," said Rivka. "That's enough time for her to drive home." She dialed Heather's number and waited. After five rings Heather picked up.

"Hello!" Her voice was higher pitched than usual.

"Hi, Heather. It's Rivka. You sound a little out of breath."

"Yeah, well, I had to run up the stairs to catch the phone. What can I do for you?"

"Dan and I are trying to locate Constable Sergeant Fenton Thorwal. It's rather important. We think he may be able to help Ivy get hold of her mother's diary. Is he by any chance staying with you?"

"Jeez, Rivka! Why the hell would you think that? You're right, of course, but no one else can know. I could get into a lot of trouble with the school board, my parents, too. It has to be kept secret. Promise?"

"I promise, Heather. Don't get your scruples in an uproar. What you do with your love life is your business. We only want to talk with your beau."

"He's right here. I told him not to answer the phone." There were muffled voices behind the hand covering the phone.

"Hello, Rivka! This is Fen. How are you?"

"I'm fine. Do you remember me and Dan?"

"I sure do, just like it was yesterday. How can I be of service?"

Rivka carefully laid out the story of Ivy's mother and how she was murdered. She explained Ivy's quest, the importance of obtaining Lainee's diary, and how she and Dan intended to use it. "The authorities acknowledged having it, but we ran into a snag. Scotland Yard refused to either release or even photocopy it."

"Again," asked Fen, "how then can I help you?"

"We thought either you or Chief Inspector Winston might have a little pull with these people so we could get our hands on a copy."

"I don't think a lowly sergeant from another city's district constabulary would have much pull at Scotland Yard. The Chief Inspector might, though. Have you contacted him?"

"My husband tried, but it seems Winston transferred out of Bath."

"The Chief Inspector has been reassigned to Scotland Yard in London. I'll make a few calls and try to locate him for you. After what you and Dan went through to locate those printing artifacts last year, I think the old man owes you one, as you chaps say."

* * * *

"Excuse me, Katie, can you hold on a minute? The wild one's trying to escape again." Thelma Katz set the receiver down on the kitchen counter. "Arnold!" his wife screamed from the kitchen sink. "Where in the heck do you think you're going at this time of night? You promised to fix the drain on this infernal sink. There must be something stuck in it."

"Tomorrow, sweetheart," Arnold said as he slipped into a leather jacket. "I've got to drive Maurine to her rehearsal. She's already late."

Maurine was already out the front door.

"Our daughter is seventeen. She has her driver's license and is perfectly capable of driving herself wherever," retorted Thelma. "What kind of lying shenanigans are you up to now, Arnold Katz?"

"I'm not up to anything, sweetheart. Why would you say something like that?"

"Then why do you need your guitar? Do you think I'm stupid?"

"Of course not. I have the utmost respect for your intelligence."

"Don't get smart alecky with me, buster. You're going over to that pub, Marmaduke's, aren't you?"

"Well, as long as I'm in the car, I thought I'd head over there and try out my new ballad on the gang. I finished it this afternoon."

"The gang, hell. I'll bet it's that tramp Fanny Lee Talbot. Does she perform in bed better than I do? Does she wiggle her *tush* to your melodies the way I used to?"

"That's enough, Thelma," he said as he and his guitar ducked out the back door.

Thelma hurried back to the kitchen and picked up the receiver. "You still there, Katie? Sorry. I didn't mean for you to tune in to all my *tsuris*. No, it's no worse. He'll be home by eleven, dragging his instrument behind. No, no, dear. I meant his guitar. I can't believe there's anything going on between them. He goes to Marmaduke's for a sympathetic ear. They sit around singing themselves into a frenzy or sit back and listen to him all evening. Sometimes he even has a paid gig there. Yeah, I'll keep a sharp eye on him. Yeah, I know it runs in the family. You call it what? The roving gene? Hah! Goodnight now."

Chapter 13

## The Leo Schwartz Families
Wednesday Evening, October 26th

Leo Schwartz sat in his office with the door closed. Shoving aside all other files, he unfolded the sheet of paper filled with sweepings and spread it out on his desk. Next he grasped his florescent lamp with its built-in magnifier and adjusted it over the sweepings. With his letter opener, he poked through the shavings until he found the tiny copper flecks of metal he suspected were there. The copper flecks confirmed that the theft had taken place at Reubens Brothers and not at the supplier's. They were the residue from slicing through the hefty wire with a hacksaw. Even though he'd discovered the presence of copper, he kept probing the little pile in the futile hope that his evidence would disappear. Eventually, he refolded the paper securely and stored it in his top desk drawer.

Glancing at his watch, Leo noticed that it was past six. The rest of the workforce had gone home to their families. It wasn't that Leo didn't have a family. He had, in fact, two fractured families and a history of wanderlust. His twenty-four-year-old son, Mark Schwartz, was all that was left of his first family. Mark was pursuing a master's degree in physics at Johns Hopkins. They saw each other a few times each month. The boy's mother had wasted away from tuberculosis after only three years of marriage. Leo's two teenage daughters, Brenda and Barri, lived with their mother, Katie. Leo and Katie had been divorced for thirteen years; neither he nor his second wife had regretted their decision to split. Katie got the West Annapolis house, and he got to see his girls several times a week.

Despite the fact that Katie had married Melvin Silvers two years later, Leo had a regular invite to Sunday dinner from them. He was actually quite fond of Mel; the two had even gone to Orioles baseball games together.

Katie, with her olive skin and gypsy eyes, was pleased with the arrangement. In some way she still wanted the incorrigible big ape, and perhaps those animal feelings were mutual. They had met and married in London, but she soon discovered that Leo was a free spirit who couldn't be tamed by any one woman, a handsome charmer, and a magnificent specimen of a lover. When the Reubens brothers brought up their proposition to move the family business to America, she championed the idea, thinking it would provide a fresh start for the both of them. Unfortunately, time and the uncontrollable Leo proved her wrong.

Leo turned out the lights in his office. Only the dimmer nightlights remained on in the rest of the building. He locked the front door and headed up Fleet Street to Church Circle, where he turned left, and found himself in front of the Maryland Inn. Leo decided to try their King of France Tavern. He slid onto an empty bar stool next to two thirty-ish blondes. He sized up both of them, and in his mind, rejected the one farthest from him right off, even though he had no intention of approaching either one.

"Hey, handsome, you got a light?" The nearer woman leaned way over toward him, close enough for him to view the ample, quite fetching merchandise. For a split second he wondered what this young woman would want with him. He looked his fifty-four years. A Sugar Daddy maybe? He hadn't smoked since he got back from serving in the British 199th light infantry in Nam in '70, but still carried a butane lighter on his keychain for just such occasions.

"You bet," he answered, as he pulled it from his pocket, flicked twice, and held it to her cigarette.

She grabbed his wrist to steady him, but she found it wasn't necessary. His hand was strong and forceful. "Thanks, mister. My name is Alice and this here is Violet. We come here a lot to listen to the music. You?"

"Occasionally."

"I mean, you got a name?"

"Sure," he teased.

"Well?" She put her hand on his left thigh.

"It's Leo, Alice." He touched the part of her fanny that didn't quite fit on the barstool and gently squeezed it.

"Whee! Whoa!" she wriggled and giggled. "Don't get me wrong, Leo. I'm not on the make."

"You sure could have fooled me," said Leo, laughing with her. "What did you have in mind?"

"You could buy me a drink, and we could talk about things and listen to the music together."

"Things?" he questioned.

"You know," she replied.

"What about Violet?" he asked softly.

Alice casually glanced over at her female companion. Violet frowned, slipped from the bar stool, and sat down at an empty table facing the other way.

Leo called to the barkeep and ordered a round of repeat drinks, laying down two twenties  against a tab. "Now let's talk about those things you mentioned. If you're out to chisel a few drinks out of me, I'm happy to oblige a round or two just for the company. If you're a pro, you and me are just gonna share a round of drinks together and call it quits. I definitely don't pay for sex. If you're not a pro and you're not too insulted, we can have a few drinks, maybe a few laughs, and go back to my place. Or not."

Alice spun the stool seat around and slid off to the floor. There were tears in her eyes, and she was biting her lower lip. "I don't do that sort of thing. None of that," she whined.

"Wait," he said. "Why then did you come on so strong to me?"

"Violet told me that was the way to attract a man."

"Bad advice from Shrinking Violet, and you listened to her? Hey, I apologize. I didn't know who or what you were." He held out his hand, and she took it. He helped her back onto the stool and pushed the fresh drink toward her. "Here, take a sip and you'll feel better."

"I'm new in town and she's the only friend I've met here. I've never done this sort of thing before—picking up dates in a bar."

"I don't recommend bar dating, but if you must find guys this way, keep it friendly and don't encourage them to buy drinks for you. It's much too aggressive for a decent young lady."

"Thank you for the advice."

"You're welcome," he said. "By the way, where do you hail from?"

"Charles County, near Waldorf, Maryland. Right off the farm to you."

For the next hour they listened to a young man with big hair playing classical piano music. Afterward, Leo paid the tab, and they both headed for the door.

"May I see you home?" he asked.

"You don't know where I live, Leo."

"You could tell me. Don't worry, Alice. I won't force myself on you. I'll be the perfect gentleman. Scout's honor." He raised his arm in pledge-like manner.

They walked toward the harbor and turned into a side street, a few houses in, and climbed a short flight of stairs. Alice put her key in the door lock and turned to face him. She had planned to peck him on the cheek, but when she got a good look at his rugged face and then his moist lips, she kissed him square on. He, in turn, put both arms around her and hugged her tightly. So tight, she could feel his heartbeat. *God*, she thought, *he's so strong. If he asks me to my bed right now, I'll have to say yes, yes, yes.* He didn't ask, and she stepped inside alone.

* * * *

The wee hours of this past night proved no different from the previous three nights. In the predawn darkness, an exhausted Fenton Thorwal sat propped up against the lumpy back of the open

111

sofa-bed. An open book lay in his lap. He had tried reading and sleeping, but both eluded him—too much on his mind. *Heather just has to be my life's mate, but am I pushing the lass too hard? I know it's sudden, but we only have so much time to connect. Perhaps the life of a policeman is too scary for her. The uncertainty of where we might live—London or Annapolis. I've wined and dined her for three days, and behaved patiently like a perfect gentleman. Still she maintains a distance between us. Kisses and embraces seem to be rationed, reserved, and restrained.* Fen put away the book he had tried reading, turned out the light, slipped out of his briefs, and slid down under the covers. He tossed and turned for the better part of an hour and then fell into a fitful sleep.

In the bedroom Heather Germain found only snatches of sleep, superficial rest. On her back and staring at the ceiling, the strands of loose auburn hair spread across the fluffy pillow. How many times this night had she tossed from side to side? Far too many. *Is Fen serious? What does he really see in me? I'm a plain woman with thousands of ugly freckles covering my whole body.* A waning self-esteem tread mercilessly into the realm of feminine attributes. *I'm way too thin and my breasts barely fill an A-cup.*

But Heather's thoughts were mostly of guilt. *What would Mama, she should rest in peace, say about the stranger in the next room? And the school board. What kind of scandal could they make out of this arrangement? The audacity of the man to put me through this. And on the basis of only one date. Well, I suppose it was a little more than that. I actually went to bed with him, didn't I? I'm thirty-one, what's so wrong about it?*

Heather's thoughts were also of loneliness and missed opportunity, the fear of making the wrong decision. This feeling, the needing to be with someone in particular, came on strong and altogether new for her. *How can I tell if Constable Sergeant Fenton Thorwal is the love of my life? Why did I so readily agree to this sleeping arrangement? What is there about Fen that I find so attractive, so compelling? Is it the mature, never-ending exchange between us?* A quick image of Fenton formed in her mind. Broad shoulders, angular face, friendly smile, alert hazel eyes and brown wavy hair. She even found his receding hairline appealing. That image, along with a growing warmth between her legs, gave her the answer, and she pressed her legs together tightly to drive the urge away. She just wasn't ready.

Suddenly, the apartment on West Street seemed so quiet. *Was it always this quiet?* Heather sat up in bed and listened intently. *Has he gone and left me without a word like the first time?* She threw the covers back and dropped her legs over the edge of the bed. She passed up the terry robe from the back of the bathroom door for the lacy blue peignoir in the top drawer of her dresser. Perhaps her subconscious knew more than she was willing to admit. Wrapping it loosely about her bare body, she stole to the living room door for just a peek at the object of all her nighttime agitation. Fenton lay on his stomach with one arm draped off the bed, the sheet revealing enough of his backside to confirm that he too slept in the buff.

Heather remembered the heat of their last encounter on that same sofa-bed just over a year ago, and now she longed to lie next to him. She regarded the peaceful look on his face, but only for a few seconds. Natural instincts overwhelmed her. The loose peignoir slipped away slowly onto the shag carpet and Heather, throwing all caution to the wind, climbed into the bed and edged close enough to fit her form to his. At first touch he turned and drew her into an embrace. Exhausted from daytime activities and sleepless nights, the two slept that way until morning and then found a feast in each other.

* * * *

A distant street lamp created only dim shadows at 2:30 a.m. The depth of the red brick alley between the buildings provided additional cover for the thieves assembled there. The latecomer leaned against a green Dumpster, while the one called Beast sat facing him on a wooden fruit crate. Shorty and Ratman were messing around playing Slap, a game with loose rules bordering on sparring, only with open hands. Being taller and having longer arms, Ratman had the advantage, but Shorty was quick and able to weave in and out of reach, so they each grunted and yelped a fair amount. Neither was aware of the exchange between Beast and the fourth member of their crew.

"Beast, I can't go through with this. Not again. It's my own family you want me to steal from."

"That's it, Stretch, no more *dust* for you then," blared Beast.

"Wait, I can pay you next week. I'll get the money. Don't cut me off."

"Hah! Next week you'll want more and you'll need more money all over again. You hopheads are all alike. Besides, this caper is too easy to pass up."

"Beast, please!"

"No! You're in too deep. We're gonna do this thing." He turned to the other two. "Hey, Ratman, get up on top of that Dumpster and do your thing."

The scuffling stopped abruptly. Ratman put his foot on the hauling cleat and his left hand on the massive hinge, and hauled himself to the top of the Dumpster. Letting go of one hand after the other, he shifted back and forth until he had achieved a comfortable balance. Then crouching, then leaping upward from one end of the Dumpster, he reached for the bottom rung of the fire-escape ladder and rode it down to the ground. Ratman held it there while the others scurried up to the roof. He followed.

On the far side of the roof Beast pulled away a huge black tarp, revealing a wide stack of roofing shingles and other materials. Between the stack and the wall edging the roof, a pair of 2-inch by 12-inch by16-foot planks and a rope ladder were hidden—left on this roof from their last caper. The four men carried the planks to the wall next to the alley and placed them so they spanned the alley and landed on the adjacent building roof, creating a kind of bridge. Shorty, carrying the rope ladder, ran across the planks to the Reubens' building. Ratman waddled across slowly and carefully, followed by Beast, who walked across casually, showing off his bravado. Stretch, terrified of heights, crawled across on hands and knees. By the time he made it, Shorty had already anchored the rope ladder to a four-inch plumbing vent pipe. Ratman had begun unscrewing the eight bolts from the hatch cover. He wrapped a scrap of cloth over each hex-head bolt so that the crescent wrench wouldn't leave telltale marks. When the last bolt was removed, the lifted hatch revealed a hole once covered by a skylight that was no longer there. Shorty threw the ladder down the hole and descended into the dark abyss. Ratman climbed down next. Beast held a three-cell flashlight to illuminate the space below.

It was Stretch who remembered this access from playing on the roof of this building when he was a preteen. Originally, an internal all-steel staircase led straight up to it. When Uncle Leo rearranged the stockroom floor to gain valued inventory space, the stairs were removed and the skylight was covered and abandoned. In a naïve mindset of trust, no one in the company had even thought to alarm this access. Nor had they ever considered it necessary to hire a nighttime guard. Stretch refused to go down the ladder. He'd already done more than enough. He had provided the layout and location of the tools needed.

Ratman and Beast knew their way only too well to Aisle Ten: the shelves holding the huge reels of copper wire. After twenty minutes of hacksawing sizeable lengths of three large-diameter electrical cables, Ratman tied their bitter ends to the rope ladder and hauled them, one by one, onto the roof.

When the two inside men finally climbed back up to the roof, they re-bolted the hatch cover and threw the cable lengths down into the alley between the buildings. The four thieves retraced their steps across the makeshift bridge. After carrying the planks and rope ladder to the far end of the roof, they again hid them under the tarp. The four scrambled down the fire escape to the alley and loaded the cable lengths onto the back of Ratman's Ford-150 pickup truck. Ratman and Shorty drove the truck away, leaving Stretch and Beast on the street.

"You done good there, Stretch," said Beast. He climbed into

his shiny black Chevy Camaro, peeled rubber, and drove away. Feeling alone and dejected, Stretch walked home.

# Chapter 14

## **A Modicum of Progress**
Friday, October 28th

Leo was always the first to arrive at the business, but this morning he found the security door already unlocked. The hour was much too early for either Hersch or Arnold, so he figured it had to be Meyer who had beaten him to work. He poked his head in the door, but Meyer wasn't in his office. *A trip to the loo, no doubt.* Disappointed, he shrugged his shoulders and dragged himself to his own office, dropping his brown bag lunch on the desk.

Leo sat down hard and heavy. He was agitated and feeling sorry for himself. *My love life sucks. I haven't had a woman in over a month now. That bitch stood me up last night. I waited all evening for her and I drank too damn much for my own good. I can still taste the morning after. Yuck! Should I have been more aggressive with Alice that first night on the front porch? Nice legs and tits, too. She didn't actually promise. She only said she might be there last night. I'll have to break down and give her a call. Maybe the hair of the dog will help.*

Leo reached into the top drawer of the desk where he kept a fifth of Johnny Walker Red. He unscrewed the cap and took a long swig of the half-full bottle and started to return the bottle when he saw the folded piece of paper containing the copper filings. It reminded him that he hadn't checked the targeted reels since Monday. Suddenly, all thoughts of Alice faded into a dim recess of his mind. He stopped long enough at Mr. Coffee outside his door to fill his Ravens football mug. *Ceila likes it too damn strong, but who am I to argue with an officer manager willing to make coffee? Besides, she's kinda cute. A skosh on the chubby side, though. Built more for comfort.* He smiled and quickly stepped through the break in Aisle Nine to reach the far wall.

Halting in front of the wire and cable inventory, Leo's stomach groaned. There in Aisle Ten, close to two of the reels of previously targeted cable, he saw two broadly dispersed piles of copper filings. *So the thieves were at it again.* He took a long draw on bitter coffee and made an ugly face. He knelt down and ran his fingers through the filings. As he looked down the aisle at that angle, he noticed that something had been dragged through one of the piles. *Most likely a sawed-off chunk of cable,* he reasoned. Leo followed the trail of filings past the Aisle Nine break and toward the center of the building. The trail did not extend toward any of the exits. It played out before reaching any place of significance that he could further explain.

Then Leo realized that the industrial tiles beneath his feet were newer than the surrounding tiles: on the exact spot where the staircase to the roof used to be. But six years ago, he had rearranged the inventory stacks to form wider aisles and accommodate the newer, larger forklifts. Leo looked up and saw the apparently undisturbed hatch cover overhead. *I don't remember if it's even alarmed. I'll have to call the Acme Alarm and Security people and find out. Who else would even know the hatch existed?*

Leo headed  for the loading platform and pushed the large red button to raise the metal overhead doors. A loud rumbling noise accompanied their travel up. He could see the street now. He walked outside, pivoted, and looked back up at the building. He couldn't make out any ladder marks, and there weren't any trees close enough to access their roof. From the loading platform it was at least thirty-five feet to the roof and the loading platform itself was five feet off the ground. He turned, walked down the concrete steps to street level, and crossed over to the other side. From that perspective he couldn't come up with anything helpful, except Old Man Miller's gravel driveway and front yard on the right. He examined the driveway for ladder depressions, but found nothing of the sort.

The ten-foot-wide alley on the left was another story. Leo found areas of displaced dirt and debris on the concrete, where something had been dropped from above. Upon closer examination, he also noticed more copper filings there. The thieves had certainly come in from the roof, but how did they get up there without leaving a trace? The three-story, six-family apartment building on the left belonged to his one-time drinking and carousing buddy, Jaimey O'Hara. Leo didn't think Jaimey would mind if he had a look at his roof, so he bounded up the staircase in the middle of the building until he was stopped by the padlocked access to the roof. The lock had enough rust on it to indicate that no one had passed this way in some time.

Leo returned to the warehouse and then to the offices. He heard voices in Meyer's office, and when he poked his head in, he saw Ceila sitting on Meyer's lap, running her hands through his salt-and-pepper hair. One "Ahem" later, Ceila sprang to her feet, straightened her skirt, and fled the room.

"It's not what you think, Leo. She was thanking me for letting her go home early yesterday. There's really nothing between us."

"Hey, cousin," replied Leo. "You're the accountant. You don't have to account for anything but money to me. I was thinking she was ripe for plucking myself, so go for it, man."

* * * *

Rivka was halfway down the stairs when the phone rang. "Can you get that, hon?" she yelled.

Ivy rushed from the poetry stack where she and Lord Byron were stocking new inventory. She arrived behind the checkout counter and caught the phone on its fourth ring. "Olde Victorian Bookstore . . . Yes, sir, just a moment please." She held the receiver out for Rivka, who had just reached the bottom step. "Sounds official," she whispered.

"This is Mrs. Rivka Sherman. Who am I speaking with? Ah, Chief Inspector Winston. Of course I remember you." She put her hand over the mouthpiece and said, "He's calling from London. Scotland Yard."

". . . My husband? No, he's out right now. Ah yes, Constable Sergeant Thorwal *is* staying with a good friend of mine. You say he intervened on our behalf? . . . You'll do that for us? Wonderful! I don't know how to thank you. You've been extremely helpful." She was about to hang up, but the inspector was intent on continuing their conversation.

Still on the phone, tucking the receiver between his ear and his shoulder, Chief Inspector Winston sprawled his name on the request document, leaned back in his heavy-duty swivel chair, and brushed aside the few strands of white hairs in the way of his vision. "My dear Mrs. Sherman, I owe *you* thanks. Your courageous part in the recovery of the Fraume artifacts played no small part in my recent promotion and relocation to London and Scotland Yard. Godspeed, ma'am." He returned the phone to its cradle.

Rivka hung up, her eyes sparkling with excitement, and turned to Ivy. "The Chief Inspector says he can't release your mother's diary, but he's going to have it copied, certified, and sent to us. It should only be a matter of days."

Tears filled Ivy's eyes as she threw her arms around Rivka in a huge hug.

* * * *

"Does Mom know what time you came in last night?" asked Josh Reubens. He was sitting at the kitchen table when his seventeen-year-old brother came through the door.

"It's none of *her* damn business or *yours* either, for that matter," said Abel. He headed for the refrigerator and pulled out a quart-sized bottle of water, upended it, and drank all but a few

120

ounces.

"How many time have I told you not to drink from the bottle? Other family members live here, too," said Esther, entering the kitchen from the opposite doorway. "You have to respect the rest of your family."

"Don't hafta anything," mumbled Abel, putting the nearly empty bottle back.

"Don't you sass me, young man. You're not so big your father can't tan your hide," Esther yelled back at her son. Suppressing tears of frustration, she fled the room.

"Damn it, Abel, why'd ya hafta go and do that? You know she's upset and worried about what the doctor is going to find."

"She'll get over it, bro," replied Abel with a deadpan expression. There wasn't an ounce of emotion in his voice. He shrugged and turned away.

Josh was four years older than his brother, but felt twenty years older. Even though he was shorter and less muscular, he grabbed Abel by the shoulders and spun him back around to face him square on. There was no mistaking the enlarged pupils and strange behavior. "You little bastard, you're high. What the hell are you on?"

"You're crazy, Josh. I don't do drugs."

"You're lying. Now shut up. We'll finish this later. Mom's coming back in and she doesn't need any more grief from you."

Esther returned to the kitchen, carrying and sorting the mail as though nothing had happened several minutes before. "All bills and advertisements. Oh, here's an invitation. It's Julie's eighteenth birthday, and her parents are having a big bash on Sunday. A cookout and open bar. Anna told me the other day she was having sixty people over." She let out a big sigh.

"Arrrrgh," bellowed Abel. "Another one of Uncle Hersch's broken-down barbeques. "I ain't going."

"Five'll get you ten you're there on Sunday," chided Josh as he nudged his brother on the arm for emphasis. "An open bar? I'd like to see you pass that up."

"Ill take that bet," boasted Abel.

"Oh, you'll be there all right," said Esther. "There's no way I'm going to let you insult your Uncle Hersch and his family. Julie's birthday is an excellent excuse for a big party. Aunt Anna always does a lot of cooking and baking for these shindigs. Beside, there'll be plenty of young people."

"Sure!" said Abel. "And all of them will be my wonderful cousins. Julie, Maurine, Brenda, and Barri." He followed the list with a loud raspberry noise.

"That's enough, young man," his mother snapped. We're a family and as long as you live in this house you'll do as I say. I'll call Aunt Anna right away and tell her all four of us will be there."

* * * *

"Where's Rivka?" Dan asked Ivy as soon as he got back from the post office.

"I'm right here," called Rivka from the Biography aisle.

"We need to talk."

"That sound ominous," returned Dan.

She ushered him toward the nearest reading room. "We got this invitation."

"You mean we're still socially acceptable? What's it to and when?"

"It's this Sunday. Anna and Herschel Reubens are throwing a big backyard bash, and we need to RSVP today."

"Is Ivy willing to work in the store alone for three or four hours?"

"That's the problem, Dan. Stuart called and invited Ivy to the same party."

"How about Heather? She's minded the fort before."

"In case you've forgotten, Heather has a house guest."

"Oh yeah, Constable Sergeant Fenton P. Thorwal."

"You like repeating that, don't you, Dan?"

"Yeah, Rivka, it's a fun mouthful. Suppose you go to the party, and I mind the store for a few hours. You're more of a social animal than I am."

"I've got a better idea. We're never that busy on a Sunday afternoon anyway. Why don't we close at noon and take half a day off? It's not as though we don't deserve a little entertainment once in awhile."

"Good idea, babe. Was that the big news?"

"No. We received an important phone call from London about an hour ago. You'll never guess who."

"So who already?"

"Chief Inspector E. Howard Winston himself. Apparently, Heather convinced Fen to get in touch with him."

"What did he have to say? The suspense is killing me."

"Winston can't release the diary itself, but he's sending us a certified photocopy. We should have it in a few days."

# Chapter 15

## One Grand Bash
Sunday, October 30th

Oh, Hersch, honey, are all the chairs set up in the yard, in little sociable groupings like I told you, not like a damned theater? Did you provide a table for each grouping, too?"

"Yes, dear."

"Did you wipe them all down? We can't have anyone sitting on dirty chairs, you know."

"Yes, dear."

"I'm so glad I had Stuart mow the lawn yesterday. It looks so much better when it's freshly cut."

Sigh. "Yes, dear."

Anna turned to Brenda Schwartz, one of Leo's daughters, who was helping her in the kitchen. "Those hard-boiled eggs don't have to be chopped so fine, sweetie." Back to addressing her husband, "Oh my gosh! It's noon already. Would you believe we've got eighty-three guests coming in less than an hour, and I've got so much to do yet." Anna took two large covered bowls from the refrigerator and slammed the door shut with her elbow. "And tell Stuart it's time to bring the beer and soda up from the basement. And that magnificent tub you use as a cooler, too."

"Yes, mine commandant!" Herschel clicked his heels in a

sham of fresh energy. He noted the flush gathering in Anna's face and decided to get out before the impending explosion. In the dining room he encountered Julie arranging fresh flowers as a centerpiece. Empty platters and serving bowls were stacked at one end of the massive table covered in a white linen cloth. An array of silver serving instruments lay next to them, at the ready like an operating room ensemble. Two folding tables sat in each of the room's corners adjacent to the bay window, one for dairy foods and paper plates for the ultra-kosher guests; the other with hot water and coffee urns. Two small armchairs sat in the remaining corners. All the straight-back upholstered chairs were on the back porch.

"Hi, Julie. Seen your brother?" asked Herschel.

"He's upstairs in his room," she replied. "I think he said something about handling a few e-mails for work, but I really think the big coward's hiding from all the commotion here."

Herschel strode to the bottom of the staircase and yelled up to Stuart.

"What's up, Dad?"

"Your mother wants you to start bringing up the stuff in the basement: beer and soda cases and, oh yeah, the big metal tub and the two Styrofoam coolers."

"But, Dad! I told Ivy I'd pick her up in fifteen minutes."

"You'll just be a little late, son. It's good to keep a woman waiting."

"You're not one to keep Mom waiting."

"You mind your own business, young man." Herschel retrieved the car keys from his pocket and slipped out the front door.

Stuart grumbled to himself. *I'm twenty-five and they still talk to me like I'm five. I'd better call Ivy. Damn, why does this always happen to me?* He slipped his cell phone from its belt holster and punched in the store numbers.

"Olde Victorian Bookstore, How may I help you?"

"It's me, Ivy. I'll be a little late. Mom has me doing some last-minute errands."

"I understand, Stuart, I can come over with the Shermans at two."

"But . . ."

"It makes more sense this way  Don't worry about me."

A disappointed Stuart clicked off.

At two o'clock the guests began to arrive, first in trickles and then in droves. By 2:15 the Shermans had stopped in front of the Georgian-style home to let off the ladies, but Abel Reubens announced that he and a friend were valet parking all the cars due to the limited parking on Prince George Street. Dan, Rivka, and Ivy pushed through the wrought-iron gate, climbed the front steps, and made their way to the living room, where they discovered the Katz family.

Thelma looked perturbed, having been shooed out of the kitchen. Arnold had settled into the sofa, pleased to have a two-hand grasp on a tall can of Coors. Their daughter, Maurine, displayed a bored look while thumbing through one magazine after another. Rivka broke up the prevailing moods by introducing Ivy. Thelma stood and gave hugs. Arnold continued his mindless grin. Maurine raised her eyes briefly, then went back to thumbing through magazines.

A tall, dark-haired young man had his back to the group, but spun around when he heard the introductions, particularly Ivy's musical voice. "Hi," he said. "I'm Mark Schwartz, Cousin Leo's first mistake."

*Mistake? What does he mean*, Ivy wondered. "Hi," she said, and held out her hand for a prim shake. While she certainly appreciated Mark's strong facial features and hunk-like appearance, Ivy trained her eyes on Arnold, scrutinizing his face. *Does he see any resemblance between me and my mother?* Rivka had purposely introduced Ivy Cohen as a recent London émigré, accenting her last name. But Arnold continued his vacant grin, adding only a slight nod of acknowledgment. Ivy couldn't decide whether his apparent numbness came from too much beer or genuine acting ability. She hid her disappointment, but her belly reacted with a brief wave of nausea. She wished her search could be simple, more clear-cut.

"Hi, Arnie," said Dan in another effort to break the ice. "Did you bring your guitar today? I enjoyed listening to your gig the other evening at Marmaduke's."

"Thanks, but Thelma made me park it in the front hall closet. She claims I can't socialize with people while I'm playing. I've been doing the Marmaduke's scene a few nights a week. It's not really a gig. I don't get paid for performing there except for tips. I like to try out my new pieces between karaoke numbers, and the management is awfully encouraging." He shifted forward in his sofa seat, thrilled by the compliment, and held out his hand.

Dan shook it and stepped back. "You mean all that great music is original?"

"Yep!"

"Any of it published yet?"

"Nope, but that doesn't mean I'm not trying. The publishing gurus haven't discovered me yet."

"If it were up to me, you'd already be published," Dan generously added.

Josh Reubens entered the living room, and Maurine suddenly popped alive. The magazine in her lap slid to the floor. She leaped to her feet and flew into his arms as though it were one smooth action, surprising everyone in the room.

Thelma glared at Arnold, but her husband had no intention of disciplining their daughter. Instead, he stood up and gave Dan a hug. "Hey, you're too kind. Can I get you a beer or anything?"

"No thanks," Dan said, as he, Ivy, and Rivka ambled into the dining room.

Dan muttered to Rivka out of the side of his mouth. "Maurine and Josh—quite a display of affection for two cousins."

"I'm just as surprised as you, Dan, but I suppose it's okay since they're related by marriage and not by blood."

"Joshua looks so much like Stuart," declared Ivy. "Maybe even better looking."

"Well, they are blood first cousins," Rivka said. "His parents are Meyer and Esther Reubens. Herschel and Meyer are brothers."

"I see," said Ivy, thinking, *Josh: another possible stepbrother in the mix.*

Anna dried her hands and greeted her guests with air kisses. "I love that dress you're wearing, Rivka. It's so, so Southwest." Turning to Ivy, "And this is Ivy Cohen. We've met at services, at the *Oneg,* but Stuart has told me so much more about you and your mission."

"But we've only had one date."

Anna appeared not to hear.

Out on the wide screened-in porch, the Shermans encountered Katie and Melvin Silvers, and Leo Schwartz, who was introduced as Katie's ex-husband. The woman seated to his left he introduced as Alice Zimmer, his date.

Ivy felt almost dizzy from the onslaught. She'd never remember all their names. "What part of London are you from?" Leo asked her. "I grew up in Tottenham. Left home from Lewisham in the eighties."

"Kensington," Ivy answered, all the while applying the same scrutiny she used on Arnold with a similar result. "Not exactly neighbors, but not too far away." She noted that Leo nodded, pressed his lips together, and raised an eyebrow. *It's not going to be easy sorting these family members out*, she thought. Besides, she couldn't imagine how a murderer should look and feel when confronted with his evil past. She felt another wave of nausea. *Good grief, am I up to the task? Four of the men most likely to have killed my mum are here today. What have I gotten myself into?* She smiled awkwardly, but felt more like crying.

"Are you all right, Ivy?" asked Leo. "Here, have a seat." He pointed to an upholstered straight-backed chair.

"Thank you, I'm fine," she managed to say. "I just need a little space and sunshine and I'll be fit." Ivy slipped out the screen door and down four steps to the spacious lawn. Choosing one of six white plastic chairs at a round picnic table, she quickly sat. Dan and Rivka joined her. They had keenly observed her discomfort.

"Something's wrong, isn't it, dear?" asked Dan.

Ivy said nothing.

"Of course there's something," returned Rivka. "She's having to face up to her mother's killer without knowing who he is. It's got to be pretty emotional, to say the least." Rivka leaned over, put her arm around Ivy's shoulder, and gave her a reassuring squeeze.

"Yup! I think she's one hell of a brave chick," said Dan, grinning.

"Daniel! You know I hate that word," scolded Rivka.

"Oh-oh! She only calls me Daniel when I'm in trouble."

"I noticed." A tiny, forced smile emerged from Ivy's thin lips. And then she saw Stuart heading across the lawn toward her.

"I like Stuart a lot even though he's a bit of a wimp," she confided to Rivka in a trembling whisper. "And, God knows, we could be related."

"There's no reason why you can't enjoy his company," Rivka advised, "as long as you stay platonic and on top of the situation. Don't let any romantic notions enter your head. You need to remain objective if you intend to learn more about the Reubens clan."

As soon as Stuart approached, he said, "Hi, Mr. and Mrs. Sherman. Hi, Ivy! Come on. I can't wait to show you off to all my friends and relatives." He took both her hands and eased her out of her chair, chatting endlessly as they moved across the lawn.

"They make a nice couple despite the dangers," said Rivka.

"I know," said Dan. "I assume he hasn't been made privy to the inter-Reubens grapevine as yet. I just wish the diary would get here already."

Rivka, in response to Dan's declaration of acute hunger pangs, followed him into the dining room. Upon approaching the kitchen, the Shermans overheard Anna's shrill voice.

"Julie, how dare you invite that *sheygets* into our home. I won't have you marrying a non-Jew."

"Mama! I'm not getting married. He's just a friend, some-one I've had two dates with. Charlie's been so nice, generous, too. I wanted to show my appreciation so I invited him over."

"This is our home and our party, and your father and I will say who's invited and who's not."

"It's my house, too."

"Shush," said Anna. "Someone's coming. They'll hear you."

The Shermans breezed through the kitchen, ignoring mother and daughter. At the dining room table, Rivka proceeded to caution Dan about taking too much food. Her caution fell on deaf ears. Happily, he loaded up on kosher barbecued turkey, stuffing, yams, three deviled eggs, two hefty pieces of gefilte fish, and a scoop of whitefish salad.

"I'll get dessert and coffee on my next trip," quipped Dan.

"And you'll complain all night about heartburn," Rivka said.

"Oh well, sometimes that's the price you have to pay." Dan was too sensitive to argue. He was actually the thin member of the family. Rivka constantly moaned about her chunky hips. Besides, he adored his zaftig wife. Back outside, they joined Meyer and Esther Reubens at a picnic table. Friends for decades, conversation bubbled, but was interrupted when Ivy strolled back to where they were sitting.

"Where's Stuart?" Dan asked.

"His mother is bent on keeping him busy, I guess," Ivy responded. "I thought she was a bit rude, too."

"What do you mean?" asked Rivka. "What did Anna say?"

"Not so much what she said. Rather, how she acted. She kept sending him on trivial errands and repeatedly looking over at me as though she didn't want me waiting for him. On the third errand I got the message and wandered back out here. Why are you making faces at me, Dan?"

*Stop gossiping already,* he was thinking. "Ivy, I want to introduce you to our friends. Esther and Meyer Reubens. This is Ivy Cohen, our newest addition at the bookstore. She's recently arrived from London. Ivy, did you know Esther and Meyer were Londoners? They grew up there."

"Really?" said Ivy.

"Oh, yes," said Esther. "I saw you at the *Oneg* last Friday. You were the prettiest young lady there."

"Thank you. I'm pleased to know you both," said Ivy, blushing and tilting her head slightly to hide her embarrassment for the compliment, but mostly for speaking so openly and negatively in front of them.

"London, eh?" returned Meyer. "There's something familiar about you. What in the world attracted you to *our* fair city? . . . Ouch!"

Esther had kicked him under the table. Her eyes rolled. She knew the answer to his question. She'd heard it at the critique meeting.

"Here we go again," Rivka whispered to Dan.

"I came to Annapolis to find my mother's murderer," replied Ivy without any sign of emotion. She honed in on and tracked his reaction carefully.

Meyer's eyes grew wider, and his brow raised a half-dozen furrows as he began to cough in short repeated hacks. His wife walloped him on the back a few times, and handed him a glass from the table in front of him. He took a swallow of the beer and tried to smile.

"Meyer?" Esther cried. "Are you all right?"

"I'm fine, now," he answered in a strained voice. He cleared his throat and swallowed twice. "It's just that I didn't expect such an explosive response. Not exactly party conversation."

Ivy had certainly evoked a reaction, but she hadn't quite anticipated the one she got. She began to mistrust her strategy, wondering whether the reaction had anything to do with real guilt or merely surprising him with such an outrageous statement.

"I know what you mean, Meyer dear," said Esther. "You could have bowled me over with a feather."

"Stop grinning, Dan," whispered Rivka. "You look like

you're enjoying this too much."

"I am," he whispered back. "I wouldn't have missed this scene for the world."

A totally composed Esther asked, "Ivy, what led you to choose Annapolis, 3,000 miles from the crime scene?"

"And don't forget twenty-three years after the fact," Ivy added. "I was drawn to Annapolis and certain families living here by specific entries in my mother's diary."

"Young lady," Meyer began, "I hope you're not making accusations."

"Of course not," interrupted Dan. "She's only making broad inquiries."

"Please forgive me for being so boorish," said Ivy. "It sort of popped out of me. If you will excuse me now, I think I'll go find something cold to drink."

"She seems very determined," said Esther, watching Ivy amble off in her periwinkle blue dress and matching macramé vest.

"Very attractive, too," declared Meyer. "Those bedroom eyes are killers."

"Extremely intelligent," added Rivka. "It only took her a few days and she had the entire bookstore routine down pat. She's polite, helpful, works hard, and then goes home to take care of her elderly shut-in landlady."

"Sounds like an angel," said Esther. "I wish my Joshua would latch onto someone like her. He's still wasting his time hanging around with his cousin Maurine."

Across the lawn, in the open-sided tent labeled The Watering Hole, Joshua Reubens pulled a Dr. Pepper from the metal tub filled with ice and cans of beer and soda and handed it to Ivy. "You look like you could use one of these."

"Yes, thank you," she said. "Have you taken over the barkeeping duties?"

"Oh, no," replied Josh. "This is a help-yourself operation. And it's a cool way to meet girls."

"I thought you had a girl. I mean the way you and Maurine

greeted each other I just assumed . . ."

"No, that's just an act to drive our parents nuts. Maurine and I are both interested in theater, and she sometimes gets a little overly dramatic. I'm single, unattached, and definitely interested in the likes of you."

"Aren't you being a teensy bit forward, Josh?"

"I have to be, if I'm going to compete with my wimpy cousin for your attention."

"That's unkind," she answered. "By the way, where is that cousin of yours? He's the one who invited me to this soirée and I haven't had ten minutes with him since we arrived."

"You see?" Josh said. "I've been more attentive already."

"I haven't seen Stuart in over an hour. Seriously, where is he?"

"I'll bet you anything Stu and Uncle Hersch are hiding from Aunt Anna this very moment. She's had those two hopping since before sun-up. If you're that serious, try the first bedroom on the right at the top of the stairs. It's Uncle Hersch's den."

"Shouldn't they be socializing with their guests?"

"Hey!" Josh replied. "I don't make the rules."

"I'll be back," she said. "Don't go anywhere."

Ivy strolled toward the house, oblivious of those around her until she reached the bottom of the stairs. She looked up the long flight and couldn't decide whether she was more angry with Stuart for deserting her and going into hiding or more angry with him for succumbing to Anna's every whim and wish. But angry she was, and she was going to tell him so.

At the top of the stairs Ivy found the room Josh had described. The television was on and the door was slightly ajar so she edged her way into the room. Herschel sat there alone with a drink in his hand, his overweight body taking up much of the plaid-covered sofa. He didn't seem surprised at all to see her.

"Sit. Sit here beside me," he said quietly. "I hate drinking by myself."

It didn't sound like a command, but his words were so

compelling that she felt obligated to obey. She sat down at the far end, knees and ankles together, hands in her lap, gripping her can of Dr. Pepper.

"Are you comfortable?"

"Yes, sir."

"Would you like a glass and ice for your soda?"

"No, Mr. Reubens."

"You can call me Hersch."

"Yes, sir."

"Why are you here, young lady?"

"I came looking for Stuart. He's been neglecting me."

"That's a crying shame. You're a beautiful woman. If I were twenty or thirty years younger, I would never, never neglect you."

"Thank you. My mother was even more beautiful than I am. Would you like to see a picture of her?" Not waiting for an answer, Ivy set her soda can on the end table. Fishing through the string purse hanging from one shoulder, she retrieved the three-by-five glossy black-and-white photo. "Here. It was taken twenty-three years ago, just before I was born."

Herschel took the photo and seemed to inhale it. "This is a trick. The photo is of you, taken only recently."

She vigorously shook her head No.

His eyes appeared watery as he handed the picture back. *Is it the alcohol?* she wondered.

"So, Ivy, why have you traveled so far from your homeland?"

"You already know the answer to that, Hersch. I told all of you on Friday night that I came here to find my mother's killer."

"But why Annapolis?"

"My mother kept a diary, an accurate account of her life and those she loved. There were numerous entries about my father's comings and goings. I'm bound to find him sooner or later."

Herschel lowered his head as if in serious thought, exposing his double chin and bald pate fringed with light brown hairs. Then raising his head, he met her gaze. "I'm not quite understanding, my dear. You said you're searching for your mother's killer. But wouldn't her diary just talk about your father? Are they one and the same?"

Her large gray-blue eyes turned watchful, mistrusting. "I have no idea, sir. Maybe, maybe not. It's too early to tell."

"If you find what you're looking for, then what?"

"Justice, and perhaps some satisfaction."

"I can see that you are extremely brave and determined."

"Yes, sir."

"Now go find my son. I won't keep you any longer." He stood, looming over her for a second, turned his back, and walked over to the bar for a refill.

She could hear the ice dropping into the empty glass as she left the room.

A few steps from the bottom of the staircase she stumbled and fell into the arms of a passing Mark Schwartz.

"All my life I've been praying for a beautiful woman like you. But I never expected you to arrive like manna from heaven, landing right in my arms."

Unhurt but all a-fluster, Ivy struggled to her feet, freeing herself from his confident grip and straightening her dress. "Sorry I'm so clumsy," she replied with a nervous giggle. "But thank God I only fell a few steps, not all the way from heaven. It was pure chance that you were here to catch me."

"Supposing I choose not to believe in chance. I'd rather think it was our karma. May I interest you in a drink?"

Ivy found the sound of his words as inviting as their meaning. His looks weren't bad either. Navy polo shirt and khakis. A little on the short side, but intellectual-looking in his owl-like glasses. "Fine, Mark, seeing as how I've been abandoned by my date."

"How tragic! We could go elsewhere. I know this quiet piano bar with an empty booth."

"No, thanks. The chairs on the lawn will be fine." *And you're too pushy.*

# Chapter 16

## Packages
### Monday, October 31st

ood morning," Rivka said as she unlocked The Dungeon door and let Ivy in. "I see you got home from the party okay. Did Stuart bring you?"

"No. Mark Schwartz drove me home. I don't want to even hear Stuart's name again. That mama's boy had no time for me the whole afternoon. I felt so neglected. It was darned near ridiculous."

"Maybe not," said Rivka. "If Anna believes Herschel is your father, wouldn't she try to break up any romance between half-siblings? I know I would."

"I see. Does that mean Herschel Reubens really is my father? I had a funny feeling about him."

"No, no, no," said Rivka. "Don't go jumping to conclusions. Anna might only have a suspicion of her husband's infidelity, and then again, she might be exerting a mother's power over a weak son. I think you shook the whole family tree at temple, possibly all four of the men and their wives. I think we're about to see a lot more fallout in the next few days. Fallout that's been part of a deep, dark secret for over twenty-three years."

"I doubt," said Ivy in a prissy, schoolmarm voice, "whether

Esther could exert that kind of influence over Josh. He seems to have more character and self-assurance than his cousin."

Rivka's lush dark-brown bangs hid a disapproving frown. *She's barely met these families and she's issuing pronouncements.* "Ivy, let me tell you: never underestimate what a mother will do or sacrifice to protect her child."

They heard a truck pull up outside and a few minutes later, a brown-uniformed UPS deliveryman rolled in a handcart stacked with small cartons. "Where do you want 'em, ma'am?"

"Over there will be fine, please," answered Rivka, pointing toward the space next to the reading room door. She watched him roll his load to the spot and wriggle the boxes free of the handcart.

"Sign on the line with the X, please. Thank you, ma'am. Have a nice day."

Rivka broke open a roll of quarters over a partition in the cash drawer. It was customary for her to close out each night; that is, remove and count all coins and bills, so it was also necessary to replenish the drawer with change the following morning.

"I finished the last of the inventory on Saturday," said Ivy.

"Do you want me to open those new boxes?"

"It's best we let Dan handle them," Rivka said. "It's the big list of books he ordered from Ingram, the distributor. He'll have to check in and record everything. I think I'll take the first turn at the register. Why don't you restock the stray books lying out in the reading rooms?"

"Okay," agreed Ivy. "Bye the bye, where is your husband this morning?"

"He's in the shed out back being the handyman. Something about a new book stack he built needing another coat of paint."

"It's all done," announced Dan as he appeared in the adjacent aisle. "And not a drop on me."

Ivy stifled a laugh even before Rivka blurted out, "Oh, no! Not your new Dockers, Dan! You've got paint all over them."

"I'll have you know I was very careful not to spill a drop."

"Look down. On your left cuff and on the edge of your

slant pocket. Couldn't you have put on a pair of your old sloppy pants or at least one of my aprons if you were too lazy to change?"

"Sorry! I don't do well in frilly aprons," he said, performing a comical curtsy.

She used to laugh when he got silly. Not this time. "First of all. I can never get you to a men's store to buy anything. And when I finally do, you go and ruin it right away."

"I said I was sorry. What more do you want?"

"For one thing, you can tackle that new delivery of boxes over there. Meanwhile, I'll consider your penance and deliver a sentence later." Rivka was trying to lighten up, but not succeeding. *I'm turning into a fishwife, and my poor husband doesn't deserve it.*

Every so often since her kidnapping ordeal last year, she'd get ambushed by unsettling feelings: crabby, edgy, even a little depressed. She recognized the bitter, negative undercurrent. She'd even gone into therapy with a good psychologist for a few weeks, but her return to normal was taking much longer than she expected. *And maybe,* she thought, *that's my problem. In some ways I'm a different person now, but that doesn't give me license to be a bitch. Dan is so sweet and he's trying so hard.* She smiled wryly and resolved to try harder herself. Helpless tears welled up in her eyes and she sniffled.

Dan reached into his jeans pocket and held out a folded hankie for her. She took it and blew her nose loudly. He made a crinkled face and broke the somber mood. "They should call it a honkie. Nobody ever hanks."

Rivka chuckled appreciatively. "Another *Whydon'tcha* for your list."

Dan then reached under the counter for his laptop and a box cutter. He opened the laptop in the reading room and brought up the new inventory forms. Cutting through the center strip and along the two perpendicular edges of the first box, he gained access to the nineteen books within. For each book he entered the title, author, bar-coded price, and ISBN. Dan's computer program provided the rest of the tagging and location data.

Upon approaching the smaller fourth box, Dan noticed the London labeling, so he tore into opening it. Inside, there were no books, only 8-1/2 x 11-inch pages in a stack at least three inches thick. A folded note on top said, "Hope this will help," signed "Mandy for the Chief Inspector." Underneath, the lightly lined pages bore a woman's cursive hand gone faint over two decades. The faded writing made for difficult reading in a few places, but all the dates were plainly legible.

"Hey girls, the diary finally arrived. Wanna have a look-see?" It wasn't long before he had one head looking over each shoulder.

"Can't wait to dig into it and see if there are any real clues to work with."

"Dan, honey, do you think maybe we should get Ivy's permission first?" asked Rivka. "After all, it did belong to *her* mother."

"There wouldn't be a diary for me at all if it hadn't been for your connections," said Ivy. "But I *would* like the opportunity to read it through first. I was only allowed forty minutes with the original in London. I could only skim through it. I promise to leave a bookmark at any passage I think has significance. You can do your thing with it when I finish. I would like the pages back as a memento, though. I may even have them bound as a book."

"Tell you what, dear," Dan said. "I have a few extra loose-leaf binders upstairs in my office. Supposing I punch holes in the pages and put them in a binder for you. I can have it ready as soon as I finish updating the new inventory. That way none of the pages can get lost."

"It's a terribly good idea, Dan," agreed Ivy. "That way I can carry it home with me at night and bring it back the next morning."

"Another thing," cautioned Rivka. "I would be extremely careful about telling *anyone* that you now have your mother's diary. It has probative value in your search. But you are dealing with a killer, and putting his back against the wall could trigger desperate measures. You're putting your life on the line, girl."

"Rivvie's right, Ivy," Dan said. "But the cat may already be out of the proverbial bag. When you attended our critique group, I remember your chapter "Love Turned Ugly." It revealed that Lainee knew her lover's real name and she was going to tell his wife. If I were the killer, I'd worry that my name was in the diary."

"I think Lainee was bluffing," said Rivka. "Otherwise, Scotland Yard would have closed the case then."

"Or my mother simply never got the opportunity to write it down. I did mention that my story facts came from a diary and the news media accounts of the murder."

"Yeah, but Arnold, Katie, and Esther are in the critique group. That means they know about the diary," declared Rivka. "I wonder how efficient that Reubens grapevine actually is?"

"What they don't know is that we are now in possession of it," said Dan.

* * * *

"My goodness, where did these things come from?" asked Rivka, staring at the three pumpkins lined up on the floor beneath the counter.

"Dan bought them at lunchtime," said Ivy, yielding her chair to Rivka for the evening shift.

"I darned near forgot. It's Halloween," said Rivka. "Oh, my gosh, the candy! Ivy, above the sink—top shelf—two glass candy dishes. One cabinet to the right of it: two bags of Hershey Kisses and a bag of mini-Snickers on the middle shelf. Would you please?"

"Of course." Ivy took the stairs two at a time and returned with the bags in tow. Shortly after, two bowls of mixed treats appeared on the corner of the counter.

Rivka immediately snitched a kiss, swirling the milk chocolate slowly around in her mouth. That's why she'd stowed the candy out of sight. In plain view, she'd have eaten half a bag by now. "The former bookstore owners had a tradition; Bernie Bender used to carve the pumpkins every year. I'm afraid I've neither the time nor the talent to do it."

"I know how to decorate jack-o-lanterns," volunteered Ivy.

"We did a lot of that sort of thing at home."

"You celebrated Halloween in the British Isles?"

"Sure!" said Ivy. "Our little community celebrated a combination of All Souls Night, Halloween, and Guy Fawkes Night. They're only a few days apart and there were lots of parties, toffee apples, baked potatoes, dress-up, jack-o-lanterns, bonfires, and fireworks."

"We don't have time to carve them, Ivy. The trick-or-treaters will be here any minute. See what you can do with Dan's Magic Markers, the ones he uses for price and sales signs."

Ivy rolled each enormous pumpkin through the first floor reading room, where she plied her inking art, then rolled them outside the front door. When she had finished, she called her employers to examine her handiwork.

"Oh, wow!" Dan said. "Amazing!" On successive pumpkins were the facial likenesses of Dan, Rivka, and herself.

"Whoa, it's seven thirty already," said Ivy. "Irma will be having a fit if I don't get home and fix dinner for her."

"Go already. What are you planning?" asked Rivka.

"Whatever TV dinners are in the freezer," said Ivy, letting go of the door behind her.

"Rivvie, shouldn't we move the candy outside to make it easier on the kids?" asked Dan. "Then we won't have to listen to that infernal tinkling of the doorbell all evening."

"I like the sound of that bell," she replied. "It usually means a potential customer is entering. Besides, we wouldn't get to see the costumes on those adorable little ones."

Dan chose to watch television upstairs, *The Twilight Zone* and one of his favorite movies, *Night of the Living Dead*. He came back down only to deliver sandwiches and milk to his wife, who stayed by the front door greeting the youngsters.

Around nine, the door tinkling slowed to a halt. Rivka intended to lock up and turn out the lights. She took the one remaining Snickers bar out of the candy dish, peeled back the paper, and stuck it between her teeth in a half-bite. With her right hand on the door lock and her left poised to pull down the shade, she hesitated. Through the beveled glass in the door, she saw a note taped to one of the pumpkins: the one with Ivy's face on it. Chomping down on the mini-candy bar, Rivka opened the door and retrieved the note. She read it, gulped down the nutty chocolate, and screamed. "Daniel Sherman! Come quick! I need you!"

Dan came bounding down the stairs. She handed him the typewritten note.

### IVY COHEN
### Go back to Great Britain and forget your
### mum's murder or suffer the consequences!!!
### *The ghost of Guy Fawkes*

"It's a threat," said Dan. "Ivy's gotten the response she sought."

"Who is this Guy Fawkes person?" asked Rivka. "I'm sure I should know, but—"

"He tried to blow up Parliament and the king in the early 1600s," said Dan. "I think they caught him and tortured him to death."

"Oh, my God," Rivka said. "Now I'm even more frightened for the poor girl. If anything happens to her, I'd never forgive myself. We have to stop with this diary business."

Dan placed his arm firmly around his wife's soft shoulders and drew her to him. "I'd be willing to stop, Rivvie, but I promised to help her. And *she* won't stop, especially now that the diary has arrived. Besides, you don't really want her to go back to England, do you?"

"Of course not, but I wish she wouldn't be so brazen. She's almost like our own child." Rivka shivered inside her favorite sweatshirt with its large illustration of Edgar Allen Poe. She could only think of their own daughter, Jenny, who'd grown up happily rebellious, stubbornly independent, questioning everything. Just like her mother.

# Chapter 17

## Love on the Opposite Side
### Tuesday, November 1st

Fenton Thorwal awoke with a start. He discovered Heather sitting up next to him, holding her knees with both hands locked around them. She had covered herself with the sheer peignoir once more, concealing little. He tried to follow her pensive gaze, but it seemed to go through the opposite wall, to nowhere, nowhere he could reach anyway.

"How long have you been up, lass?" asked Fenton, as he sat up beside her and then bussed her on the cheek.

"I slept soundly until four-thirty and I've been awake since. I just couldn't get back to sleep. My head is still going a mile a minute."

"I know what you mean," he said. "I've had nights like that. Is there something you want to tell me, lass?"

"Yes!" she said as though she'd anticipated his question and rehearsed her answer. She turned to face him and planted a long, full kiss on his lips.

"Wow! Listerine, too. Maybe I should gargle some," he said, trying to suppress his night breath. "Tell me more."

"It's Tuesday already," said Heather, both laughing and crying. "I was thinking that we have less than six days left to make one

143

hell of a big decision."

"Yes," he said. "But I've already made my decision. Say the word, and I'll request a two-week leave of absence to help you pack up and come back with me."

"What about marriage, Speedy?"

"Definitely included in the package," he answered. "Either here before we leave or in London. My mother's brother is a magistrate. Uncle Rudy would make a jolly good job of it. You'd like him, I'm sure."

"Is he anything like you?" she said as she shinnied her way down the sofa-bed until she lay prone.

"Oh, the spitting image, he is. Except he's the really good soul." He grinned and slid down to her. They embraced tightly for a few moments.

"You're so blooming sure of yourself," she said. "I only wish I could be that sure. Don't get me wrong. I know I'm in love with you, whatever that is, but is it enough to uproot either of our lives and move one way or the other across the Atlantic to live? No disrespect for your Uncle Rudy, but I've always had this big church wedding in mind. I've been planning it for years."

"Can you make it happen in the next three or four days or even in the next fortnight? Remember, I could get a leave of absence without pay for a limited time."

"Possibly, but I'm not going to rush into the biggest event of my life. First of all, I want to be as certain as you are. I need more time, dear, at least until Christmas. I should know by then, and I will come to you in London over the holidays to let you know my answer. We could even plan a June wedding if that's what the two of us really want. Sweetheart, let's put all this aside and enjoy our remaining time." Their lips came together for a long, hard kiss. Their bodies soon followed and pressed together until a more urgent, more primal need took over.

* * * *

The next day Dan and Rivka arrived at the Double T Diner

and asked to be seated in Frieda Forrester's section. Frieda welcomed them and took their orders. Poring over the massive menu, they selected roast duck, stuffing, and Hawaiian sauce for him and the egg salad platter for her. The orders came with soup or salad, and they both chose the matzoh ball soup. It was Wednesday, well after the noon rush, so Frieda hung around their table while they waited for their order.

"Is that who I think it is seated over there in the dark corner?" asked Rivka.

"It sure looks like Arnold Katz," said Dan. "But who's the cute little *shikse* with the blonde hair sitting next to him? It certainly doesn't look like Thelma."

"Oh, it's Arnold, all right," announced Frieda, "and she's that tramp from the Eastport bar he's been banging. They're in here once or twice a week. I don't like to gossip, but I seen 'em going at it in the parking lot. She's all over him. Poor Thelma. It's damn cheeky of them to display that kind of monkeyshines in public."

"Yeah," agreed Dan. "It does take a little cheek to do what their doing."

"Daniel!" Rivka tried to act shocked, but still enjoyed his irrepressible punning.

"Okay, folks, I better check on your food. It should be ready by now." Frieda ducked into the kitchen.

"It must be Old Home Week, Dan," said Rivka. "Why does that waitress look so familiar?"

"Who?" asked Dan. "Where?"

"The tall, shapely gal standing next to the dessert display case."

"You mean the one with the big boobs and the busted arm?"

"Yes, that's the one."

"Alice something. She was Leo's date on Sunday."

"Something wrong, you two?" asked Frieda, returning with their food and setting it in front of them.

"That blonde waitress over there. Alice something, isn't it?"

"Yeah! That's Alice Zimmer," replied Frieda. "She's only been here a few weeks, up from Charles County. How do you folks know her?"

"We saw her at a shindig on Sunday," said Dan. "What else do you know about her?"

"Daniel!" Rivka said in mock disapproval. "It's none of our business, but tell us anyway."

"Well, you know how I hate to gossip, guys," Frieda whispered. "But she came in to work yesterday full of bruises and red marks, claiming her boyfriend got drunk and roughed her up. Today, she's wearing a cast and sling. The only thing she can do is pour coffee and take orders."

Rivka gasped "Dear Lord! What a brute! I would never have believed it of Leo Schwartz."

"Can I get you some dessert, folks?"

"Well, seeing how it is my birthday I wouldn't say no. I haven't had a real chocolate fix in a dog's age."

"*Mazel tov!* Say no more, Rivka. I will cut you a piece myself." She returned with a monstrous, three-layer, double-chocolate cake slab on a plate. "With two forks, in case you need a little help."

* * * *

Ivy was firmly entrenched behind the checkout register for two reasons. One, business was slow. And two, Dan had invited Rivka out to lunch to celebrate his wife's fifty-fourth birthday. Alone again, Ivy pulled out the copy of her mother's diary that Dan had punched and bound in a loose-leaf binder for her. Before going home last night, she had read the last few entries, and particularly, the final entry her mother wrote early in the morning on Wednesday, March 3rd, 1982. Ivy compared the entry to her fictional chapter "Love Turned Ugly" and found that she had captured all the pertinent information.

The diary began in 1978. Early on as a schoolgirl, Lainee explained to one of her teachers her desire to become a professional fiction writer. The teacher informed her that keeping a journal was an essential adjunct.

The night before in a single reading, Ivy had gone through 1978 and '79, the first year-and-a-half of the diary. The pages periodically mentioned various affairs and beaux's names, one serious, the rest not, but she never encountered Snooks' real name.

Today at work Ivy read faithfully through another eight months of entries. She was interrupted only three times: by a patron wanting a rare copy of Jonathan Swift's *Gulliver's Travels* and a pair of customers just browsing. She continued reading.

In August of 1980 Lainee met someone. A possibility?

*Monday, August 4th, 1980:*

*I was sitting at the lunch counter, eating my usual Danish and coffee, when a man asked me to pass the sugar. As I slid the glass container over to him, I turned to face the gentleman who had made the request. I hadn't quite expected him to be so handsome and so well-dressed. I'm afraid he caught me blushing, but he did offer a smile, not so much about my blushing, friendly-like—more about discovering me. We exchanged first names and chatted a bit about weather, traffic and things. He finished his sandwich and left. The worst part was that I couldn't remember his name anymore.*

*Sally thought I acted like a ninny when I told her.*

*Tuesday, August 5th, 1980:*

*I purposely sat in the same place as yesterday, but the good-looking gent didn't show. I was terribly disappointed.*

*I saw a pair of navy pumps in the window today. Maybe next payday. Sally thinks I should save and not buy everything I see. She's right of course.*

*Wednesday, August 6th, 1980:*

*He was there today. There was a seat I was saving for him next to me. Good grief! I watched him come in and sit down at the other end of the counter instead. There was no seat next to him. I tried to wave when he looked my way, but the bloke never noticed me. On my way out I planned to stop behind him just to say 'hi,' but he was in the middle of a conversation with the counterman, and I didn't have the heart to break in.*

*Sally says I should have anyway.*

*Thursday, August 7th, 1980:*
*I had to work through lunch today.*

*Friday, August 8th, 1980:*
*He was there today, but this time I got his attention before he sat down and I motioned him over to the chair adjacent to mine. He remembered my name, but I was too embarrassed to say I had already forgotten his. Anyway, I worked around it while we talked and ate. He told me about a fair taking place on Sunday over in Hyde Park near Kensington where I live. I asked him whether that was an invitation for me to join him, and he said it was. I gave him my address and phone number. We set the time at twelve-thirty, and then he claimed that he needed to get back to work.*

*I was so excited, I couldn't wait to tell Sally.*

There was no entry on either Saturday or Sunday, But in Monday's, Ivy read that Lainee had a marvelous time on Sunday, walking among the tents and venders selling all sorts of trinkets, tchotchkes, clothing, and fast foods. They sat on a park bench and talked on and on about everything. When Lainee got hungry, they had "yummy" fish and chips wrapped in a newspaper cone from one of the venders and ate it right there on "our special bench." When it got dark, he walked her home and kissed her on the doorstep. She saw him again at lunch on Tuesday, but not for the rest of the week or throughout the start of the following week. Sally thought he'd forgotten all about her. Lainee thought she shouldn't listen to Sally.

Then on Thursday Lainee saw him again, and they made a theater and dinner date for Saturday.

Ivy skipped to Sunday, then Monday, and read one extra-long entry.

*Monday, August 18th, 1980:*

*Sally didn't want to believe we went to see "Cats," the musical, until I showed her the playbill. We had good seats, too—in the center, downstairs orchestra. God, the whole thing—the music, the dancing and the costumes were all heavenly. Then I told her we went to the Wolseley on Piccadilly and that blew her ruddy mind off. I had beef Wellington with teeny red potatoes and asparagus in, would you believe it, wine sauce. For dessert I had baked Alaska. It's ice cream with burnt meringue. They serve the bloody thing in flames.*

*We held hands under the table and blew kisses over the top. He paid me the nicest compliments—told me I was pretty and sexy and all that. On the door step, I invited him upstairs to the apartment. We sat on the settee, kissed and pet-ted awhile. He even smelled of passion, and I was just melting inside me. Soon he turned to unbuttoning my blouse. There was no one else on our earth.*

*He gathered me in his arms and carried me to my bed. I cannot rightly confess to being a virgin. But what this man did to me last night made me feel unique—as though something this wonderful couldn't have happened to anyone, anywhere before. It was dear, sweet, and honey all the way—who needed names, anyway?*

*Thursday, August 21, 1980:*

*I cooked dinner for Snooks tonight, a kidney pie—no, not as luxurious as beef Wellington, but he said he adored it. He even grabbed a towel and did up the dishes for me. After-ward, we retired to the settee again for another round of pas-sionate petting. My blouse was open, and his hands roamed freely.*

> *It was then that things became more than a little strange. I don't know why I chose that particular moment to confess that I couldn't remember his name. He said he hadn't told me his name, but really, he had. I just didn't remember it. I asked him why, and he explained to me that he was still married, but separated from his wife. He saw that I was upset, so he stood up to leave. I begged him not to go, but he insisted. He left, and I went to bed crying my eyes out for the next two hours.*

The bookstore got busy all of a sudden, and Ivy reluctantly shoved the diary under the counter. The Shermans returned just then. Dan took the register and she and Rivka went to help the milling crowd.

* * * *

It wasn't until late in the afternoon that Ivy had the chance to get back to the diary. Although she read every entry with care, she found no mention of either Snooks or the one who still remained nameless. In the entries for the next six weeks, Lainee replayed their last date many times, castigating herself over what had driven him off so easily, convinced that she had done something wrong.

Lainee had a date in mid-September with Eugene somebody. Ivy thought he sounded a little flaky. And while her mother's next few dates with a Peter B. sounded more promising, he quickly lost interest. Suddenly, her mother's tone changed. In the entries for the first week of October 1980, Ivy learned that both Snooks and the unnamed were one and the same.

Tonight was the weekly critique group meeting at The Old Victorian Bookstore. She would read those entries to the group.

"Closing time," said Rivka as she chased Ivy out of her chair to close out the cash for the day.

Ivy, with her back to Rivka, closed the loose-leaf diary and wrote something on the cover with a Magic Marker. Then she slipped it into a bookstore bag with handles and the store's Victorian logo on both sides. She threw on her heavy coat-length sweater to face the early November chill. Her next assignment: rush home to fix split pea soup and salmon salad sandwiches for Irma Riley and herself. And be back at the store by 7:30.

But there'd been no need to hurry. Irma already had the soup in the pot and the salmon salad fully mixed with mayo, vinegar, onion salt, and celery. A can's worth of mixed vegetables burbled in a second pot. The landlady was feeling much better and able to stand for short periods without crutches or a cane. She'd bathed herself and proudly put on one of her nicer dresses. Waiting by the door, she opened it when she heard Ivy come up the steps outside.

"Oh, my goodness!" said Ivy as the door swung out of the way, and Irma Riley stood in all her finery in front of her. "What's the occasion?"

"Happy birthday, Ivy," said Irma, planting a motherly kiss on her cheek.

"Birthday?" exclaimed Ivy. "It's not my birthday. That's in January."

"But I thought you said something about having a birthday on Monday morning before you left for work."

"Oh, dear," said Ivy as she removed her sweater and hung it on the clothes tree in the hall. "That was all about Rivka's birthday. I was reminding myself to wish her the tidings of the day."

"Well, no harm done," Irma said. "So you got early wishes. At least supper's ready."

"How nice. Was there any mail?"

"No, but you had three phone calls from your young men. Two of them had the same last name."

"I'll bet that name was Reubens," said Ivy. "Right?"

"Right! Joshua and Stuart, I believe."

"But who was the other from?"

"I left all the messages by the telephone table."

"They can wait. Let's sit down and eat first. I'll shower and change afterward."

* * * *

Herschel Reubens pushed himself away from the table at last. The crème brûlée was the perfect closure to onion soup, prime rib au jus, creamed corn, and baked potato à la kitchen sink. The Platza hotel dining room was half empty at nine o'clock and his waiter had been very attentive.

"Will that be all, sir?" The waiter laid the vinyl folder containing the credit slip and Herschel's Visa card on the table.

Hersch added an outrageous tip and signed the slip. "The only thing missing now is a good woman to warm my bed." He looked up at the waiter and obtained both a wink and a nod.

In a good-old-boys tone of voice, the waiter asked, "Would 10 p.m. be agreeable, sir?"

"Most agreeable," Herschel said and tucked another fifty inside with the credit slip. He left the dining room with a pleased expression on his face. Somehow, he always looked forward to these overnight business trips and Philadelphia was no exception. *Maybe it isn't all first class, but there are enough perks to keep me happy, and, best of all, Meyer never quibbles with me over the expenses. Even Anna knows what to expect from her Herschel Reubens on this long a leash.* He slipped the card key into the door lock and entered the large room. He felt at home in the semi-plush, overstuffed décor. *Anna would like it, too. Ah, Anna. Perhaps I should give her a call and put her mind at ease.* He picked up the hotel's landline, pressed eight for an outside line, and dialed his home.

"Hello," finally came at the end of a string of tones, buzzes, and clicks. It was Julie's voice.

"Hi, sweetheart, is Mom there? . . . No? Well, tell her when she comes in that I called. Tell her that I'm so wiped out I'm headed straight for bed and a good night's sleep. Hugs and squeezes and I'll see you tomorrow evening."

Herschel selected an FM radio station that played only classical music with no commercials. He showered, powdered, gargled, and applied all the outer body appointments before slipping into the hotel robe to wait. And when the expected knock finally came, the portly client opened the door and greeted Danielle. She was an attractive, brightly dressed call girl with a broad smile across her lightly lined face, placing her in her early forties. Neither Danielle nor the routine that followed was new to Herschel. She even knew him by name.

Following a sensual body dance slowly revealing all of her well-proportioned, smooth-bodied wares, Danielle joined him under the sheets and worked the age-old magic of her profession. The woman was playful and creative and at the same time, sensitive to his age and individual needs. The round, pink-bodied, middle-aged man usually enjoyed the expertly applied road to ecstasy. Yet, somehow, Herschel failed to respond to her efforts. After some time he became agitated and began apologizing. Of course, neither frame of mind was conducive to fulfillment. Danielle tried consoling him, drawing his face into her breasts and holding him there until the apportioned one-hour period was consumed. She had other business prospects that night.

Chapter 18

## Critique Group Meeting II
Thursday, November 3rd

D . . . . Patsy quickly reached out for the glass door beneath the detective's shingle, but she turned her head at the last moment to see Georgio running toward her. And in that particular instant, she slammed into a smallish man in a large overcoat with a flush face and old-fashioned spectacles. Patsy tried to free her entanglement with the homeless beggar man, but he clung onto her coat with two steel-like hands.

"I haven't eaten for days," he pleaded.

"Here!" she said, shoving two ten-dollar bills from her camel's hair coat pocket at him. "Let me go, please! There's a man chasing me. I've got to get away."

"Him?' he said. And following her nod, the beggar blundered into Georgio flying at her. The two men collided and fell on the sidewalk, floundering to recover as the grateful beggar intentionally orchestrated the same planned entanglement as before, this time engaging her pursuer. An angry Georgio watched Patsy Worth pull back the door and slip inside beyond his reach. He did not give the beggar any money.

Patsy climbed the stairs and quickly found safety in Kasper Brasse's office. Before she had a chance to say a word, the large man stood up behind his desk and walked around it to greet her. "Kasper Brasse, private investigator at your service, ma'am. How can I help you?"

He lumbered toward her, a tractor-trailer with headlight high-beam eyes, examining every morsel of Patsy from head to toe. And just before running Patsy over, he thrust out a welcome hand in her direction. She shook it, grateful her knuckles were still intact.

"I'm Patsy Worth and there's a man following me."

"I'm surprised there's only one," he said as she walked to the big window on the street side. "A former lover, no doubt. I specialize in stalking and that sort of thing, you know." He followed her to the window.

"Yes, a former lover, but he's not just stalking me. I think Georgio Gianetti wants to kill me. That's him down there on the sidewalk by the mailbox." Suddenly, she bolted back from the window. "Damn it. He's looking up at us now."

"Sit down, Ms. Worth and tell me why this Gianetti fellow would want to kill you."

Brasse eased himself into the swivel chair behind his desk. Patsy chose the straight-back chair to one side of the desk.

"He started by sitting outside my house in his car and then he'd follow me to work. Soon he was everywhere I went."

"Have you tried the police, Ms. Worth?"

"Yes, of course. After three months of this, I couldn't stand it, so I turned to the police and the courts for a restraining order."

"You mean he's violating the restraining order?"

"Yes, and because the police went to the shop where he worked to notify him, his boss fired him. He can't get another job. Now he's threatening to kill me if I go back to the police. What should I do? I need protection. I'm at my wit's end."

#

Dan picked up the latest pages of his Kasper Brasse novel and restacked them neatly before laying them down again on the table. "That's about all I could get down on paper this week, folks.

Sorry it's not a full chapter."

"It's a lot more than I got done," said Frieda.

"Ah, there she is," said Arnold as Ivy climbed to the top of the stairs and slid into an empty chair next to Dan.

Ivy removed the large binder from her shopping bag and deposited it on the table in front of her. She looked around at the familiar faces. "Hi! Sorry I'm late, everyone."

Dan took one look at the title on the cover of her binder. *The Diary of the Late Lainee Cohen.* "Ivy," he whispered, "put that away before you get yourself killed. It's much too dangerous."

"I agree," whispered Rivka, with head bent toward Ivy's ear. "All you're doing is making a target of yourself."

"Dan . . . Rivka," Ivy said aloud, "I intend to read several pertinent entries to the group and ask them if they are worthy of using in my book."

"You know damn well that's not what you have in mind," murmured Dan. "You're using yourself as bait for the killer."

"What if I am?" she snapped. "It's my life. I can do with it as I please. This is important to me."

"Hey, you three at the end of the table," called lawyer Joel. "Are you holding your own meeting down there? Let us in on what's going on, or do I have to get an injunction?"

"It's my fault, Mr. Wise," Ivy replied. "I wanted to read some entries from my mother's diary, and the Shermans seem to think I'm placing myself in harm's way by doing so."

"We feel responsible for you, Ivy," said Rivka aloud.

"Maybe they're right," said Joel. "You should listen to them."

"Hey, go for it," said Arnold with a wicked grin.

"Yeah," said Katie. "What's the harm?"

"I'm for it," joined Garry.

Ivy gathered up her slight body into an erect posture. "Then, by popular demand, I'd like to read some of the older entries and get your opinions as to whether I should include them in my story—that is, the manuscript I read from last week."

Ivy began with the August 4th through August 18th, 1980 entries, then skipped to the October 6th, 1980 entry, telling how Lainee and Snooks met and how their arrangement and his *nom d'affaire* came about. She continued with the following entries.

*Monday, October 6th, 1980:*

*In one of my lonelier moments, I got off the Tube one stop early to return to our special bench in Hyde Park. At the top of the fifty or so steps, I passed a news kiosk set near the curb. A man in a dark suit and flat peaked hat was buying a London Times. I don't know what made me turn and take a blessed second look but I did. It was him! He recognized me in the same instant. Both our jaws must have been agape. We remained silent, as he took my arm and steered me toward a little shop with tables inside and out. I think the sign said Tea and Extras.*

*At a wrought-iron table for two he ordered black tea, clotted cream, and scones for the both of us. His hand felt cool as he reached for and took my hand across the table. Then, leaning forward, looking deep into my eyes, he said the words I so much wanted to hear. He missed me terribly.*

*"If that's true why did you leave me?" I asked. "I haven't heard from you in months." I had difficulty speaking at first, then I told him I'd been miserable without him. I said "I think you owe me an explanation."*

*He nodded, yet remained speechless for the next few minutes. I might not have the words exactly right, but then he began: "I thought you were upset with me. You had every right to be—I wasn't entirely honest with you. Yes, I have a wife and I know now my marriage is sacrosanct. I will always have strong emotions for you. But my marital status cannot change regardless of how intense and sincere our feelings for each other become."*

*I told him that I truly understood. His eyes misted as*

*he spoke and I seemed more drawn into him. I saw and heard beyond his words. We two were meant to be, even if it was for only stolen precious moments. So I nervously agreed to a clandestine arrangement. I would become his mistress. He claimed he could not (or would not) reveal his true identity and I was not to press him further on the subject. He would spend weeknights with me in my apartment and the weekends at home with his wife. He promised he would pay my rent and generously provide for my expenses.*

*When I asked what name he preferred that I call him, he shrugged his shoulders and said, "Whatever." The first thing that came into my head, I spoke aloud, Snooks. As a tot, I had a stuffed monkey I called Snooks. He said that he liked the name—it had a flair and then he laughed.*

*He had to get back to work, so he left me with "See you tomorrow night at six-thirty." I watched him go down the Tube steps as I crossed the street. I lingered a tad in front of a boutique and marveled at an expensive jacket I'd love to own but couldn't afford. In the window glass I saw him come back up the stairs from the Tube and dart around the corner. He must work close by, I concluded. I had an urge to follow, but at that point, I had no desire to risk our arrangement.*

*Tuesday, October 7th, 1980:*

*I thought six-thirty would never arrive. I cooked and cleaned all day. I even washed and aired out the bedding and made room in the hall closet and the bottom two drawers of my dresser. There wasn't much I could do about the lumpy mattress. I prepared chicken cacciatore and steamed squash for dinner. I hoped he would like the plum pie I baked.*

*It was ten to six when I heard his knock at the door. His arms were so full of suits and ties, we couldn't embrace. Snooks had a large valise by his side. I couldn't lift the valise so I dragged it into the bedroom. Eventually, we got him settled in. He was exhausted from his day's work and the move, so he showered and then we sat down to dinner. It was wonderful having Snooks to myself for a whole evening. Gawd, the sex was delicious. He was so tender and attentive.*

*Wednesday, October 8th, 1980:*
*Around ten this morning, two hefty bruisers were at the door, delivering a brand new queen-sized bed, springs, mattress, and frame. They set everything up and took the old double bed away. I guess Snooks did mind the lumps even though he never complained.*

*Friday, October 10th, 1980:*
*Just before noon yesterday there was another delivery. It was a 33-inch telly. The men set it up in the living room and moved my little 15-inch telly into the bedroom on top of my dresser. Wow, what a picture—there's no comparison. At six-o'clock Snooks showed up with two arms full of groceries. Before he let me put them away he led me into the bedroom. "First things first," he said. I gave him no argument. We made love again just before turning out the lights for the night. The next night he would be going to his wife in the country.*

*Tuesday, October 14th, 1980:*
*Snooks brought me flowers yesterday and spent one glorious night with me. It looks as though I will only have him for four nights a week. I had hoped for five nights, but I'll take what I can get. We went shopping today for a coffeepot and toaster. I usually toast my muffins in a fry pan and drink tea. Last night on the way to the potty, I noticed a small pile of jewelry and change on the dresser we shared. I wasn't spying— only curious. I found a mezuzah on a chain and a ring with an inscription from his wife.*

#

Ivy closed the diary and looked up at the group. "I know it's late and I've taken up enough of your meeting time, but I thought these particular entries were important to my story. I read them tonight because I want your opinions. The last entry in particular because it establishes two things. One, Snooks is most likely Jewish. Two, Lainee now knows the name of his wife."

The room was quiet for several minutes. Esther broke the silence. "Am I to believe that you really intend to use your mother's diary to smoke out a murderer who committed a crime twenty-three years ago? It sounds a lot like you plan to accuse someone here at the table or someone very close to those here."

"Careful how you answer that," said Joel in his most authoritative voice.

"He's right," pleaded Rivka. "You've already put yourself in enough danger."

Ivy rolled her eyes and said, "That's exactly right, Esther. I intend to find my mother's murderer, wherever he is. And I do think I'm getting close. If it really costs me my life, so be it."

"Please don't talk that way, Ivy. Your life is precious to both Dan and me," said Rivka.  She got up from her chair and put her arms around Ivy from behind.

At a quarter to ten the meeting broke up. The members were still talking about Ivy's declaration of war when they walked out onto Franklyn Lane. Ivy was the last one out of The Olde Victorian Bookstore. She said goodnight to everyone as she passed them on the sidewalk. Carrying the diary under her left arm, she walked briskly away. By taunting, Ivy seemed determined to play a dangerous game.

At home, almost out of breath because of her determination to get away, she headed straight upstairs, pulled on her flannel pajamas, and fell into bed. She desperately hoped for a restful night's sleep after the upsetting reactions from the critique group. But no such luck. Her slender body flopped from side to side, her legs refused to lie still, and her heart thumped with adrenaline. Her head wouldn't leave her alone. Her brain went into overdrive. Bolting upright, she turned the bedside lamp back on and reached for the diary. Opening it, she scanned a few pages, then settled down to study them carefully and managed to finish the 1980s. But at the start of 1981 she made an unsettling discovery. Snooks had begun to travel. Now he was missing as many as two and three weeknights with Lainee. Ivy marked those entries with bookmarks and fell into a short exhausted sleep.

On Friday there was little time at work for reading. But after *Shabbat* dinner with the Shermans she did find a few minutes to discuss the diary with Rivka while the two women cleared and tidied up the dishes.

"Rivka? There's something troubling me about my mother's diary."

"What do you mean?"

"She never mentions going to work. She's not someone of means, living in a small apartment with only a few possessions. She's home during the daytime to receive deliveries, although I can't imagine that would be an everyday thing. And then there's this woman friend named Sally. Never a last name or where she knows her from. I frankly don't know what to make of all this."

Rivka dried her hands on a dish towel. "There could be all sorts of explanations, dear. You don't know if she had a family—your grandparents, possibly. They might have been supporting her. She may have had a small inheritance and was very frugal about it. She may have been between jobs or simply never wanted to talk or write about her workplace. Then again, if she had a job, Snooks may have asked her to give it up, since he wanted to support her."

"Wouldn't the police have tried to locate my grandparents? Maybe they weren't even alive. And wouldn't the police have located a bank account, unless it wasn't in my mother's real name?"

"Probably," said Rivka. "I wonder if the police even looked for a Sally. She might know a great deal more than we do." Adding to herself, *If she's still in London, and willing to talk, and even alive, for that matter.*

# Chapter 19

## Fresh Wounds
Saturday, November 5th

The first thing Leo noted when he entered the Double T Diner late in the afternoon was the striking blonde standing next to the sweets display case with a coffee carafe in one hand. Though she faced the opposite direction, he recognized the familiar curves. But to his surprise the woman had her other arm in a cast and sling. Upon approaching, he called softly, "Alice? Alice Zimmer?"

Reacting to his voice, she flashed her head around to face him, flinched, and turned blood-red. She knew he could see her swollen face heaped with layers of pancake makeup—her inept attempt to cover up multiple bruises and scratches. "Oh, God, Leo, I didn't want you to see me like this."

"Alice! What happened to you? And don't tell me you ran into a wall."

"I might as well tell you straight out. Benny, my ex-boyfriend from Waldorf, decided to punish me for dropping him. I left Charles County three months ago, specifically to get away from that bastard, but he won't let go. That goon thinks he still owns me. Not that he ever really did, mind you. When I wouldn't go back with him, he began beating on me and twisting my arm out of whack. He hurt me real bad. I had to go to the emergency room."

"You mean this Benny came all the way up to Annapolis even after you told him you were through for good?"

"Yeah! He doesn't know the meaning of No."

"Jeez, he could have killed you. How did you finally get rid of him?"

"My neighbor in the next apartment pounded on the wall and threatened to call the police. I guess that frightened him off."

"How long were you two a thing, if you don't think I'm being too nosy."

"It's been on and off since high school," she replied, "but usually he was the one breaking it off and coming back. This time I'd had enough. I decided that nothing good is ever gonna come out of that relationship. Good riddance! I'm gonna get a life for *me*."

"Do you think he'll leave you alone now?"

"I hope so."

"Do you want to press assault and battery charges?"

"No. That would only get him riled up again. I'm sorry, Leo. Would you like a table?"

"Sure, and a slab of that carrot cake in the display case," he answered as they strode toward a small booth. "Coffee, too."

Alice broke into a smile, poured his coffee, and headed for the dessert display. After she'd set his slice of the cake on the table, she hesitated, as though there was something more to be said.

Leo reached for her hand and looked up into her eyes.

"What time do you get off?"

She quickly pulled her hand back and glanced around furtively, hoping her boss wasn't watching. "Not for another two hours, but why would you want to spend your time with the likes of me— all bruised up, damaged goods and all. I can't be very pretty, hon."

"Sweetheart, it probably hurts a lot worse than it looks. Say, if I'm going to be stuck here waiting for you, maybe you had better bring me something more substantial, like an omelet."

Pencil poised. she placed the order pad in her sling hand. "What kind would you like, hon?"

"Bring me a three-egg western omelet with a couple of those chubby sausage links," Leo replied.

Alice left to put in his order, stopping only to pour coffee at another table along the way. The heavy mealtime traffic continued through the dinner hour. Suddenly, she appeared at his table sans apron, a sweater over both shoulders, clutching her purse. "I'm ready. Where would you like to go?"

Leo led her out to the parking lot and toward his pickup truck while he contemplated an answer. "We could grab a couple of drinks and listen to canned music across the street at Griffin's Bar and Grille," he said.

Alice turned to face him and looked long and deep into his eyes. "Would you like to come back to my place? It's only two rooms, but it's home to me. We could listen to music and maybe watch a little television. I got an open bottle of Johnny Walker Red, too. And Leo?"

"What, sweetheart?" he said as he opened the pickup's passenger side door.

"I want you to stay the night. I have this desperate need to be held, comforted, and maybe loved even if it's for only a little while. Could you do that, hon?"

"That's the best offer I've had in many a moon, woman." Leo shut her door, hurried around the rear of the truck bed, and slid into the driver's seat.

He noticed her rubbing her left cheek. "Does it still hurt much?" he asked.

"My jaw and cheek still hurt like hell. The doctor gave me a shot for the pain in my dislocated arm. I'm damned lucky Benny didn't knock out any of my teeth."

Leo reached Church Circle, cruised around 90 degrees, and drove down Duke of Gloucester Street.

"Turn here," Alice said, as she counted off the streets . "Look, a parking space there on the right and only half a block from my place."

A few minutes later Alice led him up a flight of worn wooden steps into her apartment. The furnishings looked like fugitives from yard sales, but he didn't care. He barely gave her time to toss her sweater over a chair before he folded her in his arms. Alice surrendered to the embrace with a cat-like purring. Struggling to look up, she admired his square chin and high cheekbones. Their lips met for a time until Leo felt an intense need for more. He reached for the top button on her blouse and had it undone before she could object.

"Not just yet, sweetheart," she said as she slipped from his embrace. "We have the rest of the evening and the whole night. God knows I have the hots for you, too, but I want to enjoy the whole you first."

Alice pushed him toward the sofa and left him sitting while she selected several CDs from her Country and Western collection and loaded them into the player. Blowing a kiss toward Leo, she disappeared into the kitchen and returned with a bottle of Johnny Walker Red and two ice-filled glasses, which she set down on the maple coffee table. Alice poured the glasses to the brim and handed one to her guest. Leaving her drink, she sat mid-sofa, pulled her feet up, and laid her head down in his lap.

The music, with its songs full of regrets and what-ifs, created a less-than-romantic mood. Leo played with her shoulder-length, ash-blonde tresses, stroking, coiling, and letting them stream through his fingers. Then a memory pushed its way through his consciousness, surfacing at just the wrong moment. Alice's hair was neither the color nor the length of the woman's he remembered. Perhaps it was the texture or the current situation that made him think of the woman he once loved. He sighed and looked down at Alice.

Her eyes locked on his. "Why the sad look? Have I said or done something wrong?" she asked.

"No, of course not." Leo worked up the curl of a smile. "It's just that you remind me of someone I knew a ton of years ago and a million miles away."

"Did she mean a lot to you?"

"At the time, *very*. But my marriage to Katie was important to me, too."

"You've been married before?" Alice blurted out. "I guess I shouldn't be surprised, but you didn't say anything at the pub. I thought you were a perennial bachelor."

"Yeah, I was married. Twice. My first wife died. Katie and I have been divorced for years."

"So . . . What about the one a million miles away? What happened to her?"

"When it was over, it was over. I don't know anything about her life now."

Alice sensed the tinge of annoyance in his voice, but she couldn't let go. "Ever think about marrying again?"

"Nope!" A frown replaced the smile. "You ask a hell of a lot of questions, woman."

"I'm sorry," she said. Actually, she wasn't. She didn't pretend to be anything but an unsophisticated farm girl, but she recognized a dead-end when she saw it. Plus, he was probably twenty years older than she. Early fifties, maybe. Still, right now she needed sex. "Let's change the subject," she murmured.

Alice took his right hand, cupped it over her breast, and pressed it there. But soon that wasn't enough for either of them. She stood up, took his hand, and led him into the bedroom, lit only by a streetlight weakly beaming through the curtains. The bedspread had been removed earlier and the covers turned down.

Gingerly removing her sling, she tossed it on the dresser, then stopped and stood still. Hampered by her cast, getting herself undressed was an arduous procedure. Leo understood and gently took care of the task for her. Blouse, slacks, bra, and pink nylon panties edged in lace. For one brief moment he reveled in her exquisite figure. Then she slid under the covers. Alice watched him undress, which he did slowly and purposely.

Their lovemaking spanned more than an hour, neither being the sole aggressor—he with extreme tenderness, respecting her pained state, and she with sincerity and warmth. It was giving and receiving, something neither had experienced in a long time.

Leo had come close to explaining himself with complete honesty only once before in his life, and this disturbed him. Was he experiencing a form of guilt or was he feeling something more positive?

* * * *

That same evening turned overcast under a heavy blanket of clouds and the moon in hiding. Ivy, with the diary under one arm and her sweater draped over it, started home after work. As she rounded the first corner toward the Riley house, she sensed the presence of someone behind her. No one she could actually see or hear, yet she imagined a face in every tall hedge and low-slung maple. She stopped and turned to check. The streetlight at the corner cast its luminescence only so far, creating shadows where it could. Not a soul was visible on this street. A few gas lamps glowed on the lawns in the next block, but emitted too few lumens to light her way. The hairs on the back of her neck bristled. She pivoted again, saw nothing, and turned back, quickening her step. Her leather soles made a slapping sound on the sidewalk. She broke into a trot, but ran into a shallow puddle, causing her to slip and slide. She slowed to get her footing and tried to convince herself she really was imagining the stalker. She turned once more. No one.

A snapping sound. A hand came out of nowhere and pushed hard on Ivy's back, thrusting her raggedly through the six-foot-high hedge that stretched along the property on her left. The pyracantha's long thorns and clusters of orange berries ripped across her face and gouged her bare arms as she was forced to the ground. She wasn't aware of when or where her sweater went, but she distinctly remembered the diary being ripped from under her arm rather than dropped. She screamed, an indescribable noise at first, and then she formed the shrill words "Help! Help me!" She crawled the rest of the way through the hedge just as the porch light came on in the nearest house.

"Who's there?" a male voice cried out.

"Ivy Cohen," she called back. "One of your neighbors from around the corner, the Riley house. I've been mugged." She struggled to her feet and found her sweater and then her purse in the grass.

Hurrying off his porch, the middle-aged man came closer. "You're bleeding, young lady. How badly are you hurt?"

Knees shaking, voice trembling, Ivy said, "No bones broken, but I'm all scratched up from being forced through your hedge and down to the ground."

"I see you still have your purse," the man said. "Is there something else missing?"

"Yes," she answered, choking back tears. "A loose-leaf binder containing my mother's diary. I can't find it anywhere. Do you have a flashlight, sir?"

"Come inside, Miss Cohen. My wife will attend to your wounds, and meanwhile, I'll come back out with a flashlight and have a look around for you."

The man took her gently by the arm and assisted her up the steps to the porch where his wife stood holding a flashlight out to him. "Here, George," she said.

"I'm Maddy Watson," she told Ivy. "Come in the kitchen where I can clean up those nasty scratches and put on some antibiotic salve and Band-Aids. What kind of bully does this sort of thing?" Mrs. Watson sat Ivy down at the table and left her for a few minutes while she retrieved her first-aid supplies. Gentle and efficient in her care, she soon had Ivy decorated in a dozen or so neat little antiseptic patches. George Watson returned inside as Maddy was finishing.

"Not a sign of anything that looks like a notebook or binder," he said, laying the flashlight down on the counter. "It appears that the diary was what the scoundrel was after, seeing as how nothing else is missing. Did you get a good look at the feller that shoved you?"

"I'm afraid I didn't get to see anybody at all," said Ivy. "It all happened so fast. I work at The Olde Victorian Bookstore and live around the corner with Mrs. Riley. I walk by here on my way home every night."

"How is Irma?" asked Maddy. "I heard she broke her leg."

"The leg is healing fine," replied Ivy "Which reminds me. I need to get home and help her upstairs to bed. She's probably falling asleep in front of the telly by now."

"I'll walk you home, Miss Cohen." George picked up the flashlight again.

"Oh! You've both been so kind already," said Ivy. "I can get home on my own, really I can."

"Nonsense," insisted Maddy. "You've had a traumatic experience. What if your mugger wanted something more from you and is still out there?"

"No! I don't think so." Ivy sighed. "I'm sure he got what he was actually after."

"How can you be so sure?" asked Maddy.

"I believe the mugger thinks my mother's diary can incriminate him." Ivy stood unsteadily and started for the door. "Thank you both so much. I won't ever forget your kindness."

George followed Ivy out. Paying no attention to her protests, he walked her home and up the steps to the Riley front door. She thanked him again and slipped inside.

Sure enough, Irma was asleep in her wheelchair in front of the TV. She picked up Irma's feet and placed them on the foot rests. Irma awoke as Ivy wheeled her to the bottom of the staircase and locked the wheels.

"I'm so glad you're here, dear," said the groggy old lady. "I'm sooo tired." Then she looked Ivy straight in the face and saw the antiseptic patches. "Good grief, girl, what happened to you?"

"I'll explain in the morning," she said, standing the old woman on her feet and closing her liver-spotted right hand around the banister. She put Irma's left arm over her shoulder and started up the stairs. Every step of the way up was dead weight. With Irma finally put to bed, Ivy stared at the second flight of stairs to her own room. Dragging one foot after the other, she reached her own bed and flopped down.

She began to sob. Now she no longer had the means to find her mother's killer. She had failed. Why hadn't she taken Dan and Rivka's advice? She doubted whether they could impose on Chief Inspector Winston to send another copy. She cried herself to sleep on a soaked pillow, still fully dressed.

# Chapter 20

## **Backed-Up**
### Monday Morning, November 7th

hat on God's earth happened to you?" asked Rivka as soon as she saw Ivy coming through the door. "You look like you've been through the wars."

Ivy choked up. Rivka tilted her head to one side and held out her arms, inviting a comforting embrace.

Ivy found her bearings. "Last night I was attacked and mugged. They're only scratches. They'll heal. But the worst part is that the mugger has the diary. The only copy. Please don't say 'I told you so.' You and Dan and Joel tried to warn me, but I didn't want to listen."

"I'm so sorry," said Rivka as she led Ivy to a chair behind the counter. "Daniel, come out here a minute," she called.

"Whoa!" said Dan upon sighting her. "Who did that to you, sweetheart?"

"I wish I knew," she wailed. "It was so very dark and the blighter pushed me through the pyracantha bushes around the corner from here. Oh, Dan, he took the diary from me. Pulled it out from under my arm. The only copy that you worked so hard to get from the Chief Inspector." Her face disappeared behind a wad of Kleenex, mopping tears and nose-blowing. "Do you think we have

171

the right to ask for another one?"

"Good news," he said, adjusting his horn-rimmed glasses. "It won't be necessary. You see, it wasn't the only copy. I had another one made and spiral-bound at Kinko's. Remember, you lent me yours to punch for a loose-leaf binder? I apologize for not telling you sooner, but I was anxious to start looking for clues myself. I must admit you've managed to read a good deal more of the diary than I have."

Rivka affectionately ruffled her husband's bushy black hair. "Thank God you made another copy. But maybe you should have asked her permission first."

"Daniel, you're wonderful," Ivy piped up. "You actually had my permission. I only said that I wanted to read it first." She jumped out of her chair and threw her arms around him.

Feeling quite heroic, he said, "I'm going to propose that I make yet another copy of Lainee's diary. One we'll keep here in the store under the counter. And the other I suggest you keep hidden at home. That way you won't have to transport it back and forth from work."

Seated in the swivel chair, Rivka assumed her favorite contemplating position. She set her elbow on one wooden arm and rested her cheek on her fist as she spelled out her thought process. "From now on we have to assume the murderer knows as much about the diary as we do. We also have to assume that Ivy has pierced his Achilles heel by zeroing in on the four men in the extended Reubens family. You've struck a nerve, Ivy. If your mother mentions Snooks' ring inscription in some later entry, we'll know our killer right off."

"The *mezuzah* tells us he's Jewish," added Dan. "And the tax rolls confirm the arrival of the family here and the start of the family business in the correct time frame."

"I've begun to catalogue the travel gaps in the entries," Ivy said. "Hopefully, they can narrow the possibilities further. Dan, is there a way we can access airline and ship's manifests for the period?"

"I don't know," he replied. "Law enforcement agencies on both sides of the Atlantic should have access, especially immigration authorities. But whether the carriers keep records for so many years or purge them on a regular basis is something we have to look into."

"Maybe your friend who's staying with Heather could help," suggested Ivy. "He helped us find Chief Inspector Winston, didn't he?"

"Yeah," Dan said, but added nothing more.

"One thing strikes me as odd," Rivka said. "All our candidates are middle-aged, fifty or older. It's hard for me to believe that any of this bunch would have the stealth and balls to pull a stunt like pushing Ivy through the hedge without getting caught."

"Leo is the oldest, but only by a year or so. He certainly looks like he's in better shape than the others," answered Dan. "What if it's Arnold? He's the youngest of the bunch, but the least ambitious. I understand he was the last to emigrate from England and join the company." Dan fixed their clerk with an eagle eye. "Until this mess is resolved, I think we'd better keep you in our sights, Ivy."

"Hey, you two," said Rivka. "Do you think we can manage to sell some books today?"

* * * *

"Hey, there, Stretch, you been avoiding me lately?"

"Naw, just busy, Beast."

"You got enough dust to last you?"

"Sure. I mean I'm trying to go easy on the stuff. My brother's getting wise and I don't want my parents to find out. I'm parceling it out so it'll last longer."

"You ain't got another supplier, have you, kid?" Beast pushed his companion up against the brick siding of the abandoned school building and grabbed him by the chin.

"No! Honest, Beast! I wouldn't do that. You're my only supplier, I swear."

"Well, Stretch, we're planning our next raid into the Reubens building. Maybe sometime next week. My fence is interested in some assorted wall switches, circuit breakers, and fancy cover plates."

"You're picking on my family's business. Can't we go easy on them? Why do you want to go back there?"

"Well, wise ass, we got the perfect way in, and they haven't figured it out yet. Besides, they haven't cried to the cops yet. Any more stupid questions?" He patted Stretch on the cheek. "And you're gonna help us."

"No! I'm out," said Stretch. "You can make the score or not, but you can count me out."

"Lemme see your wallet, Stretch," demanded Beast.

"What the hell do you want with my wallet, Beast?"

"I wanna see how independently wealthy you are, that's what. So gimme."

Stretch slowly and reluctantly pulled the wallet from his back pocket and handed it over to Beast. Beast took it and immediately started to count the wad of bills. He whistled through his teeth when he got through the first $200. There was a total of $263.

"You rob a bank or something, Stretch?" he asked.

"Nope, I did a job for someone."

"What did you have to do for that kind of money?"

"I stole a book," Stretch answered reluctantly. By now, he had started to anger at Beast's questions.

"Who'd ya steal it from?"

"None of your damn business!"

"Okay, then," said Beast as he stuck $200 in his own pocket and handed the wallet back. "Who'd you steal it for?"

"Screw you, man. I don't have to answer yer grilling me." Stretch put his wallet away.

Beast grabbed him by the polo shirt collar and slammed him against the building once more. "Don't get wise with me, you little fart. I'll work you over real good."

Beast thought Stretch had jerked sideways to avoid several blows to his stomach, but he was wrong. Stretch had made the move to raise his right foot high off the ground. Just before the next inflicted blow, he slammed the heel of his cowboy boot down on Beast's soft moccasin shoe—so hard that Beast stood helplessly upright for seconds afterward. Before the sounds of pain forming on his lips had a chance to escape, Stretch clenched his fist and delivered a sharp uppercut to Beast directly under the chin. Beast's head snapped back and his body went over backward, hitting the gravel next to the building, making a thud like a dropped bag of potatoes. He didn't move, so Stretch decided to get out of there in a hurry. His worry was not Beast's motionless state. It was that he knew Beast would extract his own heinous revenge sometime in the near future. Before taking off, Stretch stuck a hand in Beast's jeans pocket and retrieved his $200.

* * * *

Esther reached for a face-down tile in the two-high wall of ivory slabs in the middle of the table, examined it for a moment, and tucked it in her mah-jongg tray, rearranging a few others to complement it. Then she discarded another tile, a two-dot piece. "Really, Thelma, if it was my husband, I wouldn't have let it get this far."

Thelma Katz picked up her tile selection and groaned as she placed it to one side of her tray. "Oh? I don't think it's any of your Pinocchio, Esther. My Arnold has always been the kind of free spirit I haven't been able to tame, and I don't think any of *you* could do any better." On further consideration she retired the same one-crack tile she'd just picked up.

"He's never been totally *your* Arnold, Thelma," said Katie Silvers, taking her turn from the ivory Wall of China tiles spread before her. "In fact, he's never been *anyone's* Arnold. By your own words he's been incorrigible. Been that way long before you guys left England. I don't know why you've stood for it all these years." She replaced a tile in her hand and discarded an eight-bam tile.

"Because, when it's all over, he *always* comes home to me,

and things get wonderful again, even if it is only for a little while," Thelma said, wiping a tear from the corner of her eye. "And he'll come home this time, too. You'll see."

"*Pong*, ladies," said Anna, picking up the last discard. "Don't be too sure, my dear. I understand the little distraction is quite pretty." She discarded a two-crack piece.

"I saw the two of them all lovey-dovey over at the diner last week," Esther chimed in. "And you know something?"

"What?" asked Katie and Thelma in unison.

"The little tramp appeared to be a tad bit pregnant," Esther responded, exchanging one tile from the wall for one in her hand.

"How big a tad?" asked Anna with a snicker.

"Well, showing, anyway," said Esther. "But maybe not enough for him to observe it yet. I've got a flair for seeing these things, you know. Men are always the last ones to notice."

"Maybe there's hope for you yet, Thelma," declared Anna. "I know Arnold. My brother will order the bitch to abort the minute he finds out. And whether she does or not won't matter, he'll drop her like lightning afterward. This is not the first time a pregnancy got in his way. Probably won't be the last either."

"Anna, that's not fair," retorted Thelma. "He still feels like I forced him into our marriage. Thank God he's always adored our Maurine and not held it against her, as he's done with me. Still, he's the man I love and the man who surely loves me. But there's an irresponsible little boy inside him that wants to roam, carouse, and continue to punish me. He just can't help himself, and I'm not sure I want to tame the tiger in him entirely."

"That's just it," said Esther. "You're enabling that little boy to help himself all over the place, womanizing and carousing and generally making life miserable for you. I can't imagine how I'd handle that sort of thing."

"Oh, really?" replied Thelma with a swath of sarcasm. "Your Meyer has always been such a darling angel down through the years?"

"Rest assured, he hasn't always been the perfect spouse, I'll admit that. Let's just say that my Meyer has mellowed with time and resigned himself to becoming a responsible husband and father. Things have been good with us for a long time now." Esther picked the next tile, regarded it briefly, then left it face-up on the table.

"About time, woman, this game is plain dragging," said Anna. "Less gossip and pay more attention. This round is mine, so let's get on with it, ladies."

"Now don't get your bustle in a boil, Annie," said Katie. "We're moving right along."

"That you, Abel?" called Esther, hearing the front door shut.

"No, Mom, it's me," said Josh, poking his head into the living room. "Oh, hi, everyone."

"Have you seen your brother?" asked Esther.

"No. But my guess is that he's over at the old schoolyard with some of his dirt-bag friends."

Chapter 21

## Tribal Gathering
Wednesday, November 9th

bel Reubens hadn't left his room in two days. Anxiety lived within him, and he jumped with the least provocation. Rudeness prevailed, leading to scrapes with everyone in the household. He had no idea what a pathetic, frustrating picture he presented to his family. Seventeen years old, six-foot-three and 200-plus pounds, sent to his room during breakfast yesterday, like a three-year-old. He skipped breakfast on his own this morning. Abel didn't mind. The candy bars in his stash more than offset his hunger. But even his hoodie sweatshirt couldn't stop the violent shivers, the cold sweating. The vise that enveloped his head slowly squeezed into a tighter grip. If only the throbbing would stop.

Sitting on the bed, he kept eying the top left drawer of the dresser, trying to direct his attention elsewhere, anywhere, but always knowing the little white baggies hidden inside called to him. They drew him across the room like a magnet, forcing him to open the drawer and reach under the socks for one of them. He toyed with the bag, fighting himself all the way back to the bed. Sitting down again, he turned it in his fingers, over and over. Then in one bold move, he bounded from the bed, shoved the bag in his pocket, ran down the stairs, and flew out the door, despite the call from his father ordering him to stop.

Abel felt much better in the fresh air and warm sunshine. He didn't give a damn that he was a high school senior cutting another two days of classes; he had no use for the garbage they taught there. He began to walk aimlessly, not caring where he went. That is, until he heard a voice calling to him, a voice of reality. He had wandered into the streets where he would most likely find Morgan Beastrom, "Beast" they called him. But the voice belonged to Ratman. Abel had never learned his real name.

"Hey, Stretch!" Ratman yelled. "Didja hear?"

"Hear what?" asked Abel as he watched Ratman cross the street and approach him. His heart began to beat faster and louder.

"'Bout Beast. He's in the hospital with a coma in his head. I think it's called a precussion."

"What the hell happened to him?" Abel asked.

"Don't know. Poh-lice found him unconscious in the schoolyard, and they took him away in an am-bu-lance."

"Is he gonna be all right?"

"Don't know. He's not allowed visitors. You know how the poh-lice is."

"Yeah!" said Abel. "I do. Thanks, pal." He made a U-turn and hastened back toward his home. *What if Beast dies?* he thought. *He's got a concussion. Am I a murderer? At least he can't force us to break in again anytime soon.*

* * * *

"Are you finished packing yet, Fen darling?" asked Heather.

"Almost!" Fenton replied. "I came with so little, it's easy to pack. I didn't spend a whole lot on souvenirs either." He zipped around both sides of his valise.

"I guess I kept you too busy for that. Besides, you should be saving your money now." She looked straight at him as he slowly raised his head of neatly combed hair.

His eyes locked onto hers. "Does that mean you've made up your mind, lass? You'll marry me, sweetheart?"

"*Mais oui, mon amour,*" Heather said. "*Oui, oui, oui!* Mrs. Fenton Thorwal. It has such a proper ring to it." Her words could convey no more expression of love than the excitement and happiness in their tone. A blush crept in between the freckles on her cheeks.

Fenton set the valise on the floor and held his arms open for her. She leapt into them and rained kisses on his lips, cheeks, and neck. "*Je t'adore,*" he whispered in her ear. By now, both were wet with tears of happiness. He held her close to feel as much of her body as he could. And then he looked pleadingly into her green eyes.

"Do we have time for a quick one?" he asked, as he loosened his grip.

"No, Fen darling," she replied. "As much as I really want to, it's time to call the cab company. There'll be plenty of time for that when I come at Christmas. In fact, I plan to ask for a six-month leave of absence from my teaching position. I want to see if I like living in Britain. I might even let your Uncle Rudy have a go at marrying us. But I still want a big church wedding when we either come back for a vacation or a six-month trial here to see if you like living in Maryland. How does that sound to you?"

"Quite good, love. And fair, too."

Heather picked up the phone and called the cab; he laid his coat across the valise to wait.

As Fenton handed his valise to the driver, Heather called, "I love you!" He turned, blew her a kiss, and got in the cab. *I'll miss you,* she called silently after it.

* * * *

On the second Wednesday of each month either Herschel, Meyer, or Arnold hosted a family dinner—just the parents. When it was Leo's turn, he took everybody to Mama Lucia's for pasta. But it was Meyer's turn this month, and Esther made corned beef and cabbage. Anna brought apple and peach pies.

180

When the pie dishes and coffee mugs were cleared at the end of the meal, four stapled stacks of paper suddenly appeared on the table. No one had noticed who put them there and no one claimed responsibility.

Herschel reached out for one of the stacks and pulled it toward him. "It's the Cohen woman's diary!" he exclaimed. "How the hell did that trash get into this house?"

"I don't know, but you take it easy, Hersch," pleaded Anna. "You'll have a heart attack."

Others at the table reached for the remaining copies.

"My God," said Esther, at the head of the table reading the first page of cursive. "That Cohen girl has now invaded our homes with her accusations. I have news for those of you who weren't at the mystery critique group meeting. Ivy Cohen said she planned to accuse one of us sitting at the reading room table—or someone close to us—of murder."

"Actually, Esther," said Arnold, "those were *your* words. *You* said it sounded like she was going to accuse one of us. She merely said you were exactly right."

"All the same," said Esther. "She has it in that wicked little head of hers that Hersch, Meyer, Leo, or Arnold murdered her mother. I myself can't believe that anyone in our family could do such a horrible thing. I think she plans to use this diary to falsely incriminate one of our four men-folk."

"And just how would she propose to do that?" asked Leo.

"How the hell should I know?" Esther replied. "You'll have to read through it like everyone else, Leo."

"Is there anyone here brave enough to own up to such a deed?" asked Thelma. The room went silent. Many eyes moved furtively about the room, silent accusing eyes, but nothing conclusive.

"What do you think, Anna?" asked Meyer.

"I think we should stick together as a family and not let this little twerp lord it over us. Even if someone here did the deed, good grief, it's been over twenty years."

"Twenty-three years, according to her," added Esther.

"I think you're all forgetting something here," said Josh. "The killer is also her father. If what she's accusing is true, she is very closely related to this family. She could be a child to one of you. At worst, she could be a cousin, and at best, a half-sister to me."

"Josh, you watch your mouth," said his mother. "You have no right to speculate on that young woman's trashy accusations."

"The murder could have been an accident," said Meyer.

"The fathering could have been an accident, too," said Herschel.

"Maybe we should each read the damn thing first and talk about what's to be done afterward," said Leo. "All this supposition is going nowhere."

"Has anyone seen the new play at Colonial Theatre?" asked Thelma, frantic to change the subject.

Just then the front doorbell rang, silencing everyone.

Meyer got up from the table and went to the door. He turned on the outside light, looked through one of the side glass panels, and saw two uniformed policemen standing on the porch.

Meyer opened the door. "What can I do for you, officers?"

"Sir, is your son at home?" asked the shorter of the two.

"They are both at home, one's upstairs, I believe," responded Meyer. "What's this all about?"

"Does an Abel Reubens live here?" asked the same officer.

"Is he in some kind of trouble?" Meyer frowned with irritation at the avoidance of his own question.

"I can't answer that," the officer said. "We need to ask him some questions about an altercation that took place over at the old schoolyard. We found his student ID card on the ground there. Now may we talk with him?"

"Do we need a lawyer, Officer?"

"He's not being charged with anything. But if you wish an attorney to be present, we'll have to have our little talk down at the local precinct."

Meyer took a few steps back from the doorway and yelled

up the stairwell for his son. Abel appeared at the second floor landing.

"What do you need, Dad?" he said.

"Would you mind coming downstairs a moment? The police are here with some questions for you. I'm taking them into the den." He turned to the officers and guided them through the living room. "Make yourselves comfortable. He'll only be a minute."

Abel appeared at the den door in cut-off jeans and an old Grateful Dead T-shirt decorated with a rose and skull. "Hey, Dad, what's up?"

"Close the door, son, and have a seat here." It was the straight-back chair across from the two officers.

The shorter one conducted the interview. "Were you involved in an altercation with a young man named Morgan Beastrom on Monday afternoon?"

"I . . . uh . . . know him."

"All right, young man, you know him, but that's not what I asked you."

"Yes. We had a fight."

"A fight about what?"

"He wanted my wallet."

"You owed him money?"

"Nope! I mean yeah."

"You mean he was stealing from you?"

"I can't answer that."

"You mean you won't answer."

"Yessir."

"How did this fight start?"

"He slapped me around and then shoved me up against the brick wall and held me there by the neck with one hand while he punched me with the other."

"Then how did this big strapping fellow wind up in the dirt flat on his back."

"I knew he was wearing soft moccasins, so I stomped down hard on his foot. I had my cowboy boots on, and when he straightened out in surprise, I cold-cocked him under the chin and then I ran." He looked over at his father with a conspiratorial smile.

"And what's all this about? Drugs?" asked the officer.

"About my money," said Abel. "He wanted my wallet."

"Did you give it to him?"

"Yes, sir!"

"Why?"

"He had me up against the wall, and like you said, he's a lot bigger than me. What was I supposed to do?"

"How much money are we talking about, young man?"

"Exactly two hundred fifty. He took it and left me with thirteen lousy dollars. It was all mine and the bastard still has it now. I earned it."

"You earned it?"

"Yes, sir."

"How?"

"I don't know. I ran some errands."

"What kind of errands?"

"Don't know. I guess just normal errands for my family."

"That right, Mr Reubens? You gave him the money?"

"Ah . . . yes, of course. He wanted to buy some sports equipment, so I made him do some work around the house for it. By the way, how is the other youngster doing, Officer?"

"The youngster's in the hospital. In a coma induced by a concussion. They're not sure if it was the blunt force to the chin or his head contacting the hard ground. There was severe bruising in both places. Whether he dies or recovers and presses charges, a more extensive inquiry will be necessary. Thank you for your time and cooperation."

The officers stood and made their way outside to their cruiser. Abel started to leave the room when his father put his hand on the boy's right shoulder and spun him around face-to-face.

"Why did you lie to the police, Abel?"

"I didn't lie. I earned that money doing a favor for a member of *this* family."

"What kind of favor, and why couldn't you tell the police who?" Meyer put his large, hairy hands on both shoulders and began shaking his son. "What kind of favor?" he repeated.

"Okay! Okay! I pushed Ivy Cohen into the bushes and stole the notebook of the diary from her."

"Good God, what kind of son have I raised?"

"But Dad, I warned her. I sent her a note on Halloween."

"You were paid two hundred fifty to accomplish all this?"

"Yes, sir!"

"Who in hell in this family would pay you to do a stunt like that?" Meyer shook his son again. "Who, I say? Your brother?"

"No way," said Abel, still cringing in his father's grip. "He's too goody-goody for that."

"Then who?"

"Stop shaking me, Dad. I can't tell. I'm sworn to secrecy. I won't tell no matter how much you shake my *kishkes.*"

Meyer stopped and Abel wrestled himself loose.

On impulse Meyer grabbed his son, pulled him close, and hugged him. "We'll get through this, son."

"Dad, there's a bunch of other stuff I'd like to get off my chest, if you don't mind."

"Another time, son. Don't you think we've had enough revelation for one night? I know I have."

Father and son walked into the dining room together. The boy had his father's arm around his back and that felt both strange and good. *Maybe all the rest will pass and, in time, be forgotten*, Abel thought.

"What's going on with the police coming to the house?" asked Leo on his way to the hall closet for his Ravens warm-up jacket.

"Oh nothing," replied Meyer. "Abel, here, got into a scrape with another youngster. We got it all ironed out, thank you."

Chapter 22

## Arnold's Folly
Monday, November 14th

rnold found himself surviving one of the busiest weeks he'd experienced since he went to work for Reubens Brothers. All of his usual hiding places were exposed, and full partner Leo was on his back constantly. His sister, Anna, had forewarned him this was coming. She'd received too many complaints from all three partners, and Hersch refused to talk to her until she delivered Arnold his due admonishment for being so lazy.

Arnold couldn't find a moment for relaxation nor a hideaway, and as a result, his hobby composing music suffered greatly. By the end of the first week, he was exhausted, but took hope in the idea that Leo couldn't possibly continue spending this much time merely herding him from one task to another. When the harassment dragged on into the second week, Arnold decided to get even. *Hell, I'm not their slave.*

Right after breakfast on Monday, his wife, Thelma, left for her retail clerking job in the mall, and daughter Maurine left for high school. Arnold decided to play hooky from work. He pulled the telephone plug from the wall and returned to bed for almost three hours of extra sleep, figuring that someone from Reubens

Brothers would call at least three or four times by then. He thought they would encounter either a busy signal or a no connection—he didn't know which and couldn't care less.  Once up, Arnold fixed himself a sandwich and, plugging the phone in once more, punched in ten digits and munched while he waited.

A familiar female voice picked up.

"Hi ya, sweetie," he said. "I got the day off. You want to get it on?"

Fanny giggled. "My place or yours?"

Arnold thought for a moment and said, "There's no one here but me. We'll have the whole afternoon. You'll have to clear out before 3:30 when Maurine gets home, though."

"That's okay, darlin," she drawled.

"How did you like that fancy charm bracelet I sent around on Friday, sweetie?"

"I just adored it, lover boy."

"How soon can you get here?"

"I can slip on some clothes and be there in fifteen minutes."

"Why bother?" he joked. "You'll only have to take them off again when you get here."

"You're silly," Fanny giggled. "I can't go through the streets in my altogether, can I? What would the neighbors think?"

Arnold hung up and removed the wall plug from its socket again. He didn't want to be disturbed.

True to her word, Fanny Lee Talbot arrived at the front door to the Katz apartment almost to the minute. Arnold swept her inside before she even had a chance to ring the doorbell. While the two embraced, she slid open her pink raincoat to reveal nothing else hidden beneath. He picked her up and carried her to the still-mussed bed, where they reveled in every position they knew and had perfected. Then they sat side by side, touching, with their backs to the headboard while he picked tunes from his guitar and they both sang along.

This was the charming pose observed by Thelma Fitzwaller

Katz when she appeared in the bedroom doorway. The pose persisted because Arnold's eyes were rolled up in his head while he played and Fanny was fully absorbed in his music. She was the first to discover their audience. Howling and screeching, she made a stab at pulling up the bedcovers to cloak her nudity. Arnold's eyes popped opened and saw his wife of eighteen years glaring back at him.

"What the hell are you doing here," he stammered. His right hand shoved Fanny's fanny out of bed. "Git, girl. Git!" he growled under his breath.

Fanny grabbed her shiny pink raincoat and quickly wrapped it about her waning self-respect while picking her way to the bedroom door. Thelma stood to one side to let the attractive, lusciously developed teen pass. Her complaint was with *him*.

"I happen to live here too, you slime bag! This is my home. I've known for years that you've been cheating on me, but now you've the audacity to bring your whores into our house where we live and your daughter lives. Oh, put that damn guitar down and get the hell out of my bed and put some clothes on. You've slept in that bed for the last time. You've been unhappy with me since I coerced you into this marriage all those years ago."

"But . . ."

"Sure I trapped you. Now that I've said it, does that make you happy? But believe me, I didn't get pregnant just to trap you. I got pregnant because I thought you were someone worth keeping, worth spending my life with, worth making a family with. How wrong can one woman be? You turned out to be an uncaring father, a career failure, and a lousy, unloving husband. How stupid I was to stick by you. I suppose it was for Maurine's sake, but I can't see how she benefited at all. We are done. Finished. . . .Finished! Do you hear me?"

"Yes."

"So go to your whore. See if she'll wash your clothes, cook your meals, and clean up after your lazy ass. She already knows how to spread her legs for you."

Arnold pulled up his trousers and buttoned his shirt. When he sat down on the bed to put on his socks and shoes, he got another satanic eye. It was now *her* bed all right, but how else could he manage getting dressed? He could find no words now. For the first time in eighteen years, when he was about to lose the most valued thing in his life, he fully realized the impact of his loss.

Theirs was the marriage he wanted. Thelma was the only wife he needed. None of the other women could hold a feather to his beautiful Thelma with her zaftig figure, melon breasts, and bursting pink nipples. He wanted to turn the clock back, not to yesterday, but eighteen years so they could start again. But he didn't know the words, nor would she have allowed them. He slid off the edge of the bed into a kneeling position, about to beg her forgiveness, but she had already backed out of the room and out of sight to avoid his whimpering, apologetic plea.

"Get out!" she cried from the hall. "Now!" *How can he expect me to absolve him from eighteen years of faithlessness in one fell swoop? How many fancy women were there? What had he shared with them? What did they mean to him? What did I mean to him? We raised a daughter together. Didn't that mean something?*

On an ordinary day, Thelma couldn't have possibly known of this particular tryst, this invasion of their home. But today Leo had called her at her job when the Katz apartment phone and Arnie's cell phone failed to respond. Leo claimed to be concerned that Arnold hadn't shown up for work.

Thelma held her tears back until she heard the door slam shut. There was something final about it, like the pounding of a judge's gavel.

* * * *

She waited at the kitchen table until she heard Maurine at the back door coming home from school. Her mood had shifted from anger to tears and back again. *My mind is made up. I'll go it alone from here on in. I'll get a second job and, together with our meager savings, the two of us will make it until Maurine is out of school. Maybe there's a chance of child support if the bastard can manage to keep a job. I know we can make it. We have to.*

Maurine's book bag made a thump outside the door as she fumbled for her keys. Before she could put a key in the lock, her mother swung the door open.

"Mom, you look like hell. What's wrong? What's happened?"

"Your father is a damn womanizer," said Thelma.

Maurine moved into her mother's embrace. At seventeen, she had turned into a beautiful, self-assured young woman. Her light brown hair with glints of blonde cascaded about her shoulders. At this moment she seemed to be the grownup, with a quality of wisdom in her blue eyes.

"Mom! We both know that's been true for many years. He's been flaunting his girlfriends all over town. All the kids, my friends, and their parents know this. I hate it. You hate it. It's on-going. So what's so new about today?"

"Today was absolutely the last straw. The bastard brought one of his whores into my bed this afternoon—I walked in on them. The two of them sitting nude against the headboard and him strumming his damn guitar."

"What are you going to do, Mom? You know I'll stand by you."

"I've already done it, dear. I've thrown your son-of-a-bitch, no-good father out of the house."

Thelma wasted no time. By six o'clock that night a locksmith had changed both front and back door locks to the Katz apartment.

Arnold didn't learn of his new exiled status until 11:30 that night when he stumbled in from a frolicking time drinking, playing, and singing at an Eastport bar. He had taken refuge there to drown in his short-lived regret for the deed. Soon he forgot Thelma's last words. He didn't remember them until both apartment locks rejected his keys. Pounding on the front door and loudly pleading produced a rebuke from several of the neighbors, but nothing from inside the Katz apartment, where mother and daughter, lying abed locked in anxious hugs, cried silently in the dark. Too drunk to go elsewhere, Arnold curled up under the hall staircase and slept off the nightmare.

* * * *

Anna warmed up supper for her husband. Stuart was staying over in Baltimore on business. Julie had eaten early and left for rehearsals over at the high school. Herschel came home, his normally jovial face covered in an ear-to-ear scowl.

"What's wrong, dear," Anna asked, setting the plate in front of him at the kitchen table.

He picked up a forkful of brisket and set it down again. "I don't wanna talk about it," he answered with his imperfect teeth showing.

"Okay, out with it, buster," she demanded.

"Your lazy, good-for-nothing brother has gone too far this time. He doesn't show up at all for work on either Monday or Tuesday. We can't run a business that way. This morning he shows up looking like the scum of the earth, needing a shave and a change of clothes. Whew! He stunk! From alcohol as well. He looked like someone who hadn't been to bed for days. We let him sleep it off behind some of the crates. He's no good to us like that. And don't tell me you'll talk to Thelma like you always say you will—and don't."

"You haven't heard?" Anna asked.

"Heard what?" asked Herschel.

"She threw my little brother out and changed the locks to the apartment. Thelma isn't even speaking to *me* now, like this is somehow *my* fault."

"My dear wife, your little brother is forty-nine years old. I don't care how precious he is," shouted Herschel, his face red as raw hamburger. "Arnie's fired, gone, done with, poof, no more."

"Stop! Hersch, you're working yourself up over nothing. Remember your heart."

He slumped forward. "My heart," he whispered. "Ah.... There *is* a pain, a hard pressure *here* and it's getting worse." A finger on his right hand traced a line from near his neck down and across his chest. "I can't breathe." He gasped a large swallow of air.

Anna rushed to a kitchen cabinet, took down a small screw-top brown bottle, and shook out one tiny nitro pill. "Here. Stick this under your tongue and let's go to your recliner." He complied as she led him slowly into the den and his favorite chair.

Twenty minutes passed. He sat there quiet and unmoving.

Her own chest tightened as she watched him. "Do you want to go to the hospital, Hersch? I'll call for an ambulance."

"No, Anna, it's easing off now. I'll be fine."

"Do you want to finish your supper?"

"No, I'm not hungry. Too upset. Just leave me here. I want to rest."

"No. I'm putting you to bed right now, and we're calling the doctor first thing in the morning."

* * * *

Anna had been sleeping fitfully for about an hour and a half when a tapping noise disturbed her. She ignored it at first and then thought better—it might be Hersch. When Anna checked in on him, Herschel was sleeping soundly and breathing normally. Then she heard the tapping again. It sounded like someone at the back door. As she threw on a robe over her pajamas she shuffled to answer it. At first, opening only to the length of the safety chain, she wanted to slam the door shut again. She didn't recognize the unshaven, revolting, and smelly low-life standing on her back porch. The one word he whispered, "Anna," told her it was her baby brother.

"Anna, Anna, please!" begged Arnold. "I don't know where else to go. I don't know what else to do."

From the pathetic sound of the next "Anna, please!" she was reminded what had happened to make him fall to this level of disgrace. She was sympathetic, but he smelled so bad. He was disgusting.

"I can't let you in tonight," she said. "Hersch is having a

heart scare, and I'm taking him to the doctor in the morning. I can't let you stay here. He'd have another fit if he saw you. He's so fragile, Arnie, you just don't know. I can't risk it."

"But it's cold out here, sis," blubbered a shivering Arnold. "Help me!"

"I'll tell you what. Let me get my purse." She left for a few minutes and returned with a fistful of bills, an old gray overcoat of Herschel's, and a brown paper bag. "Here's $143. Get yourself a motel room and clean up. Shave, too. Meanwhile, the coat should keep you warm enough." She watched him put on the serviceable coat. There he stood, looking at her so pitifully, she wanted to reach out to him. But didn't.

Arnold didn't look in the paper bag to see that it contained a thermos of coffee and hefty wedge of apple cake. He slowly turned to face the night and descended the rear stairs into its blackness.

Anna closed the door.

# Chapter 23

## Help
### Thursday, November 17th

Isn't there some other way, Mom?" asked Abel.

"No, dear," replied Esther. "I think we both know what's best for you. We want the most complete cure: one your father and I won't have to worry that you've strayed from at any time in the future." She pulled onto the slower lane of Route 10 north and her foot eased up slightly while they talked. She still had to concentrate on her driving.

"Do you think I can still get accepted to Johns Hopkins next year?" he asked.

"Abel, what are you talking about? Apply there if you want, but your grades are lousy. You cut two days of classes just this week. Think about a community college for now. But first, you need to put all this nasty drug business behind you. So . . . the sooner you get into treatment, the sooner you can get yourself squared away."

"What if all the schools I'm applying to find out I've been on drugs?"

"That's not going to happen, because this is a private treatment facility run by real doctors, who are not allowed to reveal your medical history without your permission."

"How do I respond to college applications that ask if I've

ever used drugs?"

"You respond honestly, dear, and hope you can plead your case that you've been successfully treated. Otherwise, we'll just have to find you another, more sympathetic college."

"Mom, will I have a criminal record if Beast dies in the hospital?"

"I don't know the answer to that. We'll hire the most knowledgeable lawyer and hope for the best."

"Will I have to be institutionalized?"

"We won't know that until after today's interview at the rehab center, sweetheart. There's a chance you could be treated as an outpatient."

* * * *

Stuart Reubens rang the doorbell at his Uncle Meyer's home. Josh beckoned him in, and the two cousins walked through the house to settle into captain's chairs in the colonial kitchen.

In his charcoal-gray suit, white shirt, and striped tie, Stuart looked very much the young lawyer he was. "I heard there were some family issues going on here involving Abel. I came over to offer my legal services and any other help you guys need. Tell me, Josh, what's happening?"

"Abel has turned to drugs and then to stealing from the family business to support his habit."

"Hard drugs or pot?"

"Some of both," Josh answered. "He hooked up with his twenty-five-year-old supplier and two of his goon teenager friends to break into the family warehouse. They got in through a roof hatch and made off with a bunch of copper. The drug supplier apparently knew how to fence the stuff."

"As I see it, there are a number of questions that have to be considered," said Stuart. "First, what can we do to get Abel free of drugs? And how can we protect his future so that he isn't hampered with a drug record? Are you considering going to the police with the robbery, or has it already been reported to them? Have you confronted the remaining culprits yet?"

"Exactly my thoughts," said Meyer as he entered the room and pulled up a chair to the oak table. "I need to get my son back on track to good health and a decent education without any hint of a record. That's our first goal. Aunt Esther, Abel, and I talked it over and we're committing him to a private drug treatment facility. In fact, that's where Abel and Esther are at this moment, checking him into a facility in Baltimore."

"What about the police, Dad?" said Josh. "Do we call them in?"

"There's no crime unless we report one," said Meyer. "Isn't that right, Stu? You're the lawyer here."

"Essentially, Uncle Meyer, but your business has incurred losses and you have partners."

"True, but a few thousand in losses we can always write off some other way. Besides, it's family. I'm sure they'll see it my way. I don't give a rat's ass about those other little shysters. Let them continue in their gangster ways. They'll get their hides tossed in jail soon enough."

"What concerns me *are* those other shysters," said Stuart. "We can't ignore those little *gonifs* and let them off scot-free. If they're not stopped they might even rob our family business again. So how do we turn them in to the police without getting Abel involved?"

"We don't involve the police," emphasized Meyer. "The alarm people are coming this week. They plan to include the wayward hatch in the overall security system, along with some trip wires on the roof. I highly doubt the thieves will target our family business again."

"There's one thing we're all forgetting here," said Josh. "Morgan Beastrom, otherwise known as Beast, is in the hospital, put there by Abel, and Abel has admitted this fight in front of two policemen. You were there, Dad."

"How serious is it?" asked Stuart. "The injuries, I mean."

"The policemen seemed to think it's quite serious," said Josh.

"Deadly?"

"Yeah," said Meyer. "The drug dealer could die and never be missed by society. Good riddance, in fact. All Abel was trying to do was stop Beast from stealing his wallet and the cash he had inside it. There are black and blue marks all over Abel's neck and throat." Meyer bunched his fists, abruptly stood up, and walked to a rear window, where he stared out at the large elm in the backyard.

"I took pictures of these marks as soon as we thought of it," said Josh. "If Beast dies, we can show that Abel acted in self-defense."

"Good," said Stuart. "Choking is an overtly aggressive move that would confirm self-defense."

"But what if this Beast person survives the concussion?" asked Meyer, turning to face the others.

"Legally," said Stuart, "if Beast decided to sue Abel, he'd be opening a can of worms that would be more detrimental to himself. I doubt that he'd take that unfamiliar course anyway. Odds are, he'd come after Abel with his fists. But the longer he spends recovering, *if* he recovers,  the more time he has to cool off."

"Stuart?"

"Yes, Uncle Meyer?"

"Have you had a chance to read the Cohen woman's diary?"

"Uh . . . yes."

"Stu, is there any chance we could launch a harassment suit or at least threaten her with one to stop all this nonsense once and for all?"

"Has Ivy publicly accused anyone in the family thus far?"

Meyer shrugged his shoulders. "Not that I know of."

"I haven't heard of anything," said Josh with a shake of his head.

"If you're thinking of suing for damages," Stuart said, "so far there are none. And Ivy has no assets to speak of. We could sue to quash her inquiries. Some airline manifest data correlated with key diary dates; that data might be considered circumstantial evidence. However, a judge might consider that same evidence legitimate cause for further pursuit of her inquiries. To answer your question: No, you cannot sue her for damages. It would be better to let sleeping dogs lie. There's a good chance the impetus to continue these inquiries might peter out in time."

Meyer began pacing across the kitchen's ceramic tiles, his drawn face pale with anxiety. "What does the damn woman hope to gain from these so-called inquiries? Extradition? A murder conviction? Execution? A payoff? What would it take to buy Ivy Cohen off?"

"I don't think she can be bought off, Uncle Meyer," said Stuart. "She wants simple justice. If she can't have that, she'll probably focus all her efforts on making life miserable for her father. Once she correlates the manifests with the diary entries, she'll know the identity of her father with a good deal of certainty, a fact the rest of the family won't even know."

"That's not quite true," said Meyer. "Hersch, Leo, Arnie, and I all know which one of us is the father."

Josh nearly jumped out of his chair. "Even you, Dad?"

"Even me."

* * * *

Mark Schwartz closed the exam booklet and dropped it off in the basket on the proctor's desk at the front of the room. As he stepped out into the quad filled with fresh-mown grass, web-like crosswalks, and strolling students, he inhaled his newfound freedom. His last exam and no classes until December 5th. Even after that, it was only two weeks until the holiday break. These weeks belonged to his first major research paper, a giant step toward obtaining his master's in physics at Johns Hopkins.

This paper would be his first opportunity to add something new and original to the paper chases of academia. Of course, he'd be under the ever-watchful eye of his professor-adviser. Mark knew where he was headed with this project and had already developed the required proofs to maintain his unique proposition. Ahead of schedule, with a few days to burn, he wanted to contact that cute little bookstore clerk down in Annapolis. He could spend some much-needed time with his dad at the same time and be back at school on Monday.

"Olde Victorian Bookstore, how can I help you? . . . .Mark? Oh, Mark Schwartz. How are you? I thought you were away at school."

"I'm coming home for the weekend and I'm hopeful that you've saved an evening for me. How about tonight, Ivy?"

"Tonight is the writers' critique group that I belong to. I'm sure the others wouldn't mind if you tagged along. Some of your relatives might even be there. Esther, Arnold, and Katie, for example. Tomorrow night is *Shabbat*, and I promised Rivka Sherman I'd help with the *Oneg*. Saturday and Sunday after work are free after I feed and help my invalid landlady to bed. I'm available around 7:30."

"Let's try for Saturday night, although I might just drop in toward the end of *Shabbat* services."

"Sure," Ivy said. "See you then." She hung up and stood still for an extra thoughtful moment.

"Who was that?" asked Dan. "If you don't mind me sticking my nose into your private business."

"Mark Schwartz, Leo's son. He wants a date for Saturday night, and I accepted. If I'm going to carry this thing off, I'll need to know more about everyone who emigrated to Annapolis back then."

"You realize, of course, you're no longer invisible," said Dan. "Everyone knows what you're up to. You've declared as much to the world, at least their world. That's exactly what I'm worried about, young lady. We can't afford to train another bookstore clerk."

"And you two are precious to me as well. You needn't worry because I can take care of myself. I know what I'm doing."

"Yeah, sure," Dan said. "Like the night you were mugged and robbed."

"That took me by surprise. I won't be surprised again. I'm

going out with my eyes wide open this time."

"Hi, Ivy," said Rivka. "Are you reading at tonight's meeting?"

"No. I plan to be there, but I think I created enough commotion the last two times to hold me for a good while. I do plan to complete writing my mother's story, though. I think she deserves that consideration."

Rivka nodded. "That's a wonderful sentiment. Somehow, I think she'll appreciate it."

"Maybe you shouldn't dwell so much on such an intense subject," offered Dan. "It's possible that we might never identify your father. I don't want you turning into a depressed zombie over it. You need to live your own life, dear."

Rivka couldn't resist butting in. "Dan, honey, leave her alone. Good writing comes from intense feelings."

"What about *your* work, Rivka?" asked Ivy, anxious to change the subject. "We haven't heard from you since I started attending the meetings."

"Frankly, the store's kept me so busy I haven't had a chance to write much. I've started a bank robbery short story, but I only have a page so far. Maybe next time. I think Dan and Frieda will kick things off tonight."

"I have a concern," said Dan. "I consider Esther, Arnold, and Katie all valued members of the critique group as well as part of the Reubens family at large. As long as your father remains incognito and stands not accused, I believe they'll attend meetings just to keep in the loop. But I don't know what will happen afterward."

"Dan?" Rivka asked, her soprano voice edgy, "By *afterward* I assume you mean if he's exposed. Then . . . heaven help us all."

# Chapter 24

## **Critique Group Meeting III**
Thursday Evening, Same Day

Frieda rearranged the cowl neck of her purple sweater, squared her shoulders as if she were about to step on stage, and began reading the next chapter of her novel.

. . . .Clara lay still under the rough horse blankets, unsure whether she'd make more noise continuously breathing lightly or holding her breath to gasp periodically. The rusted hinges in the next stall squeaked louder than usual because the rest of the barn was so quiet. Ginger became skittish and backed to the rear of the stall, snorting, warning the intruder to let her be. The heavy shoes sloshed closer—between the wall and Ginger. Clara could see them in the space beneath the planks separating the stalls. She knew they belonged to a stranger. Anyone familiar with horses would be wearing some kind of farm boots. Usually a riding or mucking boot. These were hiking boots with plenty of laces to get messy.

Clara crept forward so she could see more. She used the back lighting coming through the open barn and stall doors combined. She heard sounds of leather straps flapping and metal clasps clinking. Someone was putting a walking leash on Ginger. The barn went silent again, except for three or four snorts: Ginger expressing her distaste for strangers in her stall. As the stranger tried to lead her forward, Ginger reared up on her hind legs, whinnied her loudest, and lunged forward, trying to trap and crush the intruder between the stall sideboards and herself.

"Ooof, aw, damn you, animal," Clara heard. Then a sharp slap.

Well, that's all the motive Clara needed to get out from under the blanket and onto her feet. She grabbed the pitchfork from the stall alleyway. Filling it with a chunk of straw and slippery muck, she stole toward the next stall. In the dim dawn light she saw the stranger, his back to her, still trying to pull the reluctant Ginger away from her back corner.

"Hey, you," she cried. And when the stranger turned, he got a face full of dripping muck from hair to chest, including both ears and eyes. Clara watched him pull the mess from his face as it went from surprise to anger. He took one step closer to her, and she held up the pitchfork in a threatening way. He tried to feint in one direction and charge in the other, but Clara was ready for him, managing to tear the chambray shirt away from his right arm, taking a measure of bloody flesh with it. He dropped the walking leash and his muck-filled left hand foolishly went to cover the open wound.

"What do you want with my Ginger?" she yelled at him. "Answer me!"

He stared at Clara, for she stood in his way to freedom. "A man paid me," he mumbled.

"What man?" she demanded, momentarily relaxing her stance with the pitchfork. The stranger began to remind her of someone she knew some time ago, but she couldn't quite recall who.

The stranger not only avoided an answer, but took advantage of the unguarded moment, ducked under the up-ended pitchfork, and made tracks for the barn door. The shaking Clara had no desire to pursue the intruder, so she laid the mucky weapon against the wall and ran to Ginger. She hugged and stroked her horse affectionately, looking for any harm she might have endured. There was none . . . .

#

"That's all I wrote this week," said Frieda.

"Any comments?" asked Rivka.

"I liked it a whole lot," said Katie. "Plenty of action and suspense."

"Me, too," Esther said. "I can't wait to hear more."

"Nice writing," said Ivy. "I like the idea of Clara overcoming her fear when she thinks Ginger is being harmed. But would she have actually stabbed the guy?"

"Probably," said Frieda. "Thanks, guys and gals, for the critique."

"How about you, Heather?" asked Rivka. "Got anything to contribute this week?"

"No," replied Heather, beaming with contentment. "I had a houseguest, as you well know."

"Anybody seen Arnold?" Rivka asked. "He said something about writing a new song, and needed someone to help with the lyrics. Something about a stolen bracelet, so I wonder where he is."

"I don't believe Arnold has any intention of showing up tonight," said Katie. "Thelma told me she threw the womanizing creep out on his ear—this time for good."

"Wow!" Rivka gasped. "That's a bummer. Anyone else just bursting with talent?"

"I'm still reorganizing the short story I started back in September," said Esther.

"I've got a flash short-story ready, but I'd like to go last," Katie said.

"Well, then, let's hear from Dan's Kasper Brasse and *his* adventures."

Dan opened his folder and removed several typewritten sheets. Reading aloud, he plunged into the dialogue.

. . . ."You've got quite a dilemma there, Ms. Worth."

"It's Miss, Mr. Brasse—Miss Patricia Worth, but I'm a Patsy."

"Well, yes, I'm sure you are," he said. "Try calling me Kasper."

"Can you help me, Kasper?"

"Sure, little lady, I think I know just what your friend Georgio needs—a little professional convincing." Kasper pulled open the top right desk drawer and extracted a 9mm Glock, a box of ammunition, and a pair of brass knuckles. The gun found its way into the small of his back, held in place by his belt. The ammo he fit into the side pocket of his suit jacket. The knuckles slipped easily over the fingers of his right hand. Slamming the brass into the palm of his left hand, he demonstrated a little too hard for his own sake, but squelched the appearance of pain for his client's sake.

"You won't hurt him too badly, will you, Kasper?"

"I'm an expert at knowing just how much," he boasted. "My great-grandfather, Roscoe Brasse, invented these things. Why do you think they call them brass knuckles?"

"But there's no E on the end of brass," she challenged.

"He added that to his name afterward for effect."

"Is he still downstairs watching the building?"

"Who? My great-grandfather?"

"No, Georgio."

Brasse edged up to the window from behind the curtain. "I don't see him, but we had better have a look-see anyway."

The two left the office and headed down the stairs. "Stay close," he said. And when he felt her cool breath on his neck it sent chills up his spine. "Not that close, babe!"

Out on the street under the big lamp there was little cover for them. But sure enough, Georgio was hiding in the shadows of the next doorway. "Step away from the broad and you won't get hurt, shamus."

Brasse turned toward the voice and saw the business end of a Saturday Night Special pointed right at him—so close he could see the next round in the cylinder.

#

"Hey, you're not gonna leave us there, Daniel Sherman," said Frieda.

"There'll be more for the next meeting," said Dan. "That's all the time I had this week."

"Any comments? No? Well, the coffee is ready in the kitchen," said Rivka. "Cream, sugar, and substitutes are with it. Hot water is in the kettle and the tea bags are in the jar. Plus oatmeal-raisin cookies. We'll hear from Katie just as soon as everyone settles back down again."

Fifteen minutes later, after the last person sat down at the table once more, Katie began reading:

. . . . A lone young man rode a bicycle along a dusty road. He was called Jim. All of his possessions were in the saddle bags hung over the rear wheel and in the backpack he bore on his shoulders. He rode for weeks, searching for just the right place to spend the rest of his life. He  was far from rich, but as a man with a trade, he could always afford to pay for food, drink, and lodging in moderate sums.

In the third week he came across a gray-haired man named Bill beside the road fixing his very expensive new mountain bicycle. Jim offered to help and his offer was accepted. Jim brought out a wrench and other bike tools from his saddle bags. It wasn't long before the bike was fixed and Bill flashed a wallet, fat with large-denomination bills. He pulled out a single large bill from the lot and offered it to Jim as compensation for his help. But, on impulse, Jim got greedy. With his wrench, he hit Bill over the head, stole his wallet, and left him for dead at the side of the road.

In the fifth week of riding, Jim found the little village of Hamlyn, a perfect place to spend the rest of his life. He blended easily into the local life and soon met a woman, married, and had children. There were friends galore, and he was well respected in Hamlyn. Everything would have been perfect for Jim, except he had to carry this hundred pounds' weight of guilt on his back everywhere he went. He tried to get over it by giving to charities, helping the needy, and befriending strangers. He and another man built a schoolhouse with their bare hands. As time went on, some of the guilt wore off until he felt and looked like everyone else in Hamlyn.

Meanwhile, Bill was found barely alive on the roadside and taken to a hospital to recover. It took nearly two years before he was able ride his prized bicycle again. When he finally took to the road again, it took more than five years before he narrowed his search to include the village of Hamlyn. Bill explained to the village mayor that he was looking for a man named Jim and told him what Jim had done to him. The mayor told Bill he would have to assemble their group of village elders, which, by chance, included Jim.

Not recognizing his assailant, Bill explained his quest to the group of elders and asked their assistance in bringing Jim to justice. All of the elders agreed, and before any action could take place, the real Jim stood up and said he was the Jim whom Bill sought. As Bill turned to confront him, a second elder stood and said, "No, I'm the Jim you're seeking." Then another stood and claimed the same thing. Soon every elder in the group stood and claimed to be the one and only Jim whom Bill sought. Bill became frustrated. He had Jim nearly in his grasp, but could not tell which Jim was guilty.

The mayor felt sorry for Bill, so he offered him generous compensation for his losses, five times the original amount. He told Bill that Jim was extremely remorseful for his crime. "He has more than atoned by living an exemplary life for the seven years he's lived in Hamlyn." Bill took the compensation and left Hamlyn. The long, hard search would appear to have been a waste, except that Bill was able to learn the quality of forgiveness.

#

Katie put down her pages and looked around.

"That's more of a homily—a sermon, almost—than a story," said Esther. "I felt like I was in *shul*."

"Don't you see what Katie's trying to do?" Ivy burst out. "She's trying to compare Bill's robber to my mother's murderer. That's not a fair comparison. Murder is definitely not robbery."

"I agree, Ivy," said Joel. "We all know the circumstances involved in your story, even though they're couched in fiction. I see this homily akin to a plea for anonymous status. I'm not quite sure, but I think it's an offer of bribery in return for mercy and forgiveness."

"Perhaps it is," said Rivka, "but I don't think we should turn this critique group into a court of law."

"I agree and move that we adjourn," Dan said, standing up, hoping to avoid an imminent clash. Nobody else moved.

"Wait!" said Esther. "Suppose this *is* a serious plea and offer. Consider the real truth of the matter. The person of interest, this young man, makes one awfully bad mistake in his life and spends the rest of his days regretting that mistake and proving that he's worthy of forgiveness. I agree with Ivy that murder and robbery are not equivalent. I, along with the rest of the family, believe he's telling the truth. So much so that the whole family is willing to offer Ivy considerable compensation."

Ivy jerked upright and tossed her head so sharply that her sleek black hair flopped forward, almost hiding her face. As she brushed it back behind her ears, her steely eyes shot daggers of fury.

"Esther, what are you talking about? You're saying this person of interest, Jim, made a mistake? You call what he did a mistake? He hit Bill over the head with a wrench, stole all his money, and left him for dead. How can you compare this simple-minded story with the real issue here? The murder of my mother was not a mistake. There were finger marks, strangling marks, all over her neck. In my mind there can be no compensation for murder."

Chapter 25

## A Father's Confession

Friday, November 18th

"Grab that, will you, hon?" said Dan, ringing up sales for the line of customers at the register.

Rivka dashed up the aisle to the cashier's counter and picked up the phone. "Yes, this is The Olde Victorian Bookstore. You'd like to speak with Ivy Cohen? I'll see if she's available."

"She's upstairs putting away those travel maps that just came in," announced Dan between transactions. "I'll buzz her and she'll come to the top of the stairs."

Rivka waited downstairs for Ivy to appear. "Telephone, dear. You can pick it up in the reading room. No, I don't know who it is."

"Hello, this is Ivy Cohen. How can I help you?"

"Ivy, this is your father. . . .No, wait! Don't hang up. Please give me a chance. I don't blame you. But I've got something important to say to you. No, no, no. . . .Please! Though I am directly responsible for your mother's death, I am not the murderer you think I am. What really happened was the result of a pushing-and-shoving match. I may have pushed a little too hard and she fell and hit her head. It was an unfortunate accident, and I did the cowardly thing and ran out on her. I had no idea the fall had taken

208

her life until I read the next-day account in the *London Times*."

Ivy's fair complexion turned chalky. Her small chest and narrow shoulders heaved with quickened breaths. Her skin tingled even inside her wool sweater. Her voice turned shrill. "What about the finger marks on my mother's throat and around her neck? The last I heard, death by strangulation is not caused accidentally. That's out-and-out murder. And who *are* you, you bastard?"

The man hesitated, his deep voice tired and gravelly. "You'll find out soon enough. Now what do mean, the marks on her neck? I don't know anything about that."

"You bloody rotter. I read the details in the Scotland Yard crime report. Of course, it was all in the cold-case files by the time I got to read any of it."

"The police report? There was nothing in the news saying she died of strangulation. In fact, I remember standing over her, admiring her beauty and particularly that pretty swan-like neck of milky-white flesh. There were absolutely no marks there when I left. Good grief, the police report must have said a good deal more.

"I am so sorry for the twenty-three years of anguish I have caused you. If you can't somehow forgive me, perhaps you can think the better of me for not having been Lainee's actual killer."

Ivy's cold silence spoke volumes.

The man's voice broke as he continued. "Please understand. Your mother and you represented the start of a second family, a fact I could neither support nor explain nor conceal. I tried a number of times to break off our relationship. But Lainee wouldn't have any of it. Each time, we would wind up together again."

Ivy replied, "That part is pretty well documented in her diary. But why are you confessing to me over the phone?"

"It's the coward in me. I'm not proud of it, believe me, but I don't think I could say these things directly to your face, let alone to Lainee's face. I find that your two faces—your eyes, your hair—are one and the same. I have done you a great injustice, my dear."

"You treated her miserably," Ivy retorted, her voice no longer shrill, but full of punishing logic. "When you came to her that last time you already knew you were moving everyone in the family and the entire business to America. You knew you'd never see her again. In fact, you were counting on it. I see now—that was the reason for those presents you brought from Annapolis. Before you ever walked in the door to flat 3C at 103 Devon Court, you planned to abuse this wonderful relationship you had with her, taking advantage of her innocence one more time, and then deserting her, breaking her heart. Only . . . the arrival of your daughter spoiled that plan."

"Yes," he said, "your arrival did make quite a difference. That's what we fought about. No, I didn't slug her. I don't know exactly how it happened. We were both pushing and shoving."

"And what about me? Didn't you ever wonder what had become of your blood daughter? What are you made of, sir? Didn't you think that I needed love and sustenance?"

"Sure, I thought about the daughter I'd never seen and only heard of once. You were an abstraction with neither face nor voice. I never even knew your name."

"How convenient!" Ivy spat out. "Out of sight, out of mind."

"But I already had a wife and children. What was I to do?"

"At the very least, inquire, damn it! Find out what happened to me. Arrange to pay child support, the way any ethical father would."

"But you seem none the worse for the experience."

"You call it *the experience?* How dare you be so insensitive, so callous? A child never gets over the murder of her mother, especially the mother she was deprived of ever knowing."

He took a moment, trying to rescue a shred of something positive from this ugly, negative conversation. "So I'm inquiring now."

"I was brought up by a loving set of parents, along with two siblings. Parents who made many sacrifices to educate and bring the three of us to maturity. Each sacrifice was made with devotion.

And that's all you're entitled to know."

"My dear, your long meticulous search to find me is at an end. You have found the culprit. The grand ogre of your life is exposed. Now, what do you propose to do with me?"

"Are you totally insane? I still don't know who you are. Our evidence is circumstantial right now. Am I to understand you are now willing to come forward and confess your atrocities to the authorities?"

"I would be willing to admit to desertion and abandonment."

"Ideally, killers are dealt with by the authorities and brought to justice."

"But I'm not a killer. I told you that before."

"I have only *your* word for that. Perhaps if we meet face to face, you can do a better job of convincing me."

"Perhaps, but I will need to talk to my wife first. It's a big decision. Thank you for listening to me."

Ivy took one last stab: "Who *are* you?"

He hung up.

Ivy appeared at the base of the staircase with a stunned, frantic look on her face. The last of the customers had left. "Good lord, girl, what's wrong," asked Rivka. "You look like something Lord Byron dragged in."

"Yeah! Who was that on the phone?" asked Dan. "And what did they want?"

"That was my father—at least that's what he told me. I didn't recognize his voice. It sounded like he was talking out of doors on a cell phone through the wrong end of a megaphone. Distorted tonal reception. He confessed to everything but murder." As Ivy spoke, she paced back and forth on the worn Oriental carpet in the reading room. "He tried to explain how it all happened, but I'm not sure I believe him. I still don't know which one he is. I don't even know my own father's name."

* * * *

That evening at temple neither Anna nor Julie, with their usual cache of fresh-baked goods, showed up in the kitchen to prepare for the *Oneg*. There was no explanation, just that they couldn't be there. It was a good thing Ivy had volunteered to help Rivka and Esther. Perhaps that was reason enough. As a matter of practice, left-over baked goods from at least three previous Fridays were found in the freezer. Rivka, who had brought green grapes and dried apricots, hoped the pastries would reach a chewable room temperature by the time services were finished. As soon as the platters were taken from the cabinet shelves and laid out on the counter, Stuart stuck his head in the door.

"Hi, ladies. Need any help?"

He received such an overwhelming No that he headed into the sanctuary and took a seat in the row just behind Dan. When the ladies had finished their chores in the kitchen, Esther joined Meyer, Josh, and Maurine. Dan sat between Rivka and Ivy. By the time Mark Schwartz came down the aisle and slid into the empty seat next to Ivy, Stuart was fuming. He had assumed Ivy would join him. Now all he could do was squirm and silently pout.

Afterward in the social hall, when most of the worshipers had gone home, Stuart, Mark, Joshua, and Maurine crowded around Ivy, vying for her attention. She looked quite fetching in her pink and black wool jacket and long black skirt. But her inner turmoil had bubbled to the surface and she wasted no time relaying her feelings. "I don't understand what's going on among the bunch of you. Regardless of how our eventual relationships turn out, I do wish to be on friendly terms with all of you. Until I find out which of your fathers I share with you, I need to be cautious. Oh, I dearly love being with each and every one of you. But . . . " Her eyes, more stormy gray than blue at that moment, moved from face to face. "As you can tell, I harbor extremely strong emotions about my father, and I'm not sure how that will affect my feelings toward his other children—my half-siblings, I mean."

"Let's make a pledge, then," suggested Maurine. Of all the females in the family she felt the closest to Ivy. "Let's pledge that we will all remain friends, regardless of what Ivy discovers about her father."

"Why not?" Mark asked. "I don't think any of us are guilty of our fathers' crimes."

Stuart joined in. "I'm with you, Maurine."

"I think I'd like that very much," said Ivy. "I know I would miss you guys."

"I'd like that, too," said Josh.

"What about Abel and Julie?" asked Maurine. "How come they're not here? I want them to be part of this as well. Don't you?"

"I think I can vouch for my sister," said Stuart, "although she may take some convincing. She's a daddy's girl. I hate to think what her reaction would be if it turned out my father is the one. However, I don't think he's capable of such a terrible thing."

Joshua shrugged. "Ivy, I don't know about Abel. He confessed to me that someone in the family paid him to mug you in the bushes and steal your mother's diary. He wouldn't say who. Apparently, *his* loyalties lie elsewhere. Maybe he'll come around, though."

"Oh, my God," gasped Maurine, with all the drama of a budding actress. She felt rocked by her cousin's revelation. Then she caught herself and resumed her leading role. "Then all for one and one for all, except that I don't have a sword."

The Shermans cautiously approached the group. "What's the excitement about?" Rivka asked.

"We've pledged to remain friends no matter how things turn out with Ivy's father," replied Maurine.

"Good for you!" Dan said. "It's a great and thoughtful pledge, though you might find it pretty hard to keep when reality drops in. I wish you luck."

* * * *

Much later that night Arnold tried the restroom door at the City Dock. He'd just tossed his last empty booze bottle in the outside trash barrel. It made a clanging noise over the soft nighttime stir of moored boats in Ego Alley. Entering the facilities, he found both cubicles in use. During the wait, he noticed another man finishing his shave and tossing a single-use razor in the trash. When that man left, Arnold foraged in the trash and retrieved it. Using soap from the dispenser, he managed to work up a slight lather, which he attempted to remove with the razor. His hands shook, so the stubble removal came with several painful nicks and scrapes. He washed the soap and trickles of blood off his face and ran fingers through his hair, untangling a few snarls. By then both cubicles were available. Afterward, he left the restroom and walked to a single-family home in Eastport, where he rang the doorbell. Fanny Lee Talbot came to the door in a bathrobe and scowled when she opened it.

"Arnie, don't you know what time it is?" she whispered.

"No," he said. "Who cares?"

"Sushhh," Fanny murmured. "Not so loud. It's after midnight. Fifteen minutes after, for that matter. And I ain't never been so insulted as when your wife called me those names. Whore, tramp, fancy woman. Nobody ever called me those things before."

"I'm sorry, Fanny honey. I don't know how she found out about us. You know I don't think of you like that."

"Sushhh," she repeated. "You'll wake my parents. They're both asleep."

He stepped closer, putting one foot up on the doorstep, and reached for her. That was his fatal mistake: moving into the light from the hall. She saw his rumpled appearance, the bloody nicks on his face, the deep, dark rings under his eyes. That step closer also gave her a whiff of stale alcohol and barf breath. Fanny Lee was revolted.

"Go away, Arnold," she said. "Go home to your wife and leave me alone."

"I can't," he said. "She threw me out and changed the locks. I got no place else to go."

"Well, you can't stay here. My father would kill me if he knew about us." She slowly pushed him back down the single step, shut the door in his face, and turned out the hall light.

"Who was at the door?" came a harsh bellow from the second floor.

"Nobody, daddy," she said starting up the stairs. "Nobody. Just a bum lookin' for a handout."

"A lotta nerve," grumbled her father.

* * * *

Leo and Alice were out walking in the crisp November air. They had been drinking and dancing at Fran O'Brien's bar and restaurant on Main Street. But the two had paced their imbibing sensibly so as to be nowhere near inebriated. They wanted to fully experience the easy conversations, the closeness, and the *je ne sais quoi*, the indefinable qualities that bond two people together. Each realized they now had something more than a fling going for them.

From the beginning Alice had known that Leo was not the marrying kind. After two blown marriages and any number of near misses, he believed there was no ideal woman. He was always quick to defend and protect his independence. Still, Alice had decided that even if it was only for a short ride, she was willing to go to the end of the line, whenever that came.

Leo, in fact, *had* found the ideal woman for himself, and he'd allowed her to slip through his grasp. It was one of those near misses, an early affair during his first marriage. A perfect match, a love that totally consumed him. Not wanting to think about the misstep that nearly broke his heart, he refused to mention her name even to himself. Only the memory of the woman, his virtual standard, remained. He had spent the rest of his life looking in vain for another such woman. He had tried finding solace in the synagogue, but lost hope fifteen years earlier and hadn't entered one since.

At the age of fifty-four, Leo was tired of the barroom scene and the effort expended just to get a warm body into his bed. If he couldn't find Love with a capital L, maybe he'd settle for loving, caring companionship. But that most likely meant marriage, and he feared taking that big step again. He liked Alice a lot, and he knew she loved him. They'd been dating for almost a month now, and he discovered she was more than compatible.

The two had walked without purposeful direction until discovering that Leo's apartment was just a few doors away. Before this, all their dates had ended at Alice's.

"Want to come in?" he asked. *What am I doing? I've never brought anyone home before. It must have been my subconscious.*

"Sure," she answered. "I can make us a pot of coffee, if you don't mind my invading your kitchen." They climbed the steps to Apartment 2B.

"Kitchen, where's that?" Leo kidded. "I don't use it much. I mostly eat out and on Sundays I sponge a free meal from my ex-wife and her husband." He ushered her in.

"I could change all that," Alice said. But what she was thinking was *Say the word, you big lummox.*

She headed for the coffeepot and rummaged through the cabinets for the makings. Alice hummed as she filled the filter. Leo hovered behind her; his breath tickled her neck. He slipped his hands around and cupped them over her breasts. She closed her eyes. *Please!* she thought.

"You could move in, you know," murmured Leo.

"What did you just say?" She spun around to face him, wanting to hear the words again.

"I just asked you to move in, Alice Zimmer. It's definitely *not* a marriage proposal, but who knows what the future might bring. Let's try it and see how the arrangement works out. I can't promise you anything."

"It's enough for me, Leo Schwartz. You know I love you, sweetheart. Maybe you'll find love for *me* in time."

"I don't want to disappoint you; I've been a bachelor for such a long time." He kissed her gently, then deeply, preventing another answer.

# Chapter 26

## Shaking the Tree
Saturday, November 19th

orning, Rivka," chirped Ivy as she let herself into the store with her own brand-new key. "Shall I take the first shift at the register?"

"Good morning, Ivy. Sure. I've got some housekeeping to do upstairs before the Board of Health declares the whole place out of bounds. Dan's in the other room working out some kind of schedule. He wants to get together with you this morning. Something to do with the diary. Oh, here he comes now."

Dan bounded down the stairs in his favorite uniform: faded jeans, white Oxford shirt open at the neck, and loafers. Spinning the spare secretarial chair around, he sat down and wheeled himself in beside Ivy at the register counter. There were several sheets of data in his hand. "Thanks to Special Agent Kenneth Robards of the FBI, we now have the dates, airlines, and flight numbers of our four suspects. They always used Heathrow Airport for their trips. And we even know the exact time of day when each suspect departed from London and arrived in New York, Philadelphia, or Baltimore. Ken's also our friend, by the way. He claims that both corporate and governmental bureaucracies were tremendous hurdles for him. I've already told him how grateful you are for his efforts, especially

217

since he isn't involved in our active case; it's actually out of his jurisdiction. He also said that Scotland Yard was instrumental in covering the London flights. As for the now-defunct BOAC airline information, they obtained it from British customs. Thank God for businesses and agencies being so anal—the data they retain and the hungry computers that store them."

Ivy spoke up. "I've got the two compilations we put together the other day of all the diary dates when Snooks came and left the country. Let's see how they compare with the new manifest list that your FBI man provided."

"I believe we're only interested in the London end of the data," said Dan. "Particularly the arrivals."

| | | | | | | |
|---|---|---|---|---|---|---|
| Fri. | 09-04-1981 | BOAC | Flt 690 | Herschel M. Reubens | Dep. | 09:10a |
| Mon. | 10-05-1981 | BOAC | Flt. 334 | Leo I. Schwartz | Dep. | 06:48p |
| Wed. | 11-18-1981 | Amer. | Flt 1012 | Herschel M. Reubens | Arr. | 05:28p |
| Wed. | 11-18-1981 | Amer. | Flt 1012 | Leo I. Schwartz | Arr. | 05:28p |
| Thur. | 12-03-1981 | Amer. | Flt 1011 | Herschel M. Reubens | Dep. | 11:20p |
| Thur. | 12-03-1981 | Amer. | Flt 1011 | Meyer J. Reubens | Dep. | 11:20p |
| Thur. | 12-22-1981 | Amer. | Flt 2311 | Meyer J. Reubens | Arr. | 12:06p |
| Tue. | 01-12-1982 | Amer. | Flt 1012 | Leo I. Schwartz | Dep. | 05:32p |
| Thur. | 01-14-1982 | Amer. | Flt 2311 | Herschel M. Reubens | Arr. | 11:58p |
| Wed. | 01-20-1982 | Amer. | Flt 1012 | Herschel M. Reubens | Dep. | 05:32p |
| Tue. | 02-16-1982 | Amer. | Flt 1011 | Leo I. Schwartz | Arr. | 11:31p |
| Fri. | 02-26-1982 | Amer. | Flt 1012 | Leo I. Schwartz | Dep. | 05:32p |
| Wed. | 03-03-1982 | BrAir | Flt. 1603 | Herschel M. Reubens | Arr. | 09:22a |
| Thur. | 04-15-1982 | Amer. | Flt. 1011 | Meyer J. Reubens | Dep. | 11:22p |
| Thur. | 04-15-1982 | Amer. | Flt. 1011 | Esther A. Reubens | Dep. | 11:22p |
| Tues. | 04-20-1982 | BrAir | Flt. 1618 | Herschel M. Reubens | Dep. | 11:43p |
| Tues. | 04-20-1982 | BrAir | Flt. 1618 | Anna L. Reubens | Dep. | 11:43p |
| Tues. | 04-20-1982 | BrAir | Flt. 1618 | Stuart C. Reubens | Dep. | 11:43p |

Ivy quickly scanned the chart. "Here it is, Dan. I didn't think it would be this easy. We have one person with more departures and arrivals than the others. That same person arrived at

Heathrow at 9:22 a.m. on the day of the murder."

"Didn't the diary actually say Snooks had come straight from the airport?" asked Dan.

Ivy hurriedly flipped through the pages to the last of Lainee's entries. "Yes, that's what it says right here." She pointed to the spot on the page. We've got him at last!"

"Not quite, my dear Ivy, but we sure know who Snooks is."

"What do you mean not quite?"

"It's still all circumstantial," said Dan. "All we've established here is opportunity. There's no smoking gun, so to speak. There are no eyewitnesses. There's no hard evidence. Just a collection of data showing probable geographic accessibility and a number of personal factors, such as a Jewish businessman with his family, living and working in Annapolis during the right time frame. That narrows the field considerably, but it remains nevertheless incomplete. Add twenty-three years to muddy the works. I suppose some juries could convict anyway, but it would be a long shot, with enormous repercussions if they failed."

"Couldn't we just confront him?" she asked anxiously.

"I'm afraid we'd have to consult a criminal lawyer for that," replied Dan. "There are all kinds of nasty slander and libel laws to consider. Also, the actual crime took place in another country over which the U.S. has no jurisdiction. You don't want to mess with direct confrontation."

The entrance bell tinkled. Several customers entered, whom Ivy recognized as regulars. She greeted them all warmly. Dan slid his roll-around chair back and got up. "It's starting to get busy. We'll continue this discussion later."

* * * *

Meyer picked up the ringing phone. "Hello, Meyer Reubens here."

"Mr. Reubens, this is Officer Bruce Danford from the Annapolis Police. I interviewed you and your son Abel a week ago

Wednesday at your home."

"Yes, Officer, I remember. What can I do for you?" Beads of sweat popped out on Meyer's upper lip.

"This is a follow-up to that interview. We now have further information that affects the status and role of your son in that altercation with one Morgan Beastrom."

"Has Beastrom died?"

"Yes, sir. He passed at 4:46 this morning."

Meyer's hefty body stiffened. "Does that mean you'll be bringing a manslaughter charge against my son?"

"No, sir," replied Officer Danford. "It seems Beastrom had a brain tumor about ready to burst. The doctor who filled out the death certificate told me that the altercation had little to do with his death. The bump on his head was nowhere near the cancer tumor. Beastrom was walking around with a time bomb in his brain, ready to explode at any moment, and did not need any external trauma to set it off. He had no living relatives or close friends he could call next-of-kin, and there were no possessions except for the clothes on his back. Without any witnesses to the altercation and the extreme difficulty in proving a connection between said altercation and Morgan Beastrom's death, we have no alternative but to close the case."

"Thank you, Officer Danford, thank you for your call. You've taken a tremendous load off my mind."

# Chapter 27

## No Place To Go
### Late Saturday Night

Arnold Katz spent painful hours on Saturday night on several park benches at the City Dock with only his cap for a pillow. Several benches because different policemen forced him to move along. He hadn't used Anna's motel money as she had wished. He spent it mostly on alcohol and burgers. All day he'd wandered the streets of downtown Annapolis, shuffling among the tourists and locals, panhandling whenever he managed to isolate his prey. Here it was nightfall again with no place to go. The panhandling had yielded a mere eleven dollars. He bought two large jugs of cheap wine at the foot of Main Street, and as he walked away, he checked his finances once again: one lonely single in his wallet. He shoved his hand deep into his pants pocket: thirty-seven cents, a used toothpick, and two keys. One key he knew was useless. Thelma had changed the locks. The second key should have been turned in when Leo fired him, but had been forgotten.

*There shouldn't be anyone at Reubens Brothers this late on a Saturday night,* Arnold decided, looking down at his pathetic watch. The pawnshop wouldn't even give him fifty cents for it. It was 9:30 and fully dark. He dragged his way through the streets until the building came into sight. No one saw him enter and close the door behind him. Instinctively, as he reached his favorite aisle, he grabbed one of the truck blankets off a shelf and spread it on the floor. Arnold no longer had his guitar, so he hummed and drank his way through one and a half bottles of wine, and fell into a drunken, deep sleep. So deep that he peed on the blanket at some point during the long night.

With the early light seeping in the dusty windows on Sunday morning, Arnold stirred, stretched, and surveyed his situation. He didn't like it. He didn't like himself. In fact, he hated himself. He took a long swig from his last bottle. *The hair of the dog*, he thought. Then he tried to take yet another swig and found the final bottle empty.

His eyes scanned the room until they stopped on the service crane used to move heavy crates from the far end of the warehouse to the loading dock. He stood up on wobbly feet, stumbled toward the crane, and grabbed the large hook suspended from a trolley cart that wheeled across heavy I-beam tracks attached to the ceiling. Arnold draped both arms around the hook and dragged it several feet in each direction. He toyed with the short loop of thick rope used to close the hook and secure it into a complete ring—so nothing could slip out.

A stout, two-button control cable hung from the trolley so an operator could follow his load to its destination. Arnold whacked it with his hand and watched it swing through a pendulum-like arc, taking several seconds to settle. He playfully placed his neck in the hook and quickly pulled it out—it fit all too perfectly. He stood there half asleep, dumbfounded with strange thoughts flowing through his head, until the direct sunlight from the window struck his eyes and startled him. He backed away slowly. These were scary thoughts.

*Who would miss me and say Kaddish for me? Would Maurine? My daughter loves me, but I don't know. My sister, Anna? Maybe. What have I accomplished in this world? My music? I've finished nothing and entertained few. I've never amounted to anything and I've made Thelma's life a living nightmare because I've been such a stub-*

*born mule. And that little bitch Ivy thinks I killed her mother. There's no hope for me. No place for me. I'm bad and I'll never change.*

Arnold wiped his eyes clear of tears and began to shake. He returned to the blanket and tried each of the empties once more, gleaning no more than a drop from each. His head hurt. He lay down on the blanket. Shivering and shaking, he rolled himself up in it. He slept for twenty more minutes and woke with an idea, a resolve, and a blasting headache. Arnold returned to the overhead crane and grabbed hold of the suspended two-button control box. He pushed the DOWN button first, and the hook descended to the floor. He released the button. *So far so good*, he thought. Digging into the bottom of his pants pocket, he retrieved the used toothpick. He pushed the UP button and quickly jammed the toothpick in beside the button. It stayed in the ON position. After rising a few feet, the hook stopped, suspended waist-high. *Perfect!*

A determined Arnold lifted and placed the hook around his neck. Slipping the safety loop over the catch, he pulled to see if it would hold. It did. He found the hook heavy, so he brought it up with the controls until it just slightly eased off the weight on his neck. *Here goes!* He depressed the UP button. Jamming it ON, he swung the control box into a high arc away from his farthest reach.

Arnold Katz's last split-second thought was that he had been too hasty. "I want to live!" he screamed at no one within earshot. He tried supporting his weight by pulling down on the hook with both hands, but couldn't. Extending an arm, there was no way he could reach the swinging control box. He had planned it that way. His neck twisted sideway first and then broke, long before the hook reached the motor's automatic cut-off limits above. He died in seconds. All his pain gone.

* * * *

The first one to arrive for work on Monday morning, Leo Schwartz felt light-hearted and quite chipper in his navy blazer and creased slacks. He had a serious girlfriend. There'd been no more copper wire thefts in almost a month. He unlocked the door of the Reubens Brothers Electrical Merchandising Company and strode down several aisles toward his office.

Then he discovered the suspended body. A swarm of flies eagerly buzzed about.

A shock wave traveled down Leo's spine. A bolt of nausea hit his gut. Should he try to bring Arnold down? But the body was suspended so high up that Leo couldn't even begin to reach it. He called the police.

Next he called Meyer, who rushed down to the warehouse twenty minutes later and assumed the responsibility for notifying the rest of the family. The police arrived, followed by a Homicide detective and crime scene analyst. A ladder was brought for a police officer to climb to the top and reach the crane control box. With the body finally lowered, the crime scene analyst made a preliminary finding of suicide after discovering the toothpick jamming the ON button. The accompanying Homicide detective agreed when he found the blanket smelling of urine and two empty wine jugs.

"Do you normally allow employees to sleep it off on the premises?" asked the detective.

"No, sir," replied Leo. "He wasn't even supposed to be here at all. We fired him on Wednesday. Frankly, I don't know how he got in."

"Is one of these a key to your building?" asked the detective.

Leo studied the keys in the detective's palm. "Where did you find these?"

"In the victim's pocket, along with thirty-seven cents."

Leo took the larger key and held it up. "It's this one. The secretary was supposed to collect it the day we let him go," said Leo.

"Any idea why he would take his own life?"

Leo stood tongue-tied for some seconds. His rugged square jaw felt like it was about to lock up. The muscles in his broad chest clenched and tightened. He had never liked Arnold, despised the frustration that the deadbeat family member had caused them in the business. But nobody could have predicted this. When he'd called the police, he'd been initially numbed. Now he imagined himself in the aftershocks of an earthquake. He thrust his fists into his trouser pockets before answering. "Well, aside from us firing him, his wife locked him out and changed the locks. I hate to speak ill of the dead, but Arnold was a lazy womanizer who never amounted to anything. The only reason we hired him in the first place was that he was my partner's brother-in-law."

"I'm going to tape this area off until the analyst is finished," said the detective. "You can go back to work if you want. Stick around for a couple of hours, I might have some more questions for you and the others."

Leo nodded and walked down the corridor to the row of offices. "Did you call everyone?" he asked, stopping at Meyer's doorway.

"Yeaaah!" Meyer grunted. "That's one task I don't wanna ever do again. I feel like I aged ten years in the last ten minutes."

"A nasty job. What happened?" Leo asked.

"When I called Hersch's number, I got Anna and told her. She freaked out, screamed, then I didn't hear anything. Hersch picked up and I had to tell him. He said Anna passed out and he'd have to call me back. I called home next and Esther chewed me out. Actually blamed me for firing him, for not giving him more understanding. Can you believe that? Then I called Thelma and, boy, did I get it from her. Here's what she said, quote: 'Even in death, that son-of-a-bitch managed to drench me in shame and guilt.' Unquote. Then she started swearing up a storm. I hung up on her. And now she's faced with telling Maurine."

Leo nodded in sympathy. As he entered his own office, he shook off his jacket. The underarms of his fresh shirt were soaked with sweat.

Chapter 28

## Desperate Fallout
Monday, November 21st

The British Racing Green Mini Cooper blended perfectly into the hedgerow background on the 400 block of Franklyn Lane. The strong, late-afternoon sun glistened directly on the tinted windshield. That same flash of reflected brightness served to hide the identity of the driver behind the wheel. Too many street noises masked the sound of the car's idling engine, so an occasional tap on the accelerator was necessary to prove to the waiting bundle of nerves that the car was still running. The driver unbuckled the seat belt to wait more comfortably.

The parking space allowed a complete view of The Olde Victorian Bookstore about fifty yards away, and the one sitting there knew the store routine well. Each weekday at 4:45 p.m. and on Saturday at 11:50 a.m., Ivy Cohen would leave the store with the daily snail mail: postcards notifying patrons that the book they'd ordered had arrived or was out of print. She would cross the street, deposit the postcards in the blue U.S. Postal Service mailbox with its round top, and return to the store. Ten minutes later, the little white USPS truck with red and blue stripes would make the last mail pickup of the day.

The clock built into the Mini dash revealed 4:15. Plenty of

time. *The little bitch had twenty-three years to plan her revenge. Well, I'm going to put an end to that plan in the next thirty minutes. I had to protect him then and I have to protect him now. Now, before she blabs her bloody truth to the whole world.*

*All these years he never knew what I did for him. He couldn't appreciate that I had to kill the woman and finish the job he started. And when I finally told him how I cleaned up his mess, what did that bastard husband of mine say? "You let me believe I killed Lainee. You let me live with that guilt for twenty-three years. Why the hell are you telling me this now?"*

*I had to explain that I did it for love. How many women did he know who would kill for their man? And what did the poor boob answer me? "I don't want to know." But he'll get over it. He's old, tired, and impotent. So who's going to love him if not me? I'm used to him and the life we live. That's what love's all about. Isn't it?*

The clock read 4:40. *Any moment now.* Tapping the gas pedal lightly, she heard the engine rev. She saw The Dungeon door open partway and stop. The door opened wider, and Rivka stepped out. She held one palm up to test for rain, and finding none, disappeared inside once more. At 4:43, the door opened and Ivy, carrying the mail, trotted down the steps and walked briskly across Franklyn Lane.

Suddenly, the Mini leaped into motion. Ivy, standing on the curb, slid the mail into the opened slot and released the handle. Unaware of the speeding car closing in on her, she stepped off the curb into the street. On impulse, she turned back to the mailbox and pulled the handle down once more to be sure her postcards had been swallowed up inside. The Mini, aiming for where Ivy should have been, had to veer sharply to correct its course. Ivy, now keenly aware of the charging car's engine noise, dove to the sidewalk on the far side of the mailbox. The driver, intending to deliver a finishing blow, misjudged and plowed full force into the USPS box, shearing its anchor bolts from the concrete, and driving it into the telephone pole that stood on the grass next to it. The screeching, crunching, scraping ended in a metallic clang as the mailbox buckled and burst.

Ivy, lying on the concrete beyond the telephone pole, checked herself out. A few bruises and scrapes from the fall, but nothing worse.

"Ivy, Ivy, dear Ivy!" Rivka shrieked as she dashed across the street.

"I'm fine, I'm fit," Ivy reassured her as she sat up and took notice of the wreckage around her.

"Someone tried to kill you and you're fine and fit?" Rivka helped Ivy to her feet, and the two of them took a closer look at the damaged car.

"Nonsense!" said Ivy. "It had to be an accident. Even *they* wouldn't stoop so low."

"Are you kidding? It's what murderers do," declared Rivka. "Trust me."

The Mini's front bumper hugged the destroyed mailbox like an old bosom buddy, while the whole front end was crushed into a green accordion. The hood stood open, at attention, a mouth gasping for air. The driven-back engine had penetrated the firewall. The windshield was covered with an intricate web of cracks spattered with blood where the driver's head had impacted. Peering in the driver's window, the two women saw the body of a female lying immobile across the steering wheel, her bloody head pressed to the windshield.

"It sort of looks like Anna Reubens," said Ivy, "but it's hard to tell."

"It *is* Anna Reubens," Rivka said. "I recognize her hair and her wool suit. My God, I think she's dead."

Dan appeared in The Dungeon doorway and shouted, "I called 911 and told them to hurry. Who is it? Are they alive?"

"It's Anna," Rivka shouted back, "and I don't think so."

The ambulance arrived first, followed quickly by a City of Annapolis Police navy blue cruiser. The emergency medical technicians confirmed Anna's death and immediately devoted their attention to Ivy. One of the EMTs cleaned and dressed her scrapes, while two police officers secured the scene. Shaken but clear-head-ed, Rivka spoke up. "Excuse me, Officers, I saw the whole thing. It wasn't an accident." They listened intently and one called in her information.

Twenty minutes later, a crime scene technician and Detective Enid Moran arrived. The crime scene tech took pictures and measurements, and also searched Anna's purse and wallet to iden-tify her. He relayed her identity and address to the detective, then officially released Anna's body. The EMTs gently lifted her lifeless, twisted form up onto a gurney. They rolled it to the ambulance, closed the rear door, and drove off.

Detective Moran's hair was pulled back into a no-nonsense bun. In her black pants suit, she looked thirty-ish and strong. She began by interviewing Rivka. "Did you witness this accident?"

"Yes, Detective. I was standing in the bookstore door across the street. I saw the whole thing. But as I told the officers, it wasn't an accident. The car was headed directly for our young employee."

The detective eyed her sharply, but patiently. Rivka dug a business card out of one of her cargo pants pockets, where she always carried a small supply, and handed it over.

The detective studied it. "Thank you, Mrs. Sherman. Do you know the intended victim?"

"Oh yes, she clerks for us in the bookstore. My husband and I are the owners."

"Do you know the driver of this car?"

"Yes. We weren't close friends, but I'm well acquainted with Mrs. Reubens and her family." Rivka explained their temple con-nection. "The driver is—was—Anna Reubens." She then gave an address for the Reubens residence.

Moran flipped the pages of her small spiral notebook and saw that Rivka's information jibed with the deceased's driver's li-cense. "You didn't see each other socially?"

"Not often. We did attend their backyard barbecue recent-ly."

Ivy, covered with Band-Aids and other dressings, thanked

the EMTs and slowly stepped over to where Detective Moran was questioning Rivka. "I'm the one Anna was trying to kill. She had it in for me."

"Who are you?" asked Moran.

"My name is Ivy Cohen and I'm a clerk at The Olde Victorian Bookstore across the street," she said, pointing to it. "That woman was trying to kill me with her car, but I jumped out of the way and she slammed into the post box."

"Why would she want to harm you?" asked Moran.

Ivy paled and her voice trembled. "It's a long story, Detective. She was afraid I would expose someone in her family as the murderer of my mother."

"Oh? Murder is police business," cautioned Moran, "an extremely dangerous business, as you've just witnessed. Why haven't you taken this to the police before this?"

"Detective," Rivka interjected, "Ivy's mother was murdered twenty-three years ago in a suburb of London. Scotland Yard is well aware that we are delving into one of their cold cases. My husband and I are helping Ivy."

"So you two now know who committed this murder?" Moran continued to scribble notes.

"It's only circumstantial so far," Rivka said. "We hesitate to accuse anyone without more evidence. It just wouldn't be fair. We could be subject to slander. Sorry, Detective, not just yet."

"Might I ask—what do you intend doing with the compelling evidence once you've secured it?"

"I'm not quite sure," said Ivy.

"Nothing illegal or revengeful, I hope?" asked Moran, her expression stern.

"Of course not," interrupted Rivka. "We fully intend to turn all our evidence over to Chief Inspector Winston at Scotland Yard."

"Do you know who the next of kin would be, ma'am?"

"I guess it would be her husband, Herschel Reubens. There are two grown-up children in the house as well. Stuart and Julie."

Rivka watched Moran capture all of this and start to put away her notepad. "Detective, are you going to notify the Reubens family now?"

"Yes, ma'am. Thank you for your help." She handed both Rivka and Ivy her business cards. "Please keep me in the loop."

Detective Moran and the technician returned to their police van and drove off.

The tow truck arrived and hooked up the Mini wreckage at its undercarriage, slowly pulling it up onto the tilted truck bed, and finally locking it in place. Next, the tow operator transferred the cable to the mailbox, wrapping it several times around the box's girth. The operator then engaged the cable winch once more, pulling the smashed heavy blue box up the same ramp. The box and its contents, gathered up from where the mail was strewn on the street, would be delivered to the post office distribution center. The operator then brought the ramped bed to the horizontal position and secured it. One of the police officers on the scene signed some paperwork, and the tow truck moved down the street and out of sight.

Clutching each other, Rivka and Ivy slowly walked back to the bookstore. They had stayed on to watch the towing operation. Ivy hoped her postcards would get delivered.

Dan had witnessed the entire sequence from The Dungeon doorway. Holding the heavy oak door open for the two women, he followed them inside. His dark eyes and five-o'clock shadow gave him a particularly brooding look. In silence he reflected: *Anna sure went to extremes to protect her Herschel. I didn't think she was the type. Now we know who killed Ivy's mum. Or do we?*

Chapter 29

## Our Father, Our Dad
The Same Day

The phone rang. Busy with bookstore closing chores, Rivka hesitated to pick up. Dan was upstairs sneaking in a snack. Ivy came running down the second Romance aisle to tackle the phone. "Olde Victorian Bookstore, how may I help you?"

"It's Stuart, Ivy. Our father, our dad is having a heart attack. We're waiting for the ambulance to come."

"*Our* father, *our* dad?" Ivy repeated. "That's a new one on me."

"Please. I gave him a nitroglycerin pill for under his tongue. I don't know what else to do."

"Then Herschel is the man who called me on Friday and refused to tell me his name?"

"Yes," Stuart said.

"So why are you calling me now?" asked Ivy. "I don't give a damn whether the rotter lives or dies."

"He's asking for you, Ivy," said Stuart. "He desperately wants to speak with you. Face to face, if possible. Won't you speak with him?"

"He brutally murdered my mother. Can't you get that through your thick lawyer's head? I don't want anything more to do with him."

"But you *are* my family, and I'm asking for your help. Please! I can't stand here arguing with you. I just finished talking with a detective who told me my mother is dead. I know she tried to kill you with her car. I can't help that." Stuart's voice caught in his throat. "I apologize. What more can I say? This morning Josh informed me that my cousin Arnold committed suicide last night. And on top of that, I can't find Julie anywhere."

"Okay, okay," Ivy said in a more sympathetic voice. "I'll meet you at the county medical center ER in about thirty minutes." She fumbled the receiver into its cradle.

"What was that all about, Ivy?" asked Rivka, now finished with her counting and recording chores.

Ivy explained the emergency to Rivka and told her she was going to the hospital to hold Stuart's hand.

"I don't like the sound of this, girl. You've already had one attempt on your life today. Isn't that enough? I'm worried about your safety."

"You're worrying for nothing. Anna's dead, isn't she? And Herschel's having a heart attack."

"What about Stuart? Can you really trust him?"

"Stuart has bonded with me. I can't imagine any danger from him."

"Just the same, I think either Dan or I should accompany you. I'll go upstairs and wake him. He'll be happy to drive you there."

* * * *

The hospital information desk directed Ivy and Dan to the ER waiting room, where they found Stuart pacing back and forth. At first sight he ran to her, and they embraced for several seconds. Meanwhile, Dan chose a seat within earshot. Strangely, Ivy derived unexpected comfort from Stuart's affectionate greeting.

"How is he?" she asked.

"The doctors are trying to stabilize him. They're afraid to try putting in a stent right now, because they don't think Dad can withstand the shock of the anesthesia."

A young doctor in green scrubs approached them. "His signs are all much stronger now. We have your father prepped for the operating room, but he refuses to take anesthesia until he's talked with all of you. He's been asking for all his children. Insisting, in fact. He frankly doesn't believe he'll survive this surgery, and I'm sorry to say he may be right. But he won't survive without it. We do have an operating room available in twenty minutes."

Stuart and Ivy followed the doctor through the double glass doors into a room full of curtained cubicles. They stopped at number eleven; the doctor pulled back the curtain to let them enter. Herschel lay on his back with an IV in each arm, oxygen tubes in his nose, and an oxygen sensor affixed like a clothespin to his left-hand forefinger. His softly spoken words sputtered out with a dry, gravelly sound.

"Where is my Julie?"

"I don't know," said Stuart. "She seems to have disappeared. I haven't seen her since the cop told us about Mom."

"Then I will tell you two what I have to say," Herschel replied. "Twenty-three years ago I made a great mistake. I had an extramarital affair with Lainee Cohen, whom I loved deeply. Oh, I loved Anna, too, and my children as well, but I missed the physical excitement only young love can provide. Neither of us went looking for an affair. It just happened. Certainly, I must accept blame for my own straying. It's not the affair itself, but the end of the affair that I want you both to know the facts about."

With labored breath, Herschel plodded on. "I had been making several business trips back and forth between London and Annapolis. Uncle Meyer, Leo, and myself were in the process of moving our business across the Atlantic. On the second-to-last trip, I'd been away almost a month. Because of this, I brought Lainee some ultra-personal presents from Annapolis.

"I swear before God I knew nothing of a baby when I went to see her for the last time. So you can imagine my surprise when I learned I had started a second family. True, we argued, we shouted, she cried, but ours was a battle of words. I swear to God, I never laid a hand on Lainee—I loved her too much. I had even agreed to provide for her and the baby. But during the shouting, she backed away and fell over a box and hit her head. I saw her lying there with her eyes shut. I tried to revive her. I shook her gently. I tried to find any life signs, but I knew so little about that sort of thing.

"I eventually left the apartment believing her dead and that I was responsible for her death. I was so devastated and distraught that I returned home and confessed the whole thing to Anna. I carried the full weight of guilt for Lainee's death with me every day since then. Until yesterday."

"What happened yesterday?" asked Ivy.

"Anna had wheedled Lainee's address out of me, supposedly so she could go and ensure there were no traces of me left in the apartment. Unknown to me, when she arrived she encountered Lainee regaining consciousness. I don't know what got into Anna, but she attacked Lainee. Lainee was weak, but still struggled. Anna wound up strangling her on the spot. Then she left the apartment and never said one word to me of her monstrous part in my lover's death. Only yesterday did Anna confess to me. Upon Lainee's death, there was no way I could acknowledge you as my child, my dear Ivy, without incriminating myself."

A nurse in scrubs slipped another pouch on one of the IV stands and connected it to a T joint in the plastic line. She opened the valve, and while the fluid ran, she injected a hypodermic syringe into the same line. "Time's up, folks. Mr. Reubens is on his way to Operating Room Four." They watched the gurney disappear down the hall and through the double doors at the end. Stuart and Ivy joined Dan in the recovery waiting room.

Thirty-five minutes later, the young doctor came out with a somber face and informed them that Herschel Reubens had died on the table. They left the hospital with Ivy's arm wrapped around Stuart's waist. Dan trailed along behind and, minutes later, drove them to the Reubens home. Stuart had ridden the ambulance to the hospital with his father.

A dense darkness smothered the night sky. Streetlights cast eerie images on the Reubens' street. Stuart invited Dan and Ivy in for leftovers. As they walked up the asphalt driveway, a shrill voice demanded: "Stop! That's far enough. Stop or I'll shoot!"

It was a totally disheveled Julie. Her hair stood in tangles every which way. Her half-tucked-in blouse hung in wrinkles from her peasant skirt. Dark circles accented her wet red cheeks. She held a gun, a .22 caliber target pistol. The gun hand wavered back and forth at three potential targets as she spoke.

"Mr. Sherman, Stuart, I hold no fault with either of you. Step aside and you won't get hurt." Obeying, the two men stepped off the driveway and circled onto the lawn. Ivy froze in place.

"Stuart, is Daddy alive?" Julie screamed.

Stuart stopped and shook his head, letting his eyes tell the story. "Put the gun away, Julie. It will accomplish nothing."

Dan, still on the lawn, slowly inched behind her.

Julie's voice shook with hysteria. "You, Ivy, you interfering little tramp. This morning when I woke up, I had two parents. Now neither one is alive and it's your fault. Before you came here, we were a happy family. You changed all that and you're going to pay for it, you bitch."

"Julie," answered Ivy, clutching her shoulder bag with white knuckles. "When I woke up this morning I still had one parent. Twenty-three years ago, I was a baby with two parents. A day later I had none. One was murdered, and the other deserted me. Two days ago I found the parent who deserted me and now he's gone as well. At the hospital *our* father, *our* dad explained everything to Stuart and me. He wanted you there. He asked for you, but you were nowhere to be found."

Dan closed the distance behind Julie. As he was about to grab her gun arm, Ivy shouted, "No, Dan, don't!"

As Dan reached out to force Julie's gun hand downward, she sensed his presence and spun to face him. She pulled the trigger. A bullet passed completely through his windbreaker sleeve and the fleshy part of his upper arm.

Ivy pulled a kerchief from her coat pocket and began wrapping Dan's wound to stop the bleeding. Julie dropped the gun on the asphalt and wandered aimlessly across the front lawn.

"Stuart," said Ivy. "You stay here and look after Julie. I'll drive Dan back to the ER."

"Okay," said Dan. "But give Rivka a call and tell her to meet us there."

Seated behind the wheel of the Shermans' car, Ivy suddenly blurted out, "Dan, I've never driven in the U.S. before. Everything's bloody backwards. I don't even have a driver's license."

Dan tried to calm her. "I'm sure you'll do fine. Just take your time, and I'll tell you where to turn."

"But . . ."

"Go ahead," he said. "We don't have any other choice."

Ivy started the car and backed out of the Reubens driveway. There were extra-wide turns, abrupt traffic stops, and one scuffed curb before the ER portal came into sight. She allowed valet parking to take it from there. They registered at the triage desk and sat down to wait. Rivka, having taken a cab, showed up only a few minutes later. Dan was ushered in for treatment almost immediately. Rivka accompanied him while Ivy filled out all the paperwork, including the police gunshot report, before joining them in one of the cubicles.

When the nurse first saw Dan and Ivy she said, "You two look awfully familiar. Weren't you in here earlier?"

Obviously in pain, Dan sucked up and said. "The service was so good, we thought we'd come back."

A doctor tended to the open wound, and together with his nurse, bandaged and bound it up. "You're a lucky man," he said. "The bullet went clean through with minimal damage to surrounding muscle, nerves, and tissue."

Again Dan sucked up the pain and quipped, "Good planning never hurts."

After a strange look from the doctor, a prescription for an antibiotic, and a pain pill from the nurse, the three left the hospital.

Rivka took over the driving and dropped Ivy off at Mrs. Riley's. Parking in front of their place at 10:30 p.m., Rivka turned off the ignition and reached over to Dan. Cautiously, tenderly, to avoid his gunshot wound, she hugged him and kissed his ear. "I love you, husband," she murmured, blinking back tears. "Thanksgiving's in three days. We have so much to be thankful for."

* * * *

On Wednesday, November 30th, fresh snow fell in thick flakes, blanketing the three coffins lined up in a row, as the entire Reubens family gathered for the funeral services. Meyer, Esther, and Joshua; Thelma and Maurine; Katie and Melvin; Stuart with an arm about Julie; and Leo were all there, plus a few friends and scattered business associates. Rabbi Moshe Goldstein was about to start the first of three services, when he was interrupted by an outcry.

"What the hell is that troublemaker doing here?" cried Esther when she saw Ivy walking toward the solemn group.

"She has every right to be here," said Josh. "Uncle Hersch was her father, too."

"Maybe we wouldn't be standing here if she'd stayed in England where she belonged."

"Mom, you can't put all that blame on Ivy," replied Josh. "Arnold's death had nothing to do with her. And Ivy never once accused any individual in this family. Auntie Anna was always the aggressor."

"It's true, Aunt Esther," said Stuart, overhearing their conversation. "My father confessed on his deathbed that he was Ivy's father. He also claimed that my mother confessed to killing Ivy's mother. On top of that, we all know my mother died trying to kill Ivy as well. I think her confession to my father and her subsequent actions triggered his heart attacks more than anything else. Yes, my dad was overweight and diabetic, but that only made him suceptible."

"Maybe so," Esther admitted. "But things sure started happening when that brat arrived."

Ivy, looking for a friendly face, chose to stand next to Stuart. Approaching, she had heard the bitter diatribe. Facing her accuser, she asked, "Would you prefer that I leave, Aunt Esther?"

Esther gasped and put her hand over her mouth. "No. Of course not. You're welcome as a member of the family. I apologize for what I said. I'm just so devastated."

"My friends," said the rabbi, annoyed over the family squabble, yet pleased with the outcome. "Do you think we can get started now?"

The rabbi began each service with a eulogy and followed with a prayer of mourning. Then, in unison, everyone said *Kaddish*, a prayer of praise for God and his plan for life's continuing renewal; the concept that the departed are not gone as long as they remain in the hearts and memories of their loved ones. Afterward, the three unadorned wooden caskets were lowered into the ground. Those wishing to participate, according to tradition, shoveled a symbolic mound of dirt onto the fresh graves. Stuart was first, Julie second, and, surprising everyone, Ivy picked up the shovel to be third.

* * * *

At the *Oneg* after *Shabbat* services on Friday night, Stuart drew Ivy aside, into a quiet corner. "It seems that funerals have a way of making people feel their own mortality. I've explained everything to the immediate family. They regret all that has happened and lay none of the blame on you. They wish to welcome you into their fold. That is, if you'll have them."

"Of course I will! I guess it's what I've always wanted."

"There's plenty of room for you to move into our house, if you'd like."

"I don't think so, Stuart. I'm really needed where I live now and that's something I want and need for myself. By the way, what's going to happen to Julie? She's so obviously troubled."

"Julie needs help. She's moving in with Aunt Esther. She's set up a series of appointments with a prominent therapist in Baltimore. Lucky for her, Dan's not pressing charges. He could, you know. Assault with a deadly weapon. Julie terribly regrets her actions."

Ivy persisted. "But where did the gun come from?"

"The gun was Uncle Hersch's. Julie found it in his night table. I took it upon myself to get rid of it. Gave it to the Police Department. By the way, if you look to your right, Julie's approaching Dan now."

The Shermans stood at one end of the buffet table nibbling rugulah. Dan wore a blue cloth sling on his right arm over his sport jacket.

"Excuse me, Mr. Sherman, I—"

"Call me Dan, Julie."

"Dan, I want to apologize for all the pain and suffering I've caused you. When I think of what could have happened. I wasn't myself, although I know that's no excuse."

"I accept your apology, young lady. I completely understand the extreme stress you were under. As for the accidental wound? Well, a fella needs a good shot in the arm every so often."

## THE END

# Also by Rosemary and Larry

## The Paco and Molly
## Mystery Series

***Locks and Cream Cheese***—In scandal ridden Black Rain Corners, a Chesapeake Bay mansion harbors locked rooms and deadly secrets. A wily detective and a gourmet cook tackle the case.

***Hot Grudge Sunday***—Bank robbers and conspirators derail the sleuths' blissful honeymoon at the Grand Canyon. Can they nail the suspects after they themselves become targets?

***Boston Scream Pie***—A teenage girl's nightmare triggers a sinister tale of twins, two warring families, and a blonde bombshell who hates being called "Mom."

## Available on Amazon.com, Kindle and Nook